Concilium Sanguinarius

The First Volume of the Velvet

By

Andrew M. Boylaı

I0651988

With Thanks To:

Sarah, for love and support

Thanks to all the readers, especially Mike Penny and Ian Melvin for concepts above and beyond the call, and also Kim Williams for reading through and finding mistakes no spell checker can detect.

Dedicated to David; I hope you enjoy this (when, of course, you are old enough to read it) my son.

Disclaimer: whilst some of the events and characters within the pages of this novel are historical, they have been taken out of context with the actual events and recorded histories and used in a wholly fictional way and a certain amount of poetic license has been applied.

Andrew M. Boylan asserts his moral rights to be identified as the author of this work.

ISBN: 978-0-9556909-0-7

vampire, n. [1. vámpīr; 2. væmp*ai*□]. Fr., fr. Magyar or Serbian *vampir*, also found in Russ., Bulgarian, Pol. & other Slav. Languages in various forms as *vepir, upir* &c.; prob. Fr. a Turk. *Uber*, 'witch'; the word has been borrowed fr. Slav. Sources in other European languages, as Germ. *Vampyr*. **1.** An evil, malignant spirit with the power of entering and reviving a corpse; person whose dead body is thus revived, and renews its life at night by visiting and sucking the blood of sleepers,

Universal English Dictionary

Prologue

Great Rock – The time of short shadow

Great rock dominated the vast wasteland, rising colossal in its midst. It was old then, as ancient as the most aged dream, though even great rock itself did not know how old it truly was. It did remember the coming of the People, walkers and singers, and remembered that, even then, it was old. It had stood silent and sentinel for an eternity it seemed.

From the summit the shaman could see for vast distances across the shimmering wasteland, the heat of fire eye causing the sands to appear as though they were water. To his eyes the wasteland was anything but desolate. Etched across the sands and rocks were the songs, straight lines of a vibrant hue that criss-crossed the wastes. Although he could see the songs their rhythms were alien to him now; a new rhythm had entered his heart.

Ngaut-Ngaut was outcast from the People. He had dared to explore the dream further than the elders had decreed safe. He had seen the hidden vastness of the dream and discovered secrets that the People could not know. To him they were as children wading in the shallows of the stream, whilst he was the adult, prepared to swim in new depths. Whilst exploring the depths of the dreams he had discovered new songs. He brought them back for them but the People had refused to sing, claiming his songs to be wicked. He knew the songs were not wicked. No song was implicitly wicked. They simply led to new places, tracing new paths through the dream. It was clear to him that they called wicked anything that they did not know.

The fire eye was almost at the height of its journey; soon it would begin its slow descent towards the eater. He had to begin the new song before long.

Ngaut-Ngaut walked back to the place of the new song walk. He had made all the preparations during the night before. He had taken the red clay and sang into it the songs of protection. In the new song walk would be creatures harmful to his being if he did not take precautions. Earlier, when the fire eye had escaped the eater, he had caked his naked body in the red clay. He walked carefully so that the clay did not crack at his joints, he would not break its protective barrier. The clay had tightened across his skin, making him feel powerful. He reached the point he had felt was the place to start the new song.

Not far from him was the child, trussed and gagged. The child looked at him with frightened eyes. It was probable that the child's throat burnt with thirst but when Ngaut-Ngaut had tried to give the child water, during the night before, the child had screamed. The shaman had quickly tied the animal skin back over the child's mouth to silence the scream. It was unlikely that the child's People would have heard the scream from the summit of great rock but Ngaut-Ngaut would not take the risk. The shaman had taken the child when he had strayed from a song walk, undoubtedly the men searched for him, though they may have given him up as lost to one of the waste hunters or withered below the gaze of the fire eye.

The time was upon him, he started to sing and his feet instinctively followed the path of the song. It was not straight this song, not like those of the People, which he had learnt when a child uncut. This song curved gradually, taking him in a languid spiral that would eventually reach the child. His voice twisted to produce the words of the song. They were strange these words, not the words that the People spoke, but as the song progressed so the words came to him as though they had been of his tongue for all his life. He could no longer see the plateau of great rock, he walked the depths of the dream and it was the landscape of the dream that filled his eyes. He walked far from the protection of the snake.

The creatures of the deepest dreams crowded around him, curious of this man who walked in their place. Some tried to investigate his flesh, but the clay repelled them. He walked.

Some of the creatures took the form of comely maidens, luridly offering their sex. He knew that they tried to tempt his spear, trying to make it rise and break the clay. He remained strong and the spear remained flaccid. He walked.

Some of the creatures twisted themselves into nightmarish parodies of the waste hunters, snapping at the shaman as they attempted to make him mispronounce the song or lose the rhythm, trying to make him become lost within the dream. Ngaut-Ngaut sang strongly, however, ignoring their ineffectual attacks. He walked.

Time had no meaning here, he might have walked for seconds or minutes or years. In the other place that was great rock the fire eye was reaching down, the eater ready to devour it. Finally he reached the place, the place were the Great Spirit he sought resided. On great rock he reached the child. The two realities converged.

He saw the Great Spirit then, darkness over darkness, yet the darkness was tinged with crimson. It had no form this Spirit, no shape. He saw the child, looking at him with terrified eyes. He knew what he must do to bring the Spirit into the place of great rock. He picked up the sharpened rock he had left near the child and with a swift movement slit the child's throat. He took no pleasure in the act but felt no sadness either. If he were to uncover the secrets he sought the blood spill was necessary. The fire eye was being consumed, the blood sprayed onto the red clay and spilt onto great rock and the rock soaked it into its body, devouring the red fluid. To mark the sacrifice great rock changed colour, the entire rock became red, as red as the blood from the child.

The Great Spirit manifested above great rock. It buffeted Ngaut-Ngaut, trying to take the shaman. Ngaut-Ngaut knew that it would tire and then he would dominate the Spirit, he would take its secrets.

It was as though he were caught in an intense wind, focused on him alone. His head jerked hard and he felt the clay crack at his neck. The protection was breached. He reached his hand up to cover the crack but it was too late the spirit swarmed through the crack, as sharp as polished rock, penetrating at the jugular, filling him, taking him. The Spirit's song became his own. Ngaut-Ngaut was nothing. The Spirit was all. The Spirit was nothing. Nguat-Nguat was all. They were one.

He fell to the floor on all fours and screamed. His fragile flesh was too small a container for the Great Spirit. Seven crimson Spirit sparks flew from his mouth, along the path of his scream, each spark bearing a different aspect of the Great Spirit. They shot into the night and began their relentless search for suitable vessels, other flesh containers that could bear them. They flew beyond the land of dreams searching the reaches beyond the oceans.

Ngaut-Ngaut looked at the world through eyes that burned with a fiery red. His nails extended, sharpening. His eyeteeth lengthened. He brayed at the night.

The fire eye had been devoured and he knew that when it rose it would try to burn the flesh and send the Spirit back to the depths of the dream. He knew that he could spread the part of the Spirit contained in the Ngaut-Ngaut flesh amongst other flesh. He knew that the flesh needed blood to strengthen the Spirit. He knew that time would strengthen each vessel, allowing the Spirit to grow within the flesh, allowing the Spirit to evolve and become more powerful. He knew that the Spirit could leave one vessel and merge with the Spirit in another vessel, though it necessitated the death of the flesh left behind.

He remembered when he was simply Ngaut-Ngaut, the flesh, and he also remembered when he was of Spirit only. Both aspects that had come together were equally his past. His stooped low and let his fingers run through dirt, the long talons scraped against great rock and the part of him that was of Great Spirit reveled in the feeling, the new capacity that he had for tactile sensation. Ngaut-Ngaut knew then that he would enjoy such sensations, that he would seek such sensations, but before he could feed the need to feel he knew that the flesh craved blood.

Down in the waste his new food walked along straight songs. He descended down great rock intending to feed the hunger before the fire eye escaped the eater.

Great rock sat impassive, but great rock knew that each time the fire eye was devoured great rock would change its colour to the colour of blood. Marking the time that the Great Spirit had entered the world and mourning the death of the child that had opened the door to the waking world.

Chapter one

New York City, 1999

She sat before the mirror.

The ornate silver brush pulled through her long dark hair, light from a nearby lamp catching the arabesque swirls inlayed in the antique metal, the light and shadow causing the delicate pattern to become more pronounced.

The mirror was part of an early Victorian dressing table, candles sat, unlit, on its richly varnished surface. She ceased her brushing for a moment and gazed at her reflection. How lucky, she mused, as she had done countless times, that the reflection myth was just that. How awful it would be if I could cast no reflection, if the cold mirror surface refused to hold my image. Just how would a girl's vanity survive such a curse?

She smiled, but the expression was no more than a spectre that brushed gently over her lips. She was too preoccupied to truly smile; her heart ached too much. In the mirror her rich hazel eyes, almost imperceptibly streaked with veins of scarlet, held a pain that reflected the ache in her heart.

She turned her head and looked at the ornate carriage clock, the hands making their slow march towards the midnight hour. She gently placed the brush on the dresser and allowed her slender fingers to glide across the mirror's smooth surface, gently brushing the reflection of the clock face.

Almost midnight. Almost a new millennium. In just fifty years she would be a millennium old herself, or in sixty-seven years if you counted from when she had received the Velvet Kiss.

She could barley remember her life before the Velvet Kiss, a life as a young maiden brought by her Norman father to a newly conquered England. She was unable to remember the name her parents had given her; indeed she had even forgotten their faces. Her memories were crystal clear from the moment that the vampire, who at that time had called herself Bronwen, had carried her over and, as was the custom for Fledglings, given her a new name, from that night she had been Danaan. To her life, albeit one of undeath, began in the autumn of 1067.

Nearly a millennium. Too much time for a human to contemplate and so much of that time spent in solitude. Oh she knew the cause of the ache in her heart; it was the dull pain of loneliness. Loneliness punctuated by a myriad of brief encounters. Encounters which, for some time, had failed more and more to lift her melancholy spirits.

Danaan looked over to the bed. Across the richly embroidered bedspread lay a girl, naked and quite dead. Death had claimed her because she had trusted someone called Juliana, the identity Danaan had adopted for the moment. If it had not been for a moment of carelessness, a lapse of reason, the girl might have distracted the vampire from her solitude, if only for a brief time.

It was unnecessary to kill. Other vampires did, but the undead varied in their appetites as much as the humans. Some vampires glutted themselves on each of their victims, but it was a choice not a necessity. The creatures only required a couple of pints to sustain their flesh, unless they were fighting injury or needing every ounce of their supernatural strength. Some of her kind took the attitude that to be immortal bestowed godhood upon them, giving them divine right to decide whether a donor lived or died, others simply did not care. Some took pleasure, even sustenance it was said, from causing the donor's last moments to be filled with terror, whilst others filled the donor with terrible pain. Some rationed themselves with a stable of donors to save the need for repeated hunts. A few, like Danaan, felt a desire stronger than the need to feed, they desired company.

In the last days of the twentieth century many vampires haunted the S&M clubs, willing donors could always be found amongst the submissives. Danaan preferred the neo-gothic scene. She had some fond memories of the Renaissance; she had adored the gothic movement and had taken delight in the works of the pre-Raphaelites. Yet the melting pot of culture that was the late twentieth century, moving – as the clock had reminded her – at breakneck speed towards the twenty-first century had created a rich vista of sub-cultures. The neo-gothics fascinated her with their heady mix of the macabre and the romantic. The glorification of the monotony of an industrial society underpinned with the bitter sweet agony of unrequited love both excited her and provided an easily accessed food supply.

Vampires were vogue within the movement. Some of the participants in the scene actually believed they were vampires. Okay, some of them were lunatics, but others were simply deluded, denying the fact that their twisted libidos had grown to associate blood with sex. Not that they were wrong, orgasm most definitely improved the crimson draft, but in a way that only a Child of the Velvet could detect.

Hell, vampires were so vogue that Danaan had once paraded herself around a neo-gothic club with her fangs fully extended. No one seemed the least bit shocked; one girl had even approached her and asked her for the address of her prosthetics company.

That evening, however, she had decided to be a little more reserved. She had worn a pseudo Victorian velvet dress of rich imperial purple and kept her fangs retracted. As the city fell into its millennial celebrations she had taken herself to one of the numerous neo-gothic clubs that littered New York, a place called The Raven.

She had arrived at the club long before the crowds and had almost left as a result. The few patrons consisted of the hardcore Goths. For these being neo-gothic was not a fashion statement or a phase, but a way of life. When the scene was no longer chic they would continue to dress in black and circle their eyes with kohl, they would continue to hold true to the vision.

The club was filled with an air of pretension. The patrons either sat in insurmountable cliques or stood alone and aloof. The pretension seeped from their very pores like a sweat born of a perceived superiority.

It was often the way, she had observed, when a person found something that made them feel different from the planet's thronging masses. It didn't matter whether it was a fashion or style, or the ability to appreciate literature rather than being perpetually glued to mindless soap operas on TV, or even being an immortal who imbued blood to survive. Yes, there were many vampires who carried the same air of pretension, forgetting or even denying that they had once been human. It was most common amongst the Fledglings; a phase that often caused the older vampires to despair, sometimes managing to cut the bond between Fledgling and Sponsor. It was a phase that more often than not they grew out of given time, Danaan certainly had, often but not always.

Music from the eighties Goth scene pounded from speakers, spilling over the empty dance floor. The early patrons demanded that "original" gothic music was played, yet were too aloof to dance.

Yes, she had almost left; their pretension chilled her flesh more than her empty veins. Then, around ten o'clock, the place began to fill up with the crowds and the atmosphere began to change. The melancholy, often under-produced, music faded out and modern harsh chords pounded across a quickly filling dance floor.

Danaan had spotted Eternity on the dance floor. She was a pretty young thing beneath the hair, dyed raven black, and the thick kohl eyeliner. Perhaps seventeen or eighteen, certainly too young to have legally entered The Raven, too young for the scent of alcohol that lingered on her breath. It hadn't taken long to seduce her. Another advantage of the neo-gothic scene was the willingness many of them had to flirt with bisexuality.

Danaan had crossed the floor towards the mortal girl, her movements gracefully flowing with the pounding beat. She had circled the girl, her curved hips swaying sensuously, her hands moving to the music, occasionally one of her fingers would delicately trace down the warm flesh of Eternity's arm. Soon the movements of the two girls mirrored each other, the rest of the club shrinking away until there was just the two of them.

Eternity was enthralled by the stranger's beauty. She drank in her long dark hair, held away from her face by ornate silver hairpins. She studied her face, the smooth pale skin and luscious lips that seemed to naturally form a slight pout.

The young mortal traced a hand lightly down her face, following the slight prominence of her cheekbone. She was so beautiful.

Her eyes lingered on her slender neck and then flowed down to her chest. Eternity drank in the round mound of her breasts, the purple dress allowing a hint of cleavage. As the flickering lights burst white for a moment she caught the subtle hint of veins, a pale blue just below the surface of the snow-white skin.

Before long they had slipped from the club unseen, Eternity's plans to celebrate the millennium with her friends forgotten as her sexual appetite overcame her loyalties. Later, when Eternity had not arrived home and the cops had questioned her friends, none of them could remember her leaving. None of them could clearly describe the girl she had talked to and danced with. None of them believed they would recognise her again, but all agreed she was beautiful.

All vampires found that the Velvet Kiss bestowed gifts upon them. Danaan was of the line of Shang-Di, the Child of Golden Skin. He was the oldest of her lineage, a council member, and the Dark Children of his blood could bewitch the human mind, while their bite brought ecstasy. It was not telepathy as such, but they could hide themselves within a person's memory so long as contact was limited, a simple act of smoke and mirrors, projecting images and sometimes a little more like making a voice sound different to a mortal's perception. By touching their surface thoughts they could discern what that person was thinking, but true communication was beyond younger vampires, such as Danaan. More powerfully Shang-Di's Bloodline could enter a mortal's dreams, and in doing so shape their nocturnal fantasies.

It had been an easy task to distort the memories of Eternity's friends and the doorman at the club, to make her features indistinct.

Danaan could not force her will on another however, not blatantly, although she could guide at times. Eternity had left the club willingly.

Danaan pulled up in front of a pair of wrought iron gates some six feet high. Eternity could see the mansion beyond, set deep within the grounds. "Where are we?"

"Home sweet home," Danaan smiled, proud of the building that she had called home for the last two years. A guard opened the gate and Danaan drove in. The guards were all human, but generous pay ensured both their loyalty and discretion. Danaan would not be without them, she enjoyed the feeling of security.

Eternity had been suitably impressed when Danaan had walked her to her car, an executive model with heavily tinted windows, but this new revelation was simply awe inspiring. She stared out of the window as Danaan drove slowly up the gravel driveway. The grounds were well kept and spoke of money. Eternity guessed, correctly, that there would be a pool at the rear of the house.

In the club she had been attracted to Danaan's beauty and entranced by her accent, European she guessed, but impossible to pin down. Sure the car had been impressive, but she did not ever stop to consider that the girl was this rich. She kept thinking girl, but was that correct? At first she had assumed her to be around her own age, but those eyes, those deep hazel eyes, seemed ageless. It didn't matter how old Danaan appeared to be, she was certainly a woman.

In her mind what had begun as a one-night stand, an experiment in sexual boundaries with a beautiful gi… woman, started to develop the possibilities of something more. Perhaps it would blossom into a relationship that could last a while and she could share in the apparent affluence. She was shocked by her mercenary thoughts, but the embarrassment was soon forgotten, her senses bewitched by her lush surroundings, by Danaan's pale beauty, by the delicate perfume of vanilla that permeated the air.

A large sweeping staircase dominated the entrance hall. Either side of the stairs, adorning each banister, was the statue of an eagle finished in gold gilt. Danaan leisurely ran her hand along the outstretched wing of one of the birds, feeling the cold metal under her sensitive fingertips and remembering, for a second, finding those beautiful pieces over a century earlier. She felt a pang of loneliness, as her thoughts turned to her long life. She reached out and took Eternity's hand, allowing the warmth of mortal flesh to push her melancholy lonesomeness away, and led the girl up the marble stairs. Eternity was shocked by how cold Danaan's flesh felt, but after all it was winter in New York, she rationalised.

As they climbed the sweeping staircase Eternity became more and more nervous. What if she failed to pleasure Juliana? The question haunted the girl's thoughts. She was no virgin, Carl had seen to that and several times more to make sure, but she had never slept with another woman before and Juliana seemed so confident, so experienced.

It was as though Danaan could sense the girl's unease. She paused and offered Eternity a reassuring smile before kissing her deeply, exploring the young girl's mouth with her tongue. As the vampire allowed a barely extended fang to graze lightly over the mortal's lip it was as though a jolt of electricity passed through Eternity's body, her nipples stiffened against the black PVC of her bustier even as her crotch became moist. Her nervousness was drowned within an ocean of lust. Danaan broke the kiss and continued to lead Eternity upwards.

The bedroom was absolutely beautiful, but Eternity had little time to take in the beauty. Danaan fell onto the bed, pulling Eternity onto her. The young girl had time enough to realise it was a four-poster bed with an ornate, jewel encrusted cross above the head of the bed and then their mouths met, and the room no longer mattered.

Danaan pushed Eternity's jacket off her shoulders as they kissed, allowing it to fall from her body. Expert hands ran along the young girl's spine, her fingers releasing catch after catch, causing the bustier to come away from her body, freeing her small pert breasts.

Fingers ran through shoulder length raven hair and nails scratched playfully down a swan neck, causing Eternity to gasp. Danaan's hands moved further down, cupping the girl's breasts, relishing their softness.

Eternity reciprocated, touching her lover's breasts through the sensual velvet of her dress. But her hands moved tentatively, unsure of themselves.

In response, Danaan grasped the girl's shoulder and, with a twist, Eternity found herself on her back looking up at the deep wells of Danaan's eyes.

Danaan's hand slipped behind her back and with a deft movement her dress was unfastened. She stood over the girl and allowed the dress to pool around her ankles. For a moment Eternity could do nothing but marvel at her lover's flawless body. Her eyes caressed her beautiful face, brushing down her slender neck, pausing at the small mole just below her shoulder, an imperfection on the otherwise faultless skin that served to make the woman even more perfect. Her eyes continued to her generous, firm breasts. Her vision devoured her brown nipples, the large areolas offering a contrast to the snow-white complexion. Her eyes continued their visual feast sliding down Danaan's taut stomach, lingering on the trim black hair that covered her pubis and then running down her long, toned legs.

This is heaven, she thought to herself, but how can a woman so perfect be interested in me?

With a slow, sensual movement, practically feline in nature, Danaan lowered herself and kissed the girl again. Her lips drifted over her chin and along her neck, only stopping their descent when they reached her breasts. She teased the girl's small pink nipples with her tongue, first one and then the other, as her hand slipped up Eternity's short skirt and into her soaked, flimsy underwear.

My God, Eternity sighed to herself, this woman has done this before. Danaan's slender finger had found the girl's clitoris and had started to gently flick the delicate bud.

Before long Eternity's skirt was removed as were the gossamer briefs. The young girl's pubic mound was a downy blonde, which caused Danaan a brief moment of amusement as the realisation struck her that Eternity was a natural blonde. How many blondes dye their hair dark, she laughed to herself? Then amusement turned into lust and Danaan nestled her face into the girl's crotch, her tongue lashing the clitoris as her fingers thrust in and out of the girl's sex.

Eternity bucked wildly as she felt the orgasm build through her body, her ecstatic screams rising to the heavens. This was when Danaan made her fatal mistake.

She had a rule, never feed and fuck. Orgasm always made the blood sweeter; she could taste an orgasm in the blood an hour or two after the event. But the taste of blood during orgasm was something else again, how easy it was to loose herself within the feed.

Yet at the moment the young girl screamed her joy, Danaan could smell the sweet nectar below the skin, stronger than the erotic scent of sex, she could hear it engorging the girl's vagina, drowning Eternity's screams.

Danaan felt her fangs extend, she tried to stop herself but need and instinct enveloped her caution. Her fangs sank into the girl's pudenda and the blood flowed into her hungry mouth as anti-coagulants ran along the sharp ivory.

The feel of the fangs buried deep in her caused the girl to orgasm again and again, fire burning through her exhausted body. Each orgasm enriched the blood further; causing the feed to become a frenzy that Danaan was unable to stop.

Eternity's voice had become hoarse with her joyous cries; her eyes stared up at the silk baldachin of the deepest royal blue that formed a canopy above the bed like the richest night, though in her bliss she focused on nothing, whilst tears of ecstasy tainted her cheeks with black smudged mascara and her knuckles stained white as her hands gripped the bedspread. Then silence as blood loss caused the girl to slip from consciousness. But the blood was as rich as ever and Danaan drank until there was no more.

***

Danaan stood and walked from the dresser back to the bed, sitting on the edge next to the corpse. Eternity's purse lay on the floor. In it were a couple of twenty-dollar bills that the vampire removed and placed on the bedside cabinet.

As she rummaged through the purse she found the girl's library card. In the picture she looked like an ordinary college girl, the stylistic, neo-gothic makeup was not in evidence. She looked like a regular girl with an ordinary name, Mildred Stenbock. Danaan stroked the girl's hair gently and said, "You know Mildred, Eternity suited you so much more."

The vampire let out a sigh and then continued, "The saddest thing is I really think you and I might have been happy, for a little time at least. I am sorry that I took too much… at least you died in the arms of ecstasy."

She started to pick up Eternity's clothes, ready to dispose of her corpse. But melancholy still gripped her heart and she sat for a moment, her eyes moving for a moment to the ornate cross that she had hung above her bed for centuries. In the polished metal, distorted by the embedded gem stones, was the reflected image of Eternity.

It was true, they could have been happy. Yet time stretched infinitely before Danaan and mortals were so frail, their lives so fleeting.

She needed… The realisation crashed down in a terrifying wave… She needed a companion of her own kind. She needed to create a companion. She knew that was a dangerous path, a path she had once been convinced she would never tread. Yet the loneliness was overwhelming. Perhaps, she wondered, perhaps that is what sparked Radu to do what he did and, as she thought this, she felt that for once she understood him, only in the smallest possible way, but a little at least.

Chapter Two

Concilium Sanguinarius, 1819

She stood in the Concilium's Great Hall. For the moment she had taken the name Helena, a name that she had only just become familiar with when spoken by another. In the Concilium chambers, however, she was always Danaan.

When dealing with their own kind they only used the name bestowed by their Sponsor, the name that was recorded within the Concilium Halls. In a way it saved confusion, in order to hide through the slow march of centuries they changed their names often; it made little sense to constantly memorise the assumed identities of their fellows. It was also a subtle tool used by the Concilium to exert its dominance. No vampire might bestow the Velvet Kiss without permission of the Concilium and the Concilium decreed that the Sponsor would give the Fledgling a new identity. The new name was registered within the Books of Census and the Sponsor was expected to take responsibility for the actions of the Fledgling, for at least a century, until the ancients' agreed the Sponsor's petition of growth, allowing the Fledgling to be known as a Child of the Velvet in their own right. The Concilium held the vampire race within its iron grip, they would broke no disobedience.

If one of the Children of the Velvet broke the rule of the Concilium then both judgement and punishment were swift. The Judgement was delivered by the seven ancients who ruled the Concilium; the punishment was discharged by the Praetorians, the honour guard of the Concilium. It was amongst their ranks that she stood now, wearing the black sash embroidered with the single teardrop of scarlet.

There had been an entirely singular reason for her taking the sash some two hundred years earlier. A reason she had subjected herself to the brutally painful tests of loyalty, which ranged through the physical, the mental, the emotional and the spiritual. Tests that the ancients used to ensure that those who received the honour of wearing the sash would be entirely and devotedly loyal to the Concilium Sanguinarius, tests which still caused Danaan to experience flashes of sheer terror.

One reason, though she could create others that sounded plausible. One reason and one name, Ariadnne. The one who had come to her as the sweet maiden Bronwen and seduced her into the darkness.

When Ariadnne had abandoned her after one hundred years Danaan was unable to understand why, understanding would come much later. Without the benefit of understanding, however, the abandonment hurt her to the very depths of her soul, though she hid the pain well, even from herself. Instead of mourning her loss she indulged in carnality and blood, and nursed a deep resentment for the Concilium. She resented their rules, their inescapable control. She resented the fact that they recognised and even condoned Ariadnne's rejection of her Fledgling by agreeing to the petition of growth. Greater than the resentment, however, was the fear. Though she had often spoken of rebelling, of ignoring their precious rules – had even pushed those rules to the very limit both before Ariadnne had forsaken her and afterwards - fear stayed her hand, stopped her crossing the point of no return. Fear that they would punish her, fear of the Praetorians. Fear of dying the true death and fear that there might be worse things than death.

It was not unusual, as she later discovered. Fledglings often became rebellious. They questioned the wisdom of the Concilium, unable to understand why the Children of the

Velvet remained hidden in the shadows when their power would enable them to rule humanity.

As they crossed the endless centuries they learnt. They began to realise their vulnerabilities, when before they saw only strength, until finally they recognised the danger of exposure. Danaan had borne personal witness to the potential aftermath of discovery. She had witnessed the carnage exacted by the frightened humans, narrowly escaping as she fled the scene of her crimes. She had seen insanity take a mortal lover who feared the march of years and wished to become as Danaan.

Most poignantly she had born witness to the true death of a two thousand year old vampire at the hands of a mortal mob. The tragedy was made all the more intense by the accidental nature of his demise, killed not for his nature but in a riot against their human rulers. Unable to control the baying mob and unable to extract himself from their relentless surge through the streets, he had been swept along with it as though he were nothing but flotsam caught in a strong tide. Then the mob began to riot, fighting with the nearby guards, fighting with people dragged from houses, fighting amongst themselves. The crowd thinned as the fighting began, allowing the vampire room to move, allowing him to escape the mob. He should have survived, melting into the night, but for the swing of a scythe, blindly wielded, that had bitten into the flesh of his neck, severing his head.

As his head came away from his shoulders an invisible wave of energy had exploded from the corpse, causing Danaan to clutch her temples as the pain of his passing washed through her and knocking those rioters closest to the fallen vampire to the floor.

The mob had surged forward again, trampling the fallen mortals before flowing deeper into the town like a natural disaster and Danaan had gone to the fallen vampire. She watched, horrified, as the flesh had sloughed rapidly from his decapitated head at an unnatural pace, death and decay claiming in seconds that which had been denied them for millennia. Only she witnessed the phenomena, and the horror of what she saw was compounded by both the realisation that the immortals were mortal after all and by the knowledge that she was, ultimately, responsible for his death.

As her arrogance had evaporated, so her loneliness had increased. Her trysts and affairs with mortals had sometimes been memorable but, eventually, memory was all they could ever be. Memories of lovers, aware but uncaring of her nature, growing aged and dying whilst she remained forever young. Memories of lovers grudgingly abandoned so that they would not become suspicious when her beauty remained uncorrupted by the passage of time. Although she still indulged in affairs, be they for a single night of satisfaction or for a length of a time, she did so with a heavy heart, knowing that they were doomed before they began.

She missed Ariadnne, missed her beauty still undefiled by time, she missed her understanding – an understanding which her own behaviour and arrogance had undermined.

Eventually she felt more human than she believed a mortal could ever feel and as these feelings grew in her, blossoming over long decades, so it was that she grew to understand the Concilium, so she grew to believe in its wisdom.

But what of Ariadnne, how could her love ever be restored? Danaan had strangled her love with a century of arrogance, with an inflated belief in her own self-importance. With her lack of humanity perhaps? Certainly her words spoken against the Concilium had raised Ariadnne's anger when they were still together, just as it would now raise Danaan's.

If she could serve the Concilium then perhaps she could reopen the door to Ariadnne's heart.

That was her thought. That was her reason for taking the sash. Incidents, such as the one at Kirklees, had not endeared Danaan with the Concilium or to Ariadnne. To prove her loyalty to the rule of the Children of the Velvet, to submit totally to the Concilium Sanguinarius, would be no bad thing.

Two centuries had passed. Two centuries as a Praetorian, serving the Concilium. Two centuries during which all her attempts to contact Ariadnne had met with frustration.

Two nights earlier she had received the summons of the Concilium and that very night, as she had answered the call of the Concilium Sanguinarius, she had finally seen Ariadnne once again – just beyond the mountain entrance to the chambers. Danaan's heart had leapt at the sight of her, pounding as it had done the night they had first met and kissed.

She had tried to catch her Sponsor's attention and failed to do so, and then, gathering all her courage together, she had walked boldly over to her. She had hoped for warmth, she had feared anger but she never expected to be ignored. It was as though she no longer existed, that Ariadnne could not even see her. Ariadnne looked straight through her, as though Danaan was no more than a spectre, unable to interact with the physical world. For a second she considered grasping Ariadnne's arms, thought of kissing her and forcing an acknowledgement, but the pain of her broken heart stopped the act. Although Danaan had grown over the centuries she still could not understand the reaction, she could not understand how she could have hurt her former lover so much that she had killed not only the love, but even the hatred and anger. How she could have turned Ariadnne's heart to ice?

Danaan's heartache was so great that, when she stood in the Great Hall of the Concilium Chambers, the sight of it, for once, did not take her breath away.

For once she was blind to the intricate mosaics that depicted events in history, which mortal scholars had long forgotten, the sagas seeming to come to life as the flickering illumination from candles played across the brightly coloured tiles, causing them the almost imperceptible illusion of movement. She was ignorant of the statues that stood within the colonnades, not depicting Gods, as the Roman fashion had been, but depicting the most worthy of the Children of the Velvet. Just this once she did not stand before the one statue that had long caught her eye. At a distance it appeared broken, the arm missing. Yet the missing limb and the blackening of the marble below the shoulder was part of the artist's device, capturing eternally the terrible injuries the vampire had sustained and now used as a symbol of how much a Praetorian should be prepared to suffer in defence of the ancients.

The Concilium Sanguinarius had been located deep in the Swiss Alps for countless ages. Hidden in caverns, buried deep within the mountains with the hidden entrances high amongst the peaks, its location was known only to the Children of the Velvet. Concerted efforts had been made by the Concilium to stabilise Switzerland within the European political arena, and the effort had paid off. Just four years earlier the mortals' Congress of Vienna had guaranteed Swiss neutrality for all time.

Once inside the caverns it was like stepping back through time. There had been an ancient, a millennium before Danaan's birth, one of the seven eldest and ruler of a Bloodline. The ancient had been called Uriel the Leech and he had been enamoured by all things Roman. Indeed it was rumoured that the face of Rome herself had been carved by Uriel. That he had manipulated the Empire from its conception, moulding it from the shadows for his own amusement.

It was the way of the seven that one would take leadership of the Concilium for a century before relinquishing the power to another, that way the balance between the bloodlines was maintained. Uriel had been the Concilium's Emperor when nature herself had ended his unlife, catching him within her fiery grip as the great Mount Vesuvius became the instrument of her temper and had crushed Pompeii.

His death sent shockwaves through the Concilium. An ancient had died; an unheard of event. But all things must go on, it was said. Uriel's eldest Fledgling took both his place on the Concilium and control of the Bloodline.

As a mark of respect, the Romophile elements that Uriel had introduced during his leadership became permanent features of the Concilium, thus since that time the vampire's council was named the Concilium Sanguinarius. The style of the Great Hall was that of a Roman palace, the title of the Concilium Leader became forever Emperor and the Concilium guard forever became known as the Praetorians.

Danaan had entered the Great Hall long before the appointed hour, standing alone before the thrones of the ancients, too lost in her own heartache to mingle with the Children of the Velvet. Making small talk and embroiling herself in the various plots and counter plots were the last things she wished to do.

She stood staring at the seven thrones, the seats for seven ancients, each the Bloodfather or mother of an entire Bloodline of vampires. Just a few short centuries earlier the thrones had been the focal point of myth and rumour. Seven thrones had always looked over the Concilium, but only five ancients sat upon them. Two remained eternally empty.

Some insisted that there had been seven Bloodlines once, but two had been eradicated in a bitter Bloodwar that had almost torn the heart from the vampire nation.

Others suggested that the two lost Bloodlines existed still, outcast and hidden in their shame.

Only the ancients knew the truth, they and their eldest Fledglings; but none of them would speak of it, aloof from Concilium rumour.

Then mortal man discovered the Americas, and later Australia, and the truth was finally revealed. The other two ancients, and their Bloodlines, existed in the newly discovered continents. Not outcast but separated from the heart of the Concilium by the expanse of ocean.

They had remained connected to the Concilium, the two ancients over the water secretly involved in Concilium rulings, linked not physically but psychically. In both the Americas and Australia records were kept as to the number of Fledglings, as meticulous as the Books of Census kept within the Concilium Halls. The same laws held the Children of the Velvet from these distant lands and Praetorians enforced them there as here. The hand of the Concilium Sanguinarius stretched across the face of the entire globe it seemed.

There would be five of the ancients present this night, the other two would cast their votes from across the oceans; the distance and dangers of sea travel making a physical appearance impractical.

Now, of course, new myths and rumours had emerged. Rumours that the ancient in Australia was the eldest of the ancients. That he had walked the earth with the first blossoming of humanity, but who would ever truly know?

Danaan became aware of restless movement around her. The hour that had been appointed was almost upon them and the other summoned Praetorians had entered the Hall.

For a moment she forgot her broken heart. There were so many present, at least thirty Praetorians. She had never known so many summoned at once for a ruling, never more than two or three were needed to enforce the rule of the Concilium. She saw the same puzzlement, the same questions, on the faces of her fellows. Something terrible had happened, something that caused Danaan to push aside her own heartache, all of a sudden it seemed so petty.

The five Ancients had taken their thrones. Shang-Di, Danaan's Bloodfather and the current Emperor, nodded and the accused was led into the Hall, his hands bound in a silver chain.

The chain itself was useless as a bond. Human literature had begun to be overwhelmed with a slew of vampire fictions, a symptom perhaps of the current fashion for phantasmagoria. Within some of these stories silver was mentioned as a deterrent against the Children of the Velvet but it was little more than a mortal fabrication. The chain was purely symbolic, all present knew that the real chains were invisible, they extended from the heart of this chamber, they were forged of the Concilium Sanguinarius itself and the Praetorians were the links of the chain.

As the accused came into view a startled gasp sounded around the tall columns that lined the Hall. It was Ymochel, child of Uriel. The vampire who had suffered such terrible burns in the fires of Pompeii as he endeavoured to pull his Bloodfather from Vesuvius' anger. Looking at him now it was impossible to tell. Even to Danaan, who worshipped only at the altar of Saphos, he was physically beautiful. His Nubian skin was flawless, his proud features chiselled into the face of a God; Uriel had always prized beauty in his Fledglings. Time and blood had healed his wounds but, Danaan had been told over a millennium after the event, those wounds had been terrible to behold, his healing had been slow and painful.

Danaan's eyes darted to his statue, depicting him with his arm destroyed by the fierce lifeblood of Vesuvius, and then back to the vampire, silent in his shame.

The voice of Shang-Di echoed through the Hall, "We meet at the hour appointed to judge the accused, Radu. Also to judge Ymochel as the Sponsor of Radu.

"Let it be known by the Concilium Sanguinarius that Radu has refused the summons of the Concilium and his refusal shall be added to the lists of crimes of which he is accused.

"Ymochel," Shang-Di's voice softened almost imperceptibly, "I am sure that you already know this but tradition demands that I tell you. You are the Sponsor of Radu and, despite the centuries that have passed, at no point have you petitioned the Concilium Sanguinarius that Radu be known as a Child of the Velvet in his own right.

"As such you are responsible for his crimes, as though you had committed them yourself. Although you have answered the summons willingly in the eyes of the Concilium his lack of respect is your lack of respect.

"Do you understand?"

Ymochel said nothing; he looked forward his features determined, set with courage or arrogance it was impossible to tell?

Finally, however, Danaan did understand, as she watched his impassive yet angelic features. She understood exactly what she had done to drive Ariadnne from her forever.

As Danaan watched the proud Ymochel plummet from a status within the Halls that was almost one of divinity, causing his name to be uttered in the hushed, awed tones normally reserved for the ancients, to a state of utter disgrace she understood.

Ariadnne had risked everything for Danaan. She had petitioned the Concilium for the right to bestow the Velvet Kiss and taken complete responsibility for Danaan's every action, all for the sake of love.

Each and every time that Danaan had displayed a childish fit of pique that had manifested as anger, arrogance or rebellion, Ariadnne's unlife had been put at risk. Danaan had constantly, over a one hundred year period, risked her lover's execution for the sake of her actions, yet had been too conceited to realise the cost of her actions.

Her behaviour had not been that of a lover, it had been little more than the actions of a spoilt child. Each and every action had been devoid of love and care, and had stripped another layer of Ariadnne's love away. Danaan's decision to take the sash may well have been the first responsible act she had performed, but it had been too little much too late.

If one such as Ymochel could fall so far from grace, could be brought in the silver chains before the Concilium, how easy would it have been for Danaan's attitude and actions to have caused her to fall from the tightrope she never even realised she had walked? How easy to have pulled Ariadnne down with her?

It seemed to her that as a vampire grew older their concerns moved away from the original misconceptions of power and towards the more basic concerns of survival. It had been an act of supreme love, admittedly married to a burning loneliness, Danaan now realised, that had caused Ariadnne to bestow the Velvet Kiss upon her and Danaan had, although she had not known it, thrown that love back into Ariadnne's face.

Despite herself a crimson tear fell down the snow-white skin of Danaan's cheek. It mattered not. If anyone had noticed they would assume it shed for Ymochel, only Danaan knew the truth.

The opening statement by Shang-Di had continued for a while. The ancient was an animated speaker, his arms always moving within the spacious robes of the finest oriental silks. His long, black braid whipping around as he moved his head as though it were possessed with a life of its own.

"Beyond the disrespect that Radu has shown the Concilium Sanguinarius, this very night, there are further charges that must be raised against him. That, on more than one occasion, he has bestowed the Velvet Kiss without informing, or gaining the permission of, the Concilium. Further, that he has committed the crime of then removing the blessing of unlife from some of these illegitimate Fledglings, bringing about true death, and has encouraged the same behaviours amongst his illegitimate Fledglings."

Shang-Di paused, allowing the enormity of the charges to settle in and the resultant shock to reverberate around the Hall.

The charge of creating vampires without the Concilium's consent was scandalous enough; it carried an automatic penalty of true death for the vampire who bestowed the Velvet Kiss and the illegitimate vampire, but to kill those whom he had created.

The seven ancients could kill another vampire, so long as that vampire was of their own Bloodline or in self-defence. Even they were loath to do so, at least publicly; it raised questions within the Concilium and threatened the stability of their Bloodline.

In the normal scheme of things the only vampires permitted to bestow true death upon another were the Praetorians and then only in defence of an Ancient, on the admittedly extremely rare occasions when a renegade tried to take the life of a Bloodmaster, or with the permission of the Concilium as a punishment for crimes committed.

True death amongst the vampires was seldom brought about by their own kind. More often it was the result of an accident, a natural disaster or the actions of a lucky mortal who, on stumbling upon a vampire and realising their true nature, conferred on themselves the mantle of a hunter. It was the general opinion that the reason the Concilium controlled the creation of new vampires with such vigour was because true death amongst their kind was so rare and a plague of vampires would draw unwanted mortal attention.

Danaan looked across at Ymochel, as the charges were revealed, but his expression did not change, he continued to look ahead with a kind of quiet calm.

"As Radu has deemed it fit to insult the Concilium and ignore our summons," continued Shang-Di, after allowing the shocked whispers to die away, "We must forgo asking the accused how he responds to the accusations and ask that Fenrir step forward and present his evidence to the Concilium."

To those within the Hall who had never come across Fenrir until this night his appearance seemed at once both miraculous and shocking. As Shang-Di called him he simply appeared before the ancient, seeming to melt out of the shadows where a moment before no one had stood.

To those who had knowledge of the strange vampire, the manner of his entrance caused little interest, more poignant was the fact that his entrance surely meant the end for Radu, and, by the laws of the Concilium, Ymochel.

Fenrir was the chief spy for the Concilium Sanguinarius. It was said that he had been a master thief in his mortal life, untouchable by the human authorities. It was said that it was these skills that had drawn the eye of his Bloodmother, Undjit the Serpent, and that she had ordered the mortal thief brought before her.

Undjit's bloodline was known for their ability to hide chameleon like in the night, it was said to be part of their dark gift. A useful gift when hunting humans, no doubt, and when hunted by them, but only truly effective against the most careless of vampires. The senses of a Child of the Velvet being so much more acute than those of a mortal, in the normal scheme of things they would be able to sense another of their kind, unless distracted or preoccupied.

If rumour were to be believed Undjit had performed arcane rites, so archaic that they were unknown to all but the three eldest ancients, when she had personally bestowed Fenrir with the Velvet Kiss. These rites, married with the dark gift of her Bloodline and Fenrir's mortal skills, had created a gift unknown in the Concilium. Whether the occult nature of his birth to the Velvet was true or not, Fenrir was unique amongst the vampires. He had the ability to walk unseen, hidden from all, mortal and undead, unless he chose to reveal himself. Some said that he could even remain hidden from the ancients, all except for his Bloodmother.

With his creation it seemed that the Bloodline of Undjit had suddenly developed a political edge above and beyond the other Bloodlines but, rather than tip the delicate balance of status quo between the seven, Undjit had voluntarily relinquished her Fledgling and made him the property of the Concilium. From that moment Fenrir had become the spy of the Concilium, the eyes and ears beyond the mountain caverns. He served all the Bloodlines equally, so long as their goals matched those of the Concilium. His word had grown beyond reproach.

Radu's refusal of the summons had, perhaps, sealed his fate and the fate of Ymochel. However, with Fenrir presenting the evidence it became all too clear that Radu had simply compounded his crimes. The summons was less a trial than it was a public denouncement of Radu and a judgement of punishment.

Fenrir composed himself before addressing the Concilium. He appeared a wholly unremarkable man, not bestowed with the otherworldly beauty associated with many of the Children of the Velvet, nor possessed of the inner luminescence of unlife. Rather he seemed to be possessed of the bland greyness of mortality, more so than any mortal would normally be.

Despite the matted tails of dirty grey hair that hung limply from his scalp and the long strands of greyed whiskers clinging haphazardly from his chin he seemed instantly forgettable.

His muted, tattered travelling clothes, still dirty from the roads, seemed out of place, even astonishing, when compared to the robes of rich silks and brocades that were more commonplace within the chambers of the Concilium. Yet even in these the mind seemed incapable of fixing on him, the eye moved passed him instinctively, convinced he was of no importance.

Even in a place where he should have stood out, such as upon the high dais with the ancients, when he had openly allowed himself to be seen, he seemed perfectly camouflaged. Hidden whilst centre stage.

He cast his watery eyes briefly over the ancients before turning directly to Shang-Di. His large, aquiline nose twitched momentarily and then he addressed the Concilium, his voice scratchy and yet each word was an arrow finding its mark in Radu.

"Emperor Shang-Di, the Child of Gold Skin, long may your Bloodline prosper.

"I was travelling, as is my want, and happened to find myself in the eastern principalities of Europe. As I moved from town to town I heard recent tales of what many in those regions call strigoï.

"The lands in those regions are, admittedly, filled with superstition. Their legends tell of creatures not entirely unlike the Children of the Velvet, legends that have long been used to scapegoat poverty, disease and death.

"Yet the more of these tales I heard, the more concerned I became. The stories seemed more accurate somehow than mere legend. They seemed to hold within them a kernel of truth.

"Then, as I travelled closer to the source of these tales, more detailed stories were told. Stories that hinted of a mighty Prince of Walachia who had returned to the lands as strigoï. Those who told the tales claimed that the Prince was Radu Drăculea, who had been puppet prince of the Turks some three and a half centuries before. They claimed that he had risen from his tomb and that he was in Transylvania, preparing an army of devils with which he would retake Walachia.

"In truth it seemed as though the tellers of these tales did not know what they feared the most, the strigoï or the Turks? Yet their tales were enough to cause me concern and to travel to Transylvania, which is known as the Land Beyond the Forest.

"I travelled to the Schloß that was spoken of in whispered tones; a place that I believed was now occupied by Radu of the Bloodline Remus."

Danaan glanced across to Ymochel and for a second caught a dangerous gleam sparkling in his eye, as though he was offended that Fenrir had used the new name of his Bloodline, rather than refer to it as the line of Uriel. Then, just as quickly the gleam was gone, the mask of composure had been fixed firmly back in place.

"I entered the Schloß in secrecy," Fenrir continued, "And saw that the master of the Schloß was indeed Radu, Blood Kissed by Ymochel, Bloodson of Remus.

"I stayed in the Schloß for some time. There were, at any given time, twelve other vampires, none of whom were known to me. They were ruled by Radu, who bade them call him by his mortal title of Prince. He encouraged them to indulge in Bacchanalian orgies, more often than not involving young mortals kidnapped and brought to his domain.

"Occasionally he would spy a mortal who would take his fancy, and that one would be removed and placed in a cell.

"Each week he would encourage his illegitimate Fledglings to fight amongst themselves. These battles would be brutal and, when finished, Radu would select the strongest and the weakest. The strongest would then be ordered to bestow true death upon the weakest." Fenrir paused for a moment, for dramatic effect, "In the manner of the Praetorians."

Hushed whispers again circulated around the Great Hall. For those Children of the Velvet who casually watched the events unfold the shock came from the audacity of the act. To copy the Praetorians, the honour guard of the Concilium no less, seemed to be a form of mockery that verged on the sacrilegious. It brutally satirised all that held the lives of the vampires together. Most did not know what bestowing the true death in the manner of the Praetorians actually entailed; none knew what it truly meant.

For the ancients, and the gathered Praetorians, the meaning was all too clear.

Bestowing the true death on a vampire was no easy matter. Fire would do it, though the fire would have to be devilishly hot and exposure prolonged. Sunlight would also kill, but was in itself wholly impractical. The direct light of the sun was agonising, certainly, and stole the blood strength, but it incinerated very slowly, though the speed of incineration increased if the vampire was denied blood to heal the slowly charring flesh. In practice several days' exposure might be needed in order to ensure the true death and, it was generally agreed, that any vampire who allowed that to happen deserved to die.

Some mortal legends spoke of a stake through the heart. As with all legends this was not the whole truth. The heart pumped the stolen blood, and blood gave life and strength. A piece of wood or metal rammed through the heart would prevent the organ from repairing itself, until it was removed, and would rob a vampire of the preternatural strength and dark gifts that the blood bestowed. In itself, however, it would not kill.

In more accurate folklore the stake through the heart was a prelude to the sure-fire method of bestowing the true death, decapitation. In other folklore the heart was also totally removed, a generally effective way of ensuring that true death visited the vampire.

The Praetorians killed in a slightly different way. All Children of the Velvet knew of the power of blood, it propelled them through the endless centuries. Few knew how powerful the blood of another vampire was. Of course some vampires became lovers and some of these shared blood as part of their lovemaking. In doing so they would learn of the fleeting potency of vampire blood. The ancients knew more, of course. They knew that if you drank of another, emptying their veins, and then bestowed the true death, the feeder stole the very power of the other vampire.

When carrying out a death sentence the Praetorians killed in two ways, depending on personal taste, but they always began by draining the vampire dry. Then, with their fangs still embedded in the vampire's neck, they would either rip the head from the body or tear the heart from the chest.

It was a secret the ancients had shared with the Praetorians. Carrying out an execution was a reward for loyalty and ensured that their guard were stronger than the common Fledglings. It was a secret not to be divulged, that it might become common knowledge was too dangerous. It would lead to anarchy and a loosening of their iron grip of power.

The penalty of true death for the killing of a peer helped prevent the uninitiated from stumbling across the secret; only the Praetorians were trusted to hold the secret.

Fenrir cleared his throat and then continued, "When the weakest had been despatched, Radu would select a mortal from the cells. Either the one chosen as strongest or Radu himself would then bestow the Velvet Kiss, ensuring that the Fledglings always remained twelve."

Fenrir fell silent and his silence filled the Hall.

The silence was finally broken by Shang-Di. "Fenrir, we thank you for your testimony, as disturbing to the Concilium as it was. I would like to ask you a further question."

"Of course, my Emperor."

"Did you discover, in your time in Radu's Schloß, whether any other Child of the Velvet was directly complicit in these crimes?"

Fenrir thought for a moment, his large nose twitching all the while, until he carefully answered, "To the best of my knowledge, no other Child of the Velvet visited the Schloß whilst I observed the activities there. During my time there I heard nothing which might implicate any other. So, I must answer that I cannot say if any other was directly complicit in these terrible crimes."

Shang-Di nodded, "Thank you Fenrir, you may go."

Fenrir bowed, almost imperceptibly, and faded back into the shadows, quickly vanishing from sight although he seemed to have not moved. It was as though he had never been there, though the implication of his words still hung heavy in the air.

Shang-Di had already turned his attention directly to Ymochel. "You have heard the charges against Radu, but I ask you directly, were you aware of his actions prior to Fenrir's testimony?"

Ymochel's eyes flicked across to one of the thrones, resting for a moment on Huginn of the Morning Star.

Danaan noticed and followed Ymochel's gaze. It was said that Huginn was a powerful mentalist, the ancient's eyes seemed to bore deep into the heart and he was able to know the truth of any word spoken.

Ymochel had turned his attention back to Shang-Di, whilst Danaan continued to watch Huginn. She heard Ymochel reply, "No." A second later Huginn nodded, Ymochel had told the truth.

Danaan turned her attention back to Ymochel. Throughout the proceedings Ymochel had remained silent, proud and stoic. Now Danaan saw that it was no longer the case. His single utterance had managed to break his carefully constructed mask. His shoulders had slumped and he seemed drained. Yet his innocence was proven, he knew nothing about Radu's activities, but innocence was not enough. Radu had wreaked the damage; his betrayal of the Concilium had been a more personal betrayal of his Sponsor.

Proceedings were adjourned and the ancients retired to confer. With them gone urgent whispers erupted around the Great Hall, the discussions amongst the Praetorians curtailed in case they accidentally revealed the secret which Radu had somehow discovered.

Eventually the ancients returned and a hush immediately fell upon the Hall. Shang-Di stood before the Children of the Velvet and delivered the judgement of the Concilium.

"We have heard the testimony of Fenrir and the words that he spoke were, to say the least, disturbing. They outline a crime that has no peer in the history of the Concilium, yet we have never had reason to doubt the words of Fenrir before, and no reason to doubt them now.

"Of course, we have not heard Radu's account of the events, but we have taken his insult against the Concilium as an admission of guilt.

"We therefore decree that the unlife of Radu of the Bloodline Remus, and those of his illegitimate Fledglings, be forfeit and that the Praetorians summoned before the Concilium this night shall bestow true death upon them."

He shifted his attention directly towards Ymochel, "As for you, it is normal that you would suffer the same fate of your Fledgling.

"The Concilium has discussed your fate. It is my opinion that you have brought such a fate upon yourself. I opposed your petition to bestow the Velvet Kiss upon Radu Drăculea. As Fenrir has reminded us, he was, for a short time, Prince of Walachia, although his star was eclipsed greatly by his brother. To my mind it is dangerous to bring one so well known in the mortal world into the Concilium Sanguinarius. Yet such was your standing that the majority did not share my opposition.

"You wished for Radu to maintain his mortal name, something, again, which is unique in the history of the Concilium. I reveal to you now that all of the Bloodlines had grave concerns regarding your wish, but again your standing before the Concilium swayed us.

"It seems now that we were right to harbour concerns. Radu has clung to the vestiges of his mortal past. We have heard that he demands his illegitimate Fledglings call him Prince, it seems that he tries to recreate his mortal life and mocks the Concilium as he does so, breaking our most precious laws.

"All that said, we believe you when you say that you had no knowledge of his actions – though one who wishes to remain apart from their Fledgling should attempt the petition of growth – and we have not forgotten the terrible injuries you suffered when attempting to save Uriel of blessed memory.

"It is unusual, but the Concilium may judge your sentence different to that of your Fledgling.

"It is the decision of the Concilium Sanguinarius that you witness the true death of your Fledgling and his get. Further you shall then be handed to Qutrub of the Flesh, for a period lasting no less than one hundred years, in order that you may best serve the Concilium and atone for your crimes.

"Praetorians we journey to Radu's domain in one hour and rest only for the sun. Any Child of the Velvet who might try to warn the outcast of this judgement will share the same fate as the outcast.

"This is the judgement of the Concilium Sanguinarius."

With that the ancients marched from the dais and an obviously dazed Ymochel was led away.

As soon as the ancients had left the Hall the whispers that had punctuated the proceedings exploded into a babble of excited, shocked and horrified conversations.

Some could not believe the generosity the ancients had shown in sparing Ymochel's life. A few harboured resentment that he should possess such a hold over the Concilium that he was able to escape the sentence of true death when another in his place would not.

The Praetorians knew differently. Qutrub was an ancient with a rather unique taste in pleasure. It was rumoured that he had manufactured the Inquisition but became bored when mortal man showed a distinct lack of imagination, and, of course, vampiric flesh could take so much more punishment than the fragile flesh of mortals.

For most Praetorians, their short time with the Flesh had proved the most difficult part of their initiation to the sash, the ancient had a way of devising pleasures for himself that would make the recipient awaken as the sun set, centuries later, with a scream upon their lips. If some believed that the Concilium had been generous, even benevolent, with Ymochel's sentence they were sorely mistaken. In truth they had exacted a most terrible punishment and, if asked, any of the Praetorians would have said they would prefer true death to even one night serving the darkest needs of Qutrub. It was clear that his standing with the Concilium had fallen to naught.

The Praetorians quickly left the Hall to prepare for their journey, whilst two more entered, their orders to remove forever the statue of Ymochel from the Great Hall.

Before they left for Transylvania, Danaan left a note for her former lover.

Ariadnne

I understand now. I also realise that you may never be able to forgive me for the peril I caused you and the mockery that, I now see, I made of your love. I shall probably never be able to forgive myself.

I only wish for you to know that I am sincerely sorry,

Still Yours

Danaan

It would be the last time she contacted Ariadnne; an apology made with a note, the crisp parchment smeared with a single tear of blood.

Chapter Three

New York City, 2000

"I am a stupid little whore," the words barely spoken as a tear rolled down her face. A tear of pain, humiliation or joy she could no longer tell.

She had forgotten her own name over the hour she had been at his never-tender mercy. She had forgotten the safety word. She didn't care. Strapped to the wooden Saint Andrew's cross, her clothes and undergarments ripped away.

Normally they would have beaten her by now, she seemed to recall, a memory that surfaced from a lifetime ago. The whip would have cracked and the searing pain would have sent ecstatic pulses racing through her flesh. But he was different.

He had strapped her to the cross, constraining her wrists and ankles with plain leather straps, and ripped away her clothes, but since then had not physically touched her. His cruelty came from his words and from the depths of his eyes. His eyes dripped with malice, deep brown pools of malevolence set within his handsome features, chiselled like a statue of obsidian. Cruelty seemed to radiate from his person, a miasma of sadism.

"I am a stupid whore and do not deserve your punishment."

He raised one eyebrow, an unspoken query.

"…Master." She added.

It was his eyes, she suddenly recalled, his sadistic eyes. They seemed to call for her across the club. Normally she was more careful, choosing her partners in the knowledge that they would only take her as far as she wanted. She didn't know him, normally she wouldn't have accepted his summons, but his eyes sang to her in a language of brutality that her soul yearned for.

She had become quite the regular at the club. The pounding beat of the bass driven dance music reminded her of the pounding of her heart when the whip cracked down. The room was always dark, with the darkness punctured by lasers that fanned across the dance floor and the occasional strobe lights, which captured the patrons in slow motion. You could lose yourself in the constant clinging mist of dry ice, or find yourself if that was what you chose to do.

There were no taboos to hide from, every patron was either a dominant or a submissive, and all of them had their own special ways. She had never seen him there before but he was beautiful, his dark black skin, his handsome chiselled face, the smooth dome of his head. His clothes were expensive and not the normal clothes she would have associated with the club, but it didn't matter. She could tell from his bearing that he was a Dom, a Sub could always tell.

His eyes captured her, held her. She looked into those dark wells and she saw everything she had ever wanted. It was like magic, she saw him and immediately moved to him, attracted by an irresistible force. He had grabbed a handful of her hair and drawn her violently to his mouth. He whispered into her ear, "Let's go." She obeyed.

Her memory shattered as his hand whipped out. It caught her across the face, jarring her head back. She heard the vertebrae in her neck scrape, she felt the sting of a blow far too fierce, and she felt the trickle of blood from the side of her mouth. Something in her panicked. That was too hard, far too hard, she thought as the flesh he had struck immediately started to blacken and bruise. She tried to remember the safety word again, but it was gone, lost within the evil of his words and the malice of his eyes. Yet, despite the pain, or perhaps because of it, she felt her vagina moisten and her nipples harden.

He sniffed the air and his eyes flashed. He lent across her and licked the trickle of blood and for a second, just a second, she thought his eyes had flashed red. His tongue was smooth against her aching flesh and the feel of it sent an exquisite feeling coursing through her body, causing her to squirm despite her tight bonds.

He had driven her back to his apartment. Part of her screamed no. She didn't know who he was, she didn't know if he could be trusted. Yet the larger part of her was lost in his invasive presence, the sheer animal brutality that seemed to seep out of his every pore. His movements were bestial, primitive, as though he could barely contain the power in his limbs and had to deliberately hide his strength. She obeyed that lowest, most primal part of herself that desired to be with him.

The apartment was luxurious. As they had entered his fingers flickered over a keypad, too quick to see what he had pressed, and a small red LED had flickered out to be replaced with a green one.

She was suddenly possessed with a sense of daring. She ran her hand down his arm, feeling the taught muscles, hard as steel, through the soft silk of his shirt. He glanced at her and her hand dropped away. She knew that she had invoked his displeasure from that brief glimpse of his eyes and the malicious scorn they contained. He had not given her permission to touch him, she must always ask for permission.

He led her to a room that was shrouded in darkness. As they entered his finger moved across a dimmer switch, illuminating a single spot lamp that focused on the Saint Andrew's cross placed purposefully in the centre of the otherwise bare room.

She should have known then. He did not offer a safety word as he manoeuvred her towards the apparatus and he was too forceful as he hooked the leather straps around her wrists and ankles. She was still dressed, she realised. His fingers grabbed hold of the fabric of her blouse and ripped. And again and again, with all her clothes. They dropped in tatters around her feet. She should have been angry, the clothes were designer, but the dominance of the act made her forget such things, it thrilled her to her very core.

A small voice told her that this was very wrong. In the mirror world of the S&M scene it was the Submissive who was truly in control. There was always a subtle trade in power. The Submissive dictated how far things could go; the Dominant was ultimately subject to their will. But not this time, he had total authority over her and she knew it.

"Safety word…" Her voice seemed so small, so weak, almost pleading.

He told her.

Why couldn't she remember it?

His hand flashed out again, shattering her memory once more, though this time he did not strike her. Rather, his nails clawed the soft pink flesh of her breasts, leaving trails of crimson weeping in their wake. It was like fire and she felt fear burning at the back of her throat. Again he licked the blood.

"What is your name?"

"I don't know…" She admitted.

"You don't know? You don't know! You stupid little whore."

"Yes." She confessed, "I'm a stupid little whore Master."

He looked at her for a moment, as though he was weighing something up and then he leant towards her. "You know, don't you?" He whispered, his voice rich and deep. "You know that you are going to die."

There was something within his voice, something that convinced her that his words were sincere and this was not part of a game. He intended to kill her, she knew it and part of her, the part that had screamed no when she got into his car, had always known it. She began to weep, her breath scratching in her chest.

"I promise you this, though," he added, "By the time it comes you will embrace it."

Her mind raced, searching again for the safety word, despite the fact that she now knew for certain that it was utterly useless. She felt a dread deeper than anything she had ever felt before.

He lifted his hand again; she winced awaiting the next blow. Yet, inexplicably, he stopped. He seemed to sniff the air for a moment, and then ran to the window, vanishing into darkness as he left the circle of light around the cross until he pulled the drapes open and allowed the lights of the city to catch his silhouette.

"Danaan." The word meant nothing to her, but she could hear the fury in his voice as it growled out of his throat. In that instance she realised that none of his actions so far had been fuelled by anger, the rage captured in that single word was far more terrifying than anything he had done so far. Cold shivers exploded through her body and finally she understood what total fear was.

"What is that bitch doing here? Why New York?" The shout echoed around the room. For a second she thought she was safe, that his anger for this other person would cause him to forget her. Then he reeled around and his eyes shone with fury that was all for her.

"Well... I guess I'll deal with the Praetorian later. First things first... I promised that you would embrace your death, did I not? I learnt my art from the greatest master of pain who ever lived. Truly I could do to you things so terrible that they would make death the greatest pleasure you have ever felt...

"Yet you should know that Ymochel is a great deceiver. I have lied to the most powerful of all the creatures of the Earth and they believed my words."

His voice dropped in volume so that she had to strain to hear his words and yet they rang through her soul like the loud peal of a bell. "Your time has come…."

Her tears blurred her vision, yet through them she saw him shrug out of his silk shirt and trousers with an inexplicable fluidity.

He pulled the drapes closed; they shut with a certain finality as he vanished into darkness.

Then he was approaching her, caught in the spot's soft light. He moved gracefully, slowly towards her, his massive penis erect.

His approach might have taken seconds or hours, she couldn't know, time had lost all meaning. Suddenly he was upon her.

She screamed as he forced his enormous member into her, causing a trickle of blood to run down her thigh from the torn tissue, unable to know that the pain was nothing compared to that which was to come.

He stood there, thrust deep inside her, looking at her. Her scream pierced the night as she watched his eyes turn unnaturally red and his fangs slide from his gums. A scream drowned by the next as he sank the ivory daggers into her neck. If the bite of the Children of Shang-Di could give pleasure then it was as nothing to the agony that the bite of the Children of the Leech could bestow.

As he bit deep into her smooth throat an image filled his mind's eye, a vision of memory. He saw another room, a darkened basement festooned with shadow, and in it equipment to which he was strapped. He remembered the searing agony that engulfed his entire being and then the vision was gone replaced only with anger, not burning within him but chilling his heart. Anger as cold as ice, which he channeled entirely towards his victim.

She screamed and screamed again, her voice trapped within the soundproofed apartment. The fangs were embedded deep in her neck, his mouth fixed as he suckled her blood whilst his pelvis thrust to the rhythm of her cries, hard thrusts that tore again and again at her sensitive vaginal tissue. He fed upon her agony as well as her blood, her suffering lending the crimson draft a spicy aftertaste. He enjoyed her as only a Child of the Velvet could. He enjoyed every aspect of the sadistic rape, and draining, as only a creature addicted to pure sensation was able, taking extra pleasure from the vicarious emotions imprinted chemically into her crimson lifeblood. The pain she felt was so intense that her screams continued, only ending when the last of her strength escaped her body.

As her soul fled its fleshy prison Ymochel, or Michael as he called himself presently, released his dead sperm into her ripped and bloodied sex. As he turned away his mind was already forgetting the broken plaything that hung limp on the cross, instead ice cold thoughts of revenge to be exacted flooded his mind, entwining with the sweet memories of a vengeance almost two millennium old.

Chapter Four

Pompeii – 0074

Three couches had been set out in the atrium of the villa. One was empty but on one led the vampire ancient Uriel, known as the Leech due to his significant capacity for blood consumption. He did not generally entertain human guests, but found it a necessity when he guided the direction of the Empire.

This was one such night and his guest, Senator Septimus, led upon the third couch. Uriel's concubines played the role of servant for the night, all three resentful of the fact that they were expected to wait upon a mortal. It was clear that Uriel was aware of their abhorrence of the roles they were forced to play, and the ancient enjoyed their ire. It was good to remind them of their place from time to time.

The pungent aroma of incense permeated the night air, as braziers smouldered, the smoke spiralling lazily into the night sky towards the distant stars. The Greeks claimed that the stars depicted the Gods and heroes, immortalised forever in the night sky. Other cultures had said that each star was a God looking down onto mortal man. Uriel believed neither. He had lived too long to believe in Gods. As far as he was concerned the closest thing to divinity were the seven ancients who ruled the Concilium. Immortal and powerful beings who governed the vampires and, in truth, the destiny of mortal man.

The Senator held up his cup and shook it in the general direction of the servants. This time it was not one of the vampires that approached with wine but Severus, a mortal who served Uriel during the daylight hours. He poured the sweet red wine into the Senator's cup and then backed away dutifully.

Septimus was no longer a young man but he still appreciated the finer things in life. His path had become entwined with Uriel's some ten years previously and since that time his star had been in ascendance. He ran his hand across his bald crown, wiping the sweat away and wondered when the obese merchant would finally bring up the subject of why he had been invited to the villa. Not that he minded, whenever Uriel revealed his thoughts it invariably led Septimus to more wealth and power.

The Senator reached down and picked some food from one of the trays on the floor before him. If he had noticed that his host had not eaten anything himself he was too polite and politically astute to mention it.

As Septimus pushed the salty meat into his mouth, a young man walked into the atrium. The older man was struck by the beauty of the youth. His hair was cut short, after the fashion in Rome, and his features were perfect. He was, the Senator guessed, some twenty years old. Septimus had never been one who was attracted to boys but, he mused, this one was so beautiful that he could be persuaded to explore such intimacies.

"Ah, Remus," the Vampire addressed the youth, "I wondered when you would deign to join us." Turning to the Senator he added, "Septimus, may I introduce my son Remus."

Remus took his place on the third couch, at his father's right hand. The Senator might have laughed at the pretension of the merchant, naming his son after one of the twins who had founded the glory that was Rome. He knew, however, that Uriel had played no small part in the direction of the Empire over the last decade. He was not aware, of course, that Uriel had been instrumental in making the Empire as it was for centuries.

"Now, good Septimus, I hate to bring this up but something has been on my mind of late."

The Senator nodded, waiting for Uriel to reveal his scheme.

"There is a Senator who concerns me. Do you know Litugenus?"

Septimus confirmed he did, inwardly smiling. If Litugenus had come to Uriel's attention then his days were surely numbered. "I believe he has espoused seditious ideas to the Senate, Master Uriel. He seeks to bring about the old days when the Senate had power over the Emperor." Uriel nodded, allowing the power of Rome to reside in the Senate had proven disastrous. He had guided the Empire towards a state where the rule of the Emperor was unquestioned, except of course by himself.

"Is it true that he taught a slave letters, encouraged him to think for himself?"

"I believe so, a Nubian by all accounts."

Uriel laughed deeply, "What do you make of that my son, teaching a Nubian letters, allowing him run of the household."

"It is said that these Nubian's are animals, father," answered Remus, "And cannot be taught civilised ways. I myself do not believe that and the very fact that this slave has been taught letters proves such nonsense to be untrue. However, if history has taught us anything, it is that we must not allow slaves to aspire above their station."

Septimus laughed, "You speak wisely, young Remus, but tell me, what history you speak of, exactly?"

"Why the revolt of Spartacus," Remus replied, whilst barely containing an ironic smile at being called young by the mortal, "Which, if my memory of history serves me correctly, began on the self-same Mountain that dominates the view from my father's villa." He took a sip from the cup that Severus had quietly brought him. The cup did not contain wine, but blood. As the coppery taste filled his senses Remus felt a pang of the hunger, which the blood in the cup could do nothing to abate. Once removed from the body, blood soon lost the vitality that the vampires craved. The taste of stored blood was pleasant enough and useful in situations such as this, when they wished to pass for human, but just did not satisfy. Some of the Velvet had tried animal blood, but even when taken straight from the body it did nothing to abate the hunger. Only direct feeding from a human would suffice.

"Your son knows his history well." Septimus was continuing the conversation with Uriel.

"He does indeed," replied the Leech, though he did not add that Remus should remember it perfectly for he had been forced to intervene directly, at Uriel's command, to bring the slaves' revolt to an end. "It is not, however, his liberal attitude towards his slaves which worries me. Nor his troublesome, but ineffectual, longing for the old days of power residing with the Senate. After all, if his views were any threat I am sure that Vespasian would have dealt with the situation by now," Uriel laughed as did the Senator, both knew that the Emperor would broke no serious threat from the senate.

"No," He continued, his laughter suddenly dead and the word cutting through Septimus' mirth. "These things do not cause me concern, but I believe he is a supporter of the Judean Cult which has become popular recently."

Septimus nodded, Litugenus had indeed been advocating the virtues of the cult. The Senator did not see the point of it personally; a single God was surely not enough for any religion, the simplicity of their faith betrayed it as erroneous. His eyes glanced in the direction of the mosaics of the Gods that lined the atrium and he silently thanked them for their generosity. If they had not led him to the merchant his star may have faded and died away, he may have ended his days a toothless old Senator barking ineffectually at the Empire. Now he was a force within the Senate. If he needed any evidence that his Gods were real his recent history was it.

"This cult," Uriel continued, "Is not good for Rome, but Litugenus is popular despite his faults and may persuade others that it has virtue. It would be terrible if…" He paused for just a moment. "If some scandal should befall the Senator's house."

Nothing more was said on the subject for nothing more needed to be said. Senator Litugenus' fate was sealed. Septimus was delighted, he could see his star rising higher and, now that business was concluded, the real entertainment could begin.

Two slaves were brought into the atrium and were both given tiny knives, wickedly sharp but hardly capable of penetrating deeply. On command they started to circle each other. Uriel hated to waste good food thus, but it was believed that such entertainment occurred regularly, hence the villa's need for so many slaves. Letting someone of the Senator's standing watch a brutal gladiatorial match was logical. To not do so would seem like a slight and damage the hard work Uriel put into maintaining his shadowy control over the Empire. Letting his guest see what he expected only confirmed the stories.

The slaves had been promised that the winner would enjoy their freedom. Given the value of the prize the slaves went at each other with incredible vigour, though the sharp little knives ensured that the fight would be both protracted and bloody.

Septimus brought a goblet of wine to his lips and drank deeply so as to moisten his mouth, which had become dry with anticipation. He loved gladiatorial sports, and was a frequent visitor to the games in Rome, but he loved these more intimate bouts even more. There was a palpable feeling of danger when the combatants fought so close; he knew he would be able to smell the sweat and the blood, he knew that their blows might fall upon each other within inches of him. The anticipation was almost sexual.

The two men were evenly matched, both selected for their physical prowess. Both wore small loin clothes, but were otherwise naked and, after a few minutes, both their bodies were covered in small slashes that wept blood, the sticky red fluid blending with the sweat that clung to their bodies.

The Senator was cheering loudly, his eyes fixed upon the spectacle, whilst both Remus and Uriel led upon their couches, watching impassively, containing the hunger that the sight and scent of the freshly spilt blood was stirring within them.

Uriel looked over at Augustine. The young concubine's eyes had misted over with a red sheen and his fangs protruded over his bottom lip. Uriel gestured angrily towards him, but he was oblivious to his master, so he signalled instead to Diana and pointed at the transforming male. Understanding immediately she took Augustine by the arm and led him from the atrium.

Septimus noticed them leave, luckily only seeing their backs as they disappeared from the garden; he glanced quizzically across at Uriel.

"Some of my servants have weak stomachs for such violence, Augustine finds such entertainment disturbing." He hid his ire with a laugh, "A weakness of character, I'm sure you would agree."

Septimus nodded, "That is why, my good Uriel, some of us are destined to wield power and others are not." With that he turned his attention back to the contest.

One of the slaves was flagging; he retreated from the other, backing across the atrium. His foot slipped in spilt blood and he fell heavily backwards. That was all the opening his competitor needed.

The standing slave leapt at his fallen enemy and plunged the little dagger hard into his throat, the force of the thrust causing both the blade and the hilt to rip through the hard cartilage. Blood welled up around the small blade, bubbling at the wound and then flowing freely as the weapon was wrenched out of the throat. The fallen slave immediately became limp, the light dying from his eyes. The contest had ended.

Septimus applauded loudly, whilst Uriel gestured to Mercia. Nodding to her master, she took the knife from the victor and led him away.

Severus stood before the Senator and refilled his cup. Septimus swallowed a mouthful of the wine, the red liquid spilling over his lips and splattering the white cloth of his robe. Within moments the Senator fell into a deep sleep, the cup tumbling from his fingers and clattering onto a tray of food, wine seeping around the salted fish. Severus lifted him from the couch, throwing a flaccid arm over his shoulder and grabbing the limp mortal around his waist. Stumbling, he half carried and half dragged the slumbering Senator towards his room.

Uriel invariably drugged his rare mortal guests before the night could come to an end. The vampires of the household had yet to feed and he had business to discuss with Remus. In the morning Septimus would believe he had passed out through too much wine.

"This Judean cult worries me Remus. They preach love but I see another hand in it." Uriel's chins wobbled as he spoke.

"Bloodfather, it is just another religious cult, it will pass." The cult had been a faction of the Hebrew religion, but the destruction of the temple in Jerusalem had seen the cult open its arms to all races. That, Remus would have to agree, was unusual in the Judaic cults, but even so.

"Maybe, but I believe I have looked into their philosophy a little deeper than you have." He paused for a moment. Severus had entered the atrium, busying himself about his duties. The mortal was fully aware of what his master and the rest of the household were. Uriel had needed a daylight servant and had conditioned the man well. He should have been confident in the mortal's loyalty but he was unable to bring himself to fully trust the man. Once Severus had left the garden again he continued.

"At the core of the cult is a curious ceremony that imitates the drinking of blood, blood that leads to eternal life, though wine is used to emulate the crimson draft," Uriel explained.

Humans using wine to mimic blood, much as the Velvet used blood to mimic wine when masquerading as mortal, and the promise of life eternal. It seemed too much to be a coincidence. "So you believe one of the Velvet manipulates it?"

"I suspect the Qutrub has a hand in it. If so he offends me, he meddles within the confines of the Empire."

"Why would he…"

"Why does the Flesh do anything? The cult will be directed towards acts of violence, he gains his pleasure from that. Even more so as he manipulates a message of peace and turns that message to violence. If he can cause consternation within the Empire whilst he does this then the slight against me will give him further pleasure."

Remus looked over at his Bloodfather, "Surely then the Concilium should force him to cease? They have already declared Rome yours."

"When Nero attacked the cult thirty years ago, they should have been eradicated. The fact that they have re-emerged, that they flourish even, indicates that someone manipulates them. But, before I bring this matter before the Concilium, I need proof. Return to the Halls of the Concilium, see what you can discover."

"I will do as you ask bloodfather." Remus gave a curt nod.

Uriel's smile was lost within the folds of flesh, "Then it is settled. Have Severus bring my meal to my chambers, tell him that I desire the victor of the contest first."

He stood and left the atrium.

It almost slipped his notice, his mind firmly on Qutrub and his rival ancient's never-ending games, but as he passed the room in which the Senator was sleeping he realised the door was slightly ajar.

He pushed it further open and his anger exploded.

The senator had been carefully led upon a bed, but a second figure was in the room, knelt above the mortal. Augustine had come to Septimus and Augustine fed.

The ancient charged at his concubine, his speed astounding given his weight. The younger vampire was oblivious, lost within the joy of feeding.

Uriel pulled the young vampire sharply from the mortal and, on recognising his master, Augustine's face twisted into a mask of fear. The ancient threw him against the far wall of the room, the young vampire's head smashed against the partition, leaving a sticky trail of blood down the plaster as he slid to the floor.

Remus ran into the room.

"Get him out of here!" Uriel pointed at Augustine.

Remus pulled the vampire to his feet by his toga.

"Wait," Uriel walked over to them and looked at the concubine through narrowed eyes, his voice dropped into a dangerous whisper, "Augustine, I have given you life eternal, but remember that I can also take it away.

"During the slaves' fight you threatened to destroy our charade and now you feed from a mortal important to me. Luckily he lives still.

"Hear me now. If you break the rules of my house again I will bestow the true death upon you.

"Remus, have Severus tidy that up," he pointed at the wall and the cracks which had spread through the plaster from beneath the smear of blood, "And then have him tend to Septimus' wounds. I want him cleaned up before he awakens.

"Once the Senator has left I want that, "he indicated towards Augustine, "To spend a day caught in the sunlight. Let us see if a day trapped in the burning rays of Helios can improve his behaviour."

Panic brimmed in Augustine's eyes. A day would not kill him, but the pain would be unbearable. He thought for a second that he might try to plead clemency, but the furious look in Uriel's crimson eyes was enough to seal his mouth. He considered that he might search for an opportunity to run, but the ancient vampire would find him and his suffering would be so much worse than a day exposed to the sun, he knew that he would eventually pray for true death to release him from Uriel's retribution.

Remus looked at the young vampire and could only think that Augustine had been incredibly lucky to escape from Uriel's fury so lightly.

Chapter Five

The Land Beyond the Forest, 1819

The children of Radu writhed in the centre of the great hall. Twelve vampires had merged into an indistinguishable mass of bodies, legs and arms, excited genitalia, fangs and blood. Careful feeding and powerful sex, an orgy fit for the Sultan's palace. Perhaps the Sultan would have disagreed; twelve was barely an orgy after all. Then he would have looked closer and as his eyes caressed the scene he would have been forced to agree. If the Sultan had prized any two things above all else, they were the beautiful and the exotic. Each vampire in Radu's get was beautiful, the beauty of a human was a pre-requisite for him to turn one rather than consume one, and could the Sultan have ever found a creature more exotic than the nosferatu?

Of course the Sultan had long been dust, but the appetites that Radu had developed during his childhood incarceration in the Turk's court lived on into his unlife.

The orgy had lasted two hours so far, beginning when the sun had fallen behind the lofty Carpathians. Within minutes of starting the first orgasm had sounded, echoing loudly through the dusty halls. More and more followed. As a vampire became spent he or she would bite another, the orgasm fuelled blood of their fellows causing the excitement to blossom anew, lending fresh strength.

The orgy would continue for hours to come, Radu knew. He had both participated in the bacchanalian marathons, and, like tonight, had patiently observed them, carefully watching his children and absorbing the waves of orgasmic energy that reverberated around the room, feeling his own sexual tension growing until it felt that it might snap him in half. Eventually they would tire beyond a point were even the taking of blood could revive them. Then, as the sun threatened return, he would select one of his get. Tonight one would be sacrificed to his glory and power. One would give of their unlife and fall into the dust of true death.

For a second Radu became aware of something, an uninvited presence that flickered across his senses for a brief second. Yet that was impossible and he tried to dismiss the feeling. Then they appeared, and the impossible had become suddenly possible.

He should have sensed them as they encroached upon his lands, rather than the flicker that had just occurred. He should have been prepared.

The Praetorians stood around the hall, surrounding him and his, blocking all the possible paths of escape. Fear ran the course of his spine, a sensation almost alien to him, yet his get were oblivious in their ecstatic rutting, ignorant of the danger.

Why had his senses failed him? His bloodline was more sensitive to their own kind than most; he could normally perceive another vampire anywhere within a mile of himself. Perhaps it was the orgy, the waves of sexual energy produced, that had distracted his senses so.

Then he felt them, their presences unmasked. The Ancients. Shang-Di and Undjit. The witch bitch must have used her sorcery to conceal their approach. Radu's fear dissolved into despondency when his gaze fell across Ymochel, his Sponsor's eyes downcast, hands ceremonially chained by the thin silver links.

It was not meant to be this way.

He had known that he played a dangerous game, but had always believed that fate favoured the bold. The

Concilium should not have discovered his get, not yet. When he had received the summons, the telepathic death knell, he had realised that their suspicions had been raised. In all probability they had heard rumours born of peasant tales.

But to appear in such numbers, to invade his Schloß in such a way... They must have discovered his plans. But Radu, ignorant of Fenrir's visit and subsequent testimony before the Concilium, could not understand how.

Surely not Ymochel, surely after all that had happened his Sponsor had not betrayed him? No, he mused, wise in the ways and rules of the Concilium. Ymochel had just as much to loose. More than that, Ymochel, he knew, loved him.

It was not meant to be this way... his thoughts kept returning to that one simple phrase. He had been, was still, a Prince after all. Though Radu was oblivious of the judgement of Shang-Di, the Ancient had been correct in his assumption that the vampire still clung to the position he had held in his mortal life, that he continued to think in a mortal way despite the centuries that had passed. In his mortal life the act of ignoring the summons of a greater Power would not have elicited such an absolute show of strength, not at first, nor would his act of breaking the rules of such a Power.

In the mortal world a subtle game of political chess would have unfolded first, envoys would have been despatched. Envoys that could have been dealt with, secrets hidden from them, lies whispered in the night and perhaps seduction to his cause attempted. In the mortal world he would have been given time to prepare his troops for battle, time to consolidate his position.

He had squandered his time once, not believing that Rome and Bucharest would place his brother upon the throne of Walachia again, not conceiving that the Turks would abandon him.

They came and took his crown and he had looked for a way to escape the imprisonment that faced him. He had called out to the endless night and Ymochel had answered his call. Beautiful Ymochel with skin like midnight. Ymochel with the beautiful voice, his words dripping a seductive power that had led him from the path of the sun and into the soft embrace of the Velvet. A path Radu had never regretted walking, a path that offered infinitely more power than he lost with the spilling of his mortal blood. That power, he then discovered, was held by the Concilium. Not only held but also jealously guarded and this he had found distasteful. After all, he was a Prince and they were… older, nothing more. Thus the plan had been conceived. A plan that would give him the power their age had bestowed, that would furnish him with an army of vampires loyal only to him and strong enough that he might face the Concilium and their Praetorians. Eventually, he had hoped, strong enough to rule the Concilium.

His plans were young, however, too young. The Concilium was not meant to be aware of them yet. He looked around the dusty hall, frantically searching for a means of escape, but no path opened before him and he began to feel another long lost emotion stir within his heart. He felt panic.

Radu's eyes glanced across to Ymochel, the once proud vampire now humbled. This time he would not offer Radu a means of escape, this time he could not elevate the Walachian Prince above his enemies.

Radu knew his reaction was useless, and as that realisation came his panic fell abruptly away, replaced only with an icy hatred that clawed at his immortal heart. Some of his children had begun to stir, the presence of the Ancients pulling their senses away from the ongoing carnality, causing confusion as they began to acknowledge the vampires surrounding them.

It was not meant to be this way. The thought flashed in his mind once more, but no matter how true the sentiment it was a useless thought, there was only one path left, the path of defiance. Radu's voice was shrill, "Defend me, my children!"

The get of Radu rose. Those who had escaped the sexual snare earlier sprang to their feet; the others rose slowly, abandoning their copulations grudgingly. Yet all of them were prepared to fight, fang and claw. They looked at the new enemy, sizing the new vampires, assessing them. The Praetorians, however, needed no such preparation. The Praetorians, as one, struck and Radu could do naught but watch and cling to the vain hope that his outnumbered vampires might strike a blow deep into the heart of the Concilium. The prospect of a Pyrrhic victory was all he had left.

The hope proved not only vain, but also short lived. The battle was over almost before it had begun.

Outnumbered by vampires trained to hunt and kill their own, Radu's get fell quickly, each death marked by a small burst of psychic energy, the members of the get not old enough for their deaths to register beyond the hall. Laszlo lasted the longest. He was the most powerful of the get, he threw himself into the fray catching a female's hair and pulling her head back sharply. His mouth seized upon her throat and he ripped viciously backwards, causing her sluggish blood to ooze down her tunic, staining the white fabric with blood so dark it appeared black. The Praetorian fell, but Laszlo had only torn the fleshy front of the neck, enough to kill a mortal, but the neck was not severed and the flesh had begun to slowly heal as the stolen blood she had ingested that night forced the tissue to grow and knit together. Her mouth twisted into a silent scream as the healing began, intense pain flashing through her body as the flesh remade itself, unable to vocalise the scream through the torn throat and decimated larynx. Two more Praetorians fell upon Laszlo, quickly draining and decapitating the vampire.

Finally there was only Radu. Two Praetorians walked to him and took his arms. Radu shrugged them aside with ease, throwing them across the hall and shocking them with the immensity of his strength. Radu had fed upon his own, and fed well. He had selected only the strongest, stealing their life-force, their power. If all had gone to plan he would have devoured Laszlo's strength that very night.

He walked proudly to the centre of the carnage, head held high. Despite his great strength he knew that he could not defeat so many. He was doomed, of that he was sure, but he would face true death with a regal dignity. He knelt on the grey slabs of granite that formed the floor of his hall amongst the corpses of his get, so young that decay was only now taking its accelerated hold, forcing the flesh to slough into a dust that billowed around the fallen vampire Prince.

Shang-Di nodded to a Praetorian who circled the Prince. As she moved behind him he felt his muscles tense, his instincts wanting nothing more than for him to strike at the little bitch. Somehow he kept the temptation at bay, still determined to face his death with decorum.

Danaan stood above Radu's kneeling form. She too felt a tension, like her entire being was coiled ready to explode. He had shrugged the two Praetorians away as though they were mortals. Tentatively she placed her hands on his shoulder, feeling the tightness in his muscles. Yet despite it he made no attempt to move.

There was a pretension of nobility to his resignation, a notion, perhaps, that the Concilium might be able to break his body but never his spirit. She recognised the attitude, a pride shared by hundreds of minor nobles who had claimed the myriad regions of Eastern Europe over the centuries.

Folly, she thought, what good is pride when dead is still dead? She had known many of the nobles herself and they were all now dust, pride had not spared their mortality. Her head flashed through the air and her fangs pierced Radu's regal neck.

As he became weaker, as she stole his precious blood, his nobility and pride crumbled. The instinct to live took control. He tried to struggle, but the struggle was in vain, she had already tipped the balance between them. She had taken too much. She had his strength now and her hands forced his shoulders down, holding his body fast as she continued to drink his life away.

Then the blood slowed and became nothing but a sluggish trickle; she had reached the heights and could already feel his stolen strength ebbing away.

Her hands slipped around his waist, rising sensuously to his breast. Her fingers dug deep into the flesh, curling below the rib cage. The breastbone ripped as though it was paper and her hand snaked through the gore to clutch his weakly beating heart. With a gesture it was torn from his torso. Danaan squeezed, the final drops of Radu's blood running down her snow-white wrist, the heart calcifying and then crumbling to dust as his life became permanently hers.

Yet Danaan did not notice the organs decay, or the rapid corruption of Radu's fallen body. It was as though a star had exploded in her mind, as power coursed wildly through her veins. She had bestowed true death once before as part of her duties, but the life-force she had taken then was nothing like Radu's. When she would look back at the moment she would realise the true immensity of the power she had stolen. She would understand why such a creature would be a threat to the Concilium, that he had used the blood of his get to rapidly evolve himself to something she guessed was more akin to one of the older vampires than a mere fledgling. And now that power was hers. Shang-Di had been shrewd in choosing her to bestow the punishment. The Emperor had ensured that the power Radu had created was now of his bloodline, the honour he had bestowed upon Danaan was no more than the necessity of politics.

As her mind cleared she looked up and her eyes met Ymochel's. Their gazes locked and she felt a smoldering hatred, as fierce as Radu's blood had been powerful, and the hatred seemed reserved exclusively for her.

Eventually she was able to stand and make her way cautiously out of the Schloß. Her legs shaking with each step, unused to the new strength she possessed.

Chapter Six

Pompeii – 0079

The sun beat down, casting its fiery glow into the villa. The Nubian vampire named Ymochel stood in the bright rays, still bemused by the fact that his skin did not blister and burn, though he had stood in the bright rays many times before.

His master, Uriel, had grudgingly entrusted him with the secret, as he had desired a daylight servant and yet found himself unable to fully trust mortals more and more, though he meddled often enough in their affairs. The Leech had told him to guard the secret under pain of death, it was not known by many, even the Praetorians had not divined the truth. If enough blood was ingested then the sun would not burn. It took many victims, the draining of at least four before the night was finished. The other vampires in the household did not know why Ymochel gorged himself so, nor why Uriel the Leech allowed it, and jealous that the master had elevated him to favourite they had begun to name him Little Leech.

In truth it should have been an easy secret to discover. All the Children of the Velvet had, at one time or another, gorged themselves. Yet still it remained a guarded secret, for if one gorged too much, as Uriel often did, the excess blood would force a deep stupor upon the vampire. The secret was to take just enough, and then be brave enough to walk into the sun, knowing it should slowly and painfully reduce their preternaturally animated body to ashes. It was this need for reckless bravery that successfully guarded the secret. Ymochel, himself, had not been brave the first time; he had been forced into the searing sunlight by Uriel, fearing his master's wrath more than he feared the destructive rays of Helios.

Ymochel stood in the bright sunlight and considered the bittersweet story that had been his life. He was still a youth when his father had sold him to the slavers. He should not blame his father, he supposed in his more generous moments, for he had been the second son and his family were poor. Though still a youth, he was large for his age and the slavers had given his father many coins for a boy who could one day serve in a galley or fight in the arenas. He remembered that his mother had cried and begged his father, in the name of the ancestors, not to do this thing, but his father had been determined.

Fate had, at least, cast a wan smile upon him for a while. His first master recognised that he was not slow of wit, despite his size, and had taught him letters. He wanted a slave who could help run the household, who could deal with traders and maintain order. For a short time he had been happy, his master treated him well and he had responsibility, if not freedom.

Then the scandal came, his master fell from grace and his property was seized. Every fibre told him to run, but an escaped slave was as good as dead and a gladiator, for he believed that is what he would be forced to become, could survive as long as he could fight and maintain the favour of the baying crowd.

But the arena was not to be his fate. He was bought by a wealthy patriarch, who lived below the great Mount Vesuvius. Perhaps the new master would recognise my skills, he thought, perhaps I will serve as I served my former master. Such thoughts vanished as he was placed in the slave pen and the stories were whispered of how slaves would be removed, night after night, never to be seen again.

His fellow slaves had come to believe that those who were taken each night were forced to fight bloody gladiatorial battles for the patriarch's amusement. Indeed this was the story told to the numerous slavers that sold the household the innumerable slaves needed in the villa. Little did they know that their fate was to feed Master Uriel's unending appetites.

Ymochel had been lucky. Uriel had wanted a vampire to govern his household during the sunlight hours, distrustful of the human, Severus, whom he relied upon and unwilling to turn him. At times Ymochel mused that it was his strength, or his knowledge of letters, that had caused the ancient to choose him. In truth, however, it was his beauty, for Uriel prized beauty above all else in his get. It was for this reason that Severus had become food rather than being transformed into one of the Velvet. Though he was by no means ugly, his physical beauty did not match the ideals that Uriel demanded of his Bloodline.

So it was, some five years earlier, that Ymochel had been brought into the Velvet. Uriel quickly instructed him with regard to his duties, and the laws that seemed to govern him, but not his master. He taught him the secret of day-walking and gave him charge of the villa.

"In many respects", he muttered to himself, "I was lucky, though I am still no more than a slave".

This, of course, was true. Indeed all the get of Uriel within the villa were little more than slaves, none of them free to leave their Bloodfather of their own volition. The others were concubines, two female and a male, playthings to feed Uriel's sexual appetites. Less bound, in some respects, than Ymochel, as Uriel's cravings switched from blood to flesh rarely. Ymochel had, at first, been astounded that the undead could feel sexual desire. He quickly learnt that, in truth, sex and death were just two sides of the same coin. He also learnt that he too had these desires and would from time to time avail himself of one of the mortal slaves before feeding upon them.

In time they would all have to leave the villa, everyone in the household knew that though none spoke of it. Uriel's endless need for slaves had not gone unnoticed. Though none could care what a master did with his property, it caused mortal eyes to cast towards the villa. Also Uriel had been in residence for several years, it would be prudent to vanish, to leave the legend of the villa to the mists of time and take residence elsewhere.

Wherever they went, Ymochel ruminated, he would still be a slave. He would still have to perform the same role for the bloated ancient. Perhaps it would have been better if he had become nothing more than fodder for the Leech's bloodlust. His servitude stretched out before him through the endless millennia. He hated his Bloodfather with a passion he had never been able to find for the human slave owners of the empire.

He ran a hand over his bald crown. They had kept his head shaved when he was mortal and that hair would never grow now. The skin of his head was smooth and dry; the fierce sun could not coax a sweat from undead flesh all it could do was burn. His hand moved down and stroked his stomach, rock hard and muscular beneath his fingers. He had gorged himself the night before and still wondered why, as he had the first time, his stomach did not distend. It was as though the blood was absorbed into every pore of his body, like a sponge soaking water. Even a sponge expands, he mused, why not the body of Velvet?

His reverie was broken as his sharp awareness sensed the approach of humans walking towards the villa. The slaver had returned.

Ymochel strode purposefully into the atrium of the villa, awaiting the slaver's entrance. As he waited he gazed at the mural of Priapus. The image signified Uriel's great wealth, the enormous phallus thrusting from between the God's legs bestowing fertility upon the household, or so the priests would have had them believe. In truth, thought the Nubian vampire, what fertility could there be in the house of the dead? If anything this was a place that sucked the very life out of the Empire, drop by crimson drop.

His eyes were still upon the statue when Daedalus entered the atrium, hailing Ymochel as he came. "Ah, good Sir," the slavers words a rasp, the pain of calling a slave he had sold to the household by an honorific was obvious in his voice, "Surely the Gods smile upon us today, Priapus in particular." He nodded subtly at the mural Ymochel had just studied.

Ymochel turned to face the human, his eyes working across the weathered features, pausing, imperceptibly, at the delicate pulse that throbbed tantalisingly at the slavers neck. Ymochel's fangs instinctively strained at his gums, but his will overcame instinct. His time in the sun had caused the hunger within him to stir, despite the four he had drained the night before. It was another skill the slave had been forced to develop, an exquisite self control beyond that considered normal amongst the Children, more so amongst his Bloodline.

"May I poor you wine Daedalus?" Ymochel's voice was rich and filled with better humour than his thoughts.

The slaver wiped his hands across his weather-stained toga, and then smiled. "Wine, good Ymochel, would be most welcome."

"Tell me," the slaver continued as the vampire passed him a goblet brimming with wine, "Would it be possible to speak to your master."

The impudence, thought Ymochel, but his words of reply were sweet, "I regret that cannot be, my Master is indisposed, but if you have any problems I am able to deal with them for you."

"I was hoping to be able to visit your master one evening."

A strange request, Uriel had been careful to ensure that these slavers knew he prized his privacy. "For what purpose?"

The slaver slapped at an insect that had settled on his neck before explaining. "Ymochel, I have been pleased to deal with your master for many years now. Indeed the business he offers me is so great that he has become my sole customer. Rumours abound regarding his... entertainment, the fights to the death that he puts his purchases to. All believe that these must be great spectacles, yet none have seen them."

This was not entirely true. Uriel always ensured that Senators visiting Pompeii were invited to the villa, and entertained them as though he were a human host, it was the vampire's way of ensuring that his plans for the Empire were enacted.

Ymochel looked impassively at the squalid human before him, as the trader took a large gulp from the goblet, and then helped himself to more wine from the pitcher. Daedalus looked up and, on seeing the expression on the Nubian's face added, "It would be a great honour for me if I were to be allowed to visit his entertainment, I would even bring special gifts for Master Uriel."

Ymochel raised an eyebrow, "Special gifts?"

"I may be able to acquire gladiatorial stock destined for Rome, I am sure that they would add much to the evening's entertainment."

Ymochel had considered dismissing the man out of hand, but these mortals sounded interesting. Strong, with good blood no doubt. "Daedalus, I am sure that they would be impressive specimens, but you are aware that my Master values his privacy. I cannot agree your request myself, but I will promise you I will communicate it to my master and send word as soon as he makes his feelings known. Now, should we to business?"

With that he directed the slaver back down the vestibule, out towards the slaves he knew would be waiting. The Children of Uriel were not known for their mentalist abilities, but even Ymochel, such a young Fledgling, could feel the smugness emanating from the slaver. He had expected to be refused out of hand, quite obviously, and now felt that Ymochel had, if not opened the door, at least left it ajar.

*****

The sun had reached its zenith by the time Ymochel had placed the twenty new slaves in their cells. The cells had been bedrooms once, overlooking the villa's peristylium. The view of the small trees, the colonnades and statues, was probably a blessing for the slaves, a last view of paradise before they descended into Tarterus; though how grateful they were for this was debatable.

Daedalus had returned to Pompeii, some fifteen or so miles along the coast. Ymochel had discovered that he was not going to stop in Pompeii but continue along the coast to Herculaneum. The vampire had promised to send news of his master's decision to there.

It seemed for a second that the world's voice had been stilled. The birds had grown suddenly silent; the drone of insects had quietened to nothing. Ymochel's acute senses were aware that something was amiss, though he knew not what. Then all was a cacophony, as the world seemed to vibrate. Loose roof tiles fell into the peristylium and statues began to sway. The waters in the fountains, which sat in each corner of the garden, started to slosh, pouring over the marble bowls and spilling onto the ground. The slaves started to scream in their cells, begging their new master to free them.

Ymochel ran through the villa and out onto the road. He had heard tales of the times when the earth would tremble, as though the land were a giant, shaking off his sleep and trying to rise. Nothing could have prepared the vampire for what he actually saw.

The great mountain that towered above the landscape was throwing plumes of smoke into the air; its slopes were littered with fires. The smoke was billowing into a mushroom and spreading out, creating a cloud that darkened the skies above Pompeii.

Ymochel was stunned, unable to move, unable to comprehend the vista before him. Seconds stretched into hours, in his perception. It seemed that rain started to fall upon the distant city, though in truth it was ash and blackened stones that rained onto the streets and rooftops of Pompeii.

Uriel. His master's name came unbidden into his mind, though it was not the ancient's safety he was concerned for, but surely he would understand what was happening? The ancient would know what to do.

Ymochel ran back into the villa, through the atrium and into the peristylium. As he entered the open garden a large statue of Priapus fell forwards, its collapse snapping off the huge, erect marble phallus. Undeniably it was a bad omen.

The slaves had stopped screaming, but now wept and wailed. One repeated over and over that the world was ending.

Ignoring them, Ymochel strode across to the door to Uriel's chambers. Despite all that was happening he knocked at the door and waited to be summoned, but no summons came. After a few moments he steeled himself, gripped the door handle and pushed inwards. He waited a few seconds more, resisted the mortal habit of taking a deep breath, and strode into the Bloodfather's lair.

Once the daylight sleep stole upon the Children of the Velvet it was difficult for them to be roused from their death-like stupor. Difficult, but not impossible, depending on the vampire in question. Some fell into the stupor as soon as the sun kissed the horizon and refused to wake until it vanished again. Others could fight the stupor, staying awake as the sun stretched its hand over the landscape. Some roused before it set, whilst others could not wake until it had totally vanished from the sky. However, a rude awakening from the stupor could prove disastrous to the one who roused the slumbering vampire. Instincts firing before consciousness could take hold, the sleeping vampire might well tear the offending throat out. A gentle approach was assuredly the safest.

Whilst their Bloodline were not strong mentalists, by using physical contact it should have been possible for Ymochel to enter his Bloodfather's thoughts and rouse the sleeping ancient. No matter how he tried, however, Uriel refused to wake. In desperation the Fledgling grabbed his master's shoulders and began to shake him, heedless of the danger, and the fact that the anger of the mountain, which shook the villa still, had failed to rouse Uriel from his stupor.

Eventually the Fledgling gave up, realising that the master had gorged on so many slaves the previous night that awakening him would be all but impossible. Instead he sat by his master and studied the ancient as he slept.

Uriel had never been a small man, as a mortal he had partaken of all that he could. When he had come into the Velvet, in a time so long before only the ancients were able to remember the history, his undead body had kept the bulk gained as a mortal and the appetites as well. Ymochel did not know how the ancients had become cursed, as he saw it though they would say blessed, with unlife. None shared such information with the younger vampires, but Uriel's dark parent must have been one possessed of a particularly wicked humour. Why else create such an epitome of gluttony for all eternity?

The Leech's frame was vast with blubber, his eyes and nose lost within the lunar expanse of his face. His fangs seemed small, pressed over his thick lips and his lank hair clung in grey lumps to his domed head. He was the antithesis of the rest of the Bloodline; as though the beautiful, lean creatures he created were in some way a recompense for his vast ugliness.

Ymochel knew only too well, however, the preternatural strength that crept through his jelly like arms. The blood of millennia ran sluggishly through the Leech's veins. He could snap a Fledgling like Ymochel in half, yet in that moment he lay as helpless as a child in his gluttonous trance.

The door flew open and Ymochel span around to see Augustine, Uriel's male concubine.

"What is happening?" The vampire's voice was shrill was terror.

"Calm yourself Augustine…" Ymochel's voice was surprisingly steady, the Nubian unwilling to allow the concubine to know that he was as confused and as scared as the other.

"Calm! Calm little Leech! I awake to find the villa shaking around me. The sky is black, yet I sense no night. The girls sleep still. It woke you too, didn't it, it woke you!"

"Yes," he lied, "It woke me too."

"Where is Severus?" Referring to the mortal daylight guardian before Ymochel had been given the Velvet Kiss. His services no longer needed, Uriel had gorged upon his blood but the concubines had not been informed of that, they believed he still served the villa during the day and left, at Uriel's command, at dusk.

"He's not here."

"What! Unprotected whilst the world ends around us!"

"The world is not ending, see our Master sleeps peacefully, if we were in danger he would surely rise." Ymochel wished he could believe his own words.

A particularly strong tremor struck the house causing a vase in the Master's chamber to tumble over and smash upon the mosaic floor, shards scattering like seeds on the wind across the network of cracks that spread through the delicate tiles. "Safe!" Shrieked Augustine, "No… not safe… the Master… you've done something."

In an instant Augustine's demeanour changed, his fangs extended and his nails grew into talons, his eyes flashed red and he leaped at the younger Fledgling. It should have been over in an instant, the concubine had over a century of unlife more than Ymochel, the blood growing stronger with each passing year.

Augustine was not as well fed as the Nubian, however, he had been waken from his sleep and was not used to functioning within the hours of the sun, though the cloud of ash gushing from Vesuvius had all but turned the day into night.

Ymochel avoided the lunge and, like a flash, was on the concubine's back. He buried his fangs into the neck of the vampire and began to feed. The feeling was unlike anything Ymochel had experienced. Feeding from a human offered strength, but nothing like the power Augustine's blood gave him. The concubine's body became limp, he submitted to the Nubian who, eventually, let him fall.

Where there had once been derision, there was now only timidity. Ymochel had gained dominance over the concubine. "Return to your room, and do not emerge until the Master awakens."

Augustine looked up at him with defeated eyes, nodded and slunk away.

Ymochel positioned himself on the floor next to the Leech. He wished he could be as confident as he had sounded, yet part of him felt Augustine had been right, it felt as though the world was ending. Unable to know what else to do he sat patiently waiting for the Bloodfather to awaken, enjoying the power he had stolen from Augustine, though it was quickly evaporating, and wondering what Uriel's blood would feel like running through his undead veins. Knowing it had once had the power to pull him from the abyss of death, and contemplating what power it would bestow to him now.

Chapter seven

New York – 2000

Beatrice looked from the row of figures on the VDU, to the papers on her desk and then back again. It was no good, the numbers continued to swirl in front of her, figures jumping from column to column in her vision. As hard as she stared, she just could not persuade the figures on the screen and those on paper to reconcile with each other, it was as though they purposefully conspired to frustrate her efforts. She pushed a hand through her shoulder length blonde hair and removed her thin-framed glasses, placing them gently on the desk. Her fingers, tipped with well-manicured, red painted nails, gently squeezed the corners of her eyes, as though that could make them focus upon the work at hand. In her heart she knew it was no good, she had burned out for the day and could do nothing more constructive on the project. If she continued working she would simply make mistakes. She needed sleep.

She pushed the glasses back onto the bridge of her nose, took the mouse in hand and saved the work, then she shutdown her PC. The ringing of the phone made her jump involuntarily. Who the Hell, she thought to herself. It was New Years day; no one should be calling the office on New Years day. For God's sake, she shouldn't be working on New Years day.

She picked up the receiver, "Hello…"

"Hi babe," the voice of Steve, her boyfriend, broke through her tired greeting, "How's it going?"

"Oh okay I guess, I'm dead beat though," She replied.

"I'm not surprised, what sort of asshole makes his staff work on New Years day?"

Beatrice sighed, Steve had not been happy with the fact that she had gone into work. He insisted that she had been forced to when, in truth, she had chosen to work. She honestly felt that the project was more important than the holiday, even if it was a holiday that would only come around once in a thousand years.

"The work is important…"

"Yeah, yeah… So important that you had to have a shit time last night, and miss out on a holiday today?"

He was right, the millennium celebrations had been somewhat of an anti-climax. Because she knew she was working the next day Beatrice had only allowed herself a couple of glasses of wine. Steve on the other hand, and their friends, had become very drunk. Memories of drunken revellers, as seen through sober eyes, came flooding into mind as did the remembrance of feelings of frustration and irritation that had marked her New Year. If the night before had been a disaster, she decided, it was more down to his drunken state than anything else. She said as much.

"Oh come on. Once in a lifetime babe…"

"It's just not so much fun being around drunks when you're sober."

"And whose fault is that?"

"Steve, this project is damned important to me, it could mean a promotion." So yeah, she added silently, I will work rather than party. I intend to make something of my life.

"So you've got to give up on all the fun in life to get on then, doesn't sound worth it to me." There was a peevish edge to his voice.

"Well that figures," her voice had become icily cold, "You've never stuck at anything in your life."

"I've stuck at you, though God only knows why…" His voice had raised, anger creeping into his tone.

"Well if that's how you feel…"

His voice dropped slightly, "Look I didn't want to argue, I just wanted to see if you were alright and arrange to come over to your place."

It was an olive branch of sorts she supposed, "I'm sorry honey, I just would like a little support you know…"

"Yeah, I know." His voice became more up beat, "So how about it, I'll come over, what about nine?"

"Steve, I'm dead on my feet."

"Yeah, so I'll bring take out. You've got to eat babe."

"Okay," there was resignation in her voice, food sounded all too tempting, "Come round about nine, but just don't expect me to be the life of the party."

Nothing new there then, thought Steve, but with uncharacteristic tact simply said, "I'll see you then…"

The receiver let out its annoying disconnected tone and she placed it back on its cradle. Damn him, she had just wanted to go home, take a bath and go to bed. The thought of food caused her stomach to growl, however. Jeez, she realised, he didn't even ask what I wanted to eat.

Ten minutes later she was walking through the office, past cubicles that were all empty and darkened. He was right, she supposed, no one else had worked that day, and it wasn't as though the senior partners would reward her toil with an overtime payment. But the Jackson account was important; she had been trusted with it. She wasn't going to let them down. Not for Steve, not for some dumb-ass party. Beatrice Johansson was going to succeed.

As she entered the elevator she looked at her reflection in the full sized mirror that backed the cab. She certainly looked the corporate part. Her navy blue suit was professional, and yet feminine. The pencil skirt was actually quite flattering to her figure. Her hair was nicely cut, and still fairly tidy despite the amount of times she had tried to pull it out during the course of the day.

She should have been pleased with what she saw, but instead she frowned. Her eyes looked so tired. Once the project was over she would take a vacation, she promised herself. Acapulco maybe. No, Europe. She had always wanted to visit Europe.

The thought of a vacation almost lifted the frown, but then it deepened as the familiar nag of a headache crossed behind her eyes. She leaned over to the control panel and pushed the button for the ground floor.

By the time she crossed the lobby her headache had grown from a worrying nag to a constant pain. She managed to smile wanly at the security guard as she passed the main reception desk, her heels clacking on the tiled floor in rhythm to the pulse of pain behind her eyes. Drawing her coat tight around her she passed through the automatic doors, abandoning the warmth of the lobby for the brisk breeze that blew through the New York evening.

For a second she looked around the unusually empty street, trying to catch sight of a cab. It seemed that even the New York cabbies had thought better of working on a holiday. She turned briskly to head for the cross street, with hopes of better luck in catching a cab, and collided with a young woman.

It seemed like an eternity, as her lips fumbled to supply an apology, and her eyes met those of the strangely beautiful brunette. The girl seemed to be of teenage years, though immaculately dressed in a sophisticated way that belied her years. But her eyes, those deep eyes that held Beatrice tight, they seemed ageless, filled with wisdom beyond the grasp of a teenager. It was the eyes that stopped Beatrice thinking of her as a girl, she was, without a doubt, a woman. Those beautiful hazel brown eyes held her gaze and it was as though there were a moment of contact, a meeting of minds. Then, it was gone.

"I'm sorry," mumbled Beatrice.

"That's quite alright," The girl's voice was exotic. Beatrice tried to place the accent, definitely European, but she couldn't place her finger on where in Europe. It was as though she came from all over that far off continent, and yet from nowhere.

Then she was gone, continuing her journey. Beatrice shook her head, her blonde hair swaying in the cold January air, and then the woman was forgotten. She didn't even notice that her headache had fled.

Danaan continued down the street, the contact with the woman Beatrice Johansson had lasted no more than a second, but it had been enough. She had noticed the girl coming out of the office and had felt a stirring in her heart that she had not felt in a long time. Just in that first glimpse she felt the languescence begin to lift from her soul.

She had ensured that the woman bumped into her, opening up a point of contact, allowing the mortal to see her and know her. She had managed to search through the woman's thoughts and knew enough about her. She was very pretty, thought the vampire, and she seems to have a gentle soul. That was enough for her. That moment of contact had created a decision. She would have Beatrice, she would bestow the Velvet Kiss and the woman would be her companion for the ages.

It was rash, she knew that, devoid of any of the patience she had tried to cultivate during her long life, or at least over the recent centuries. Yet it was thrilling as well, to want someone so totally after just a few moments. It made her feel alive again; it was a feeling akin to the ecstasy of the feed. She succumbed to the feeling, allowing the emotion to grow in her heart.

Beatrice had been thinking of home and so the vampire had discovered her address whilst in her mind. She had also discovered that the girl believed herself to be purely heterosexual but, given how she seemed struck by Danaan's beauty, an appreciation devoid of petty jealousies, the vampire believed she was seducible.

As she had flitted out of Beatrice's mind she had removed the stress headache, unwilling to have her future companion plagued by pain.

As she walked down the street, the manner of Beatrice's seduction was played out over and over in her mind. She didn't even notice that she was being observed.

Ymochel stood in the shadows watching the Praetorian walk down the street. Something had just occurred, though his lack of mentalist powers made it impossible to ascertain what. He would just have to be patient, and let the bitch get on with her plans. When he knew more he could consider the best way of exacting his revenge.

Chapter Eight

London – 1815

George, the Prince Regent, was finally asleep. He'd had trouble sleeping for some time. As the years had progressed he found that he was suffering more and more from the gout and the pain often kept him awake. But worse than the physical pain were the pressures placed upon him. Ever since his father had been declared insane, and he had been named Regent, life had become unbearable. Gone were the days of carefree gambling and comely wenches.

The Whigs expected him to honour his pledges, but the pressure brought to bear in order to force his support for the Tories was excruciating, his advisors simply would not allow him to follow the more progressive policy lines. That same pressure was being applied to the question of Catholic Emancipation. His good friend Charles Fox had turned against him, believing that he had betrayed their views. In truth he still believed that Catholics, and Protestant nonconformists, were terribly discriminated against, but the weight of office prevented him from publicly saying so.

Then there was the spectre of Princess Charlotte, his estranged wife. Parliament had forced him to marry the damn girl or they would not authorise the payment of his debts. In truth he missed Maria, his first wife. The same Parliament that forced his marriage to Charlotte had declared that marriage illegal because Maria was a Catholic. How could Charles believe he had turned away from the cause? Didn't the damn fool realise that he still loved Maria dearly, in fact still considered her his spouse, but to speak out in favour of the Catholics would be seen by Parliament as self-serving, simply an attempt to get his first wife back.

For all these reasons and more the Prince Regent slept badly each night, but this night sleep had come to him quickly and both pain and worry had ebbed away so that his slumber might steal upon him more easily.

He dreamt.

It seemed so real.

He was young again, the weight had fallen from his bones, he was athletic and the pain of gout had completely vanished.

He walked through the grand hall, decorated in the style of the India sub-continent. Red silks hung from the ceiling, causing delicate, semi-transparent transitions that fell lightly to the polished oak floor. Gold gilt covered the faces of Hindu Gods intricately carved into the ceiling and cornices.

He walked through the sea of silk until he reached a window, his heels clicking on the hard wooden floor and echoing hollowly through the hall. Through the glass was a beautiful garden with well-tended topiaries and winding pebble paths. A fountain sprayed into the air from the mouth of a carved fish and peacocks displayed their majestic tail feathers.

It might have been his imagination but he thought he could hear the sound of children laughing and playing in the distance, their voices full of joy. The thought that they were outside, happy and carefree filled him with elation. Something caused him to realise that they were his own children, but how could that be? Yet the knowledge was so real they were the children that he and…

A noise in the room broke his chain of thought and caused him to spin around.

A figure came through the silks, running and laughing, spinning through the partitions as the silk wrapped around her and then slid away. It was mesmerising, like watching a nymph parting waterfalls of red, shimmering water. As she drew closer he recognised Maria and his heart leapt. She saw him and ran to him, her long skirts rustling around her feet. She threw her arms around his neck and kissed his lips hard.

As they broke the kiss he whispered, "How?"

"My husband, my prince, we are together, that is all that is important." Her words were light and airy, chasing his doubts away.

A light waltz began to play, though he could not see the musicians who produced the phantom melody. George and his love danced through the hall, the silk parting like water before the bow of a ship, never interfering as they spun and spun. Maria's face was full of joy, lit by the bliss at being with her husband once more.

He was not tired, he realised. The dancing should have exhausted him but he was full of energy, he could dance forever.

Their exhilarating dance brought them to a doorway. They stopped and he reached for the two handles, pushing the ornate doors open with a flourish. In the room beyond was a beautiful four-poster bed. Transparent linen hung from the posts, allowing nothing more than a glimpse of the sumptuous bedspread. Maria took his hand and led him to the bed. Though her actions were forward, her face, half tilted towards him, seemed coy and full of girlish shyness.

He parted the canopy and laid her gently on the bed. On the cloud soft mattress they loved.

Then she was gone and he stood alone in a pool of blackness, once more he wore the clothes that he had believed ripped away in the exuberance of lovemaking.

A figure approached him, another woman though he did not recognise her. Despite her beauty, there was something sinister about her; it was as though he were a sheep and she the wolf stalking him. It seemed, for a moment, that he could detect the subtle hint of a vanilla fragrance. It was her movement and her bearing that lent her such a sinister air, he suddenly realised. She moved in a way that was far too fluid.

Suddenly he became painfully aware that it had all been a dream and, worse, he was still trapped in sleep. He tried to rouse himself but could not, his eyes gazed at the woman fearfully and he felt trapped. It is nothing more than a dream, he reminded himself, and nothing can hurt you in your dreams. Yet even as he thought this he did not believe it, a small part of him knew that he could be hurt and that the pain could be terrible.

"Good evening your Highness."

It was all so strange, but he responded in kind.

"My name is Danaan and I think you know that you dream."

"I do." He admitted.

"Good, but know that I am real and I wish to make you an offer." She smiled and her eyeteeth seemed a little too sharp, her eyes a little too red.

"What kind of offer?"

"In this dream you are young again, healthy and fit. You are also with your true love. It seems as real as life itself, does it not?"

"It does."

"We will bring you this dream once a month, until you die, for a small price."

It was so outlandish, negotiating his dreams, yet in some ways it felt natural, "What price?"

"The Congress of Vienna meets very soon. They discuss many things, including the fate of Switzerland. It has been proposed that Switzerland be made neutral territory."

The Regent nodded, he had been briefed on this just a few days before.

"You will tell your diplomat to accede to this plan and the dreams will come once a month. Once a month you will be with your beloved Maria."

He shook his head as though he could shake the notion away, he was the Prince Regent, and he would be King. Who was this dream phantasm to come to him and make demands on Britain's foreign policy? "If I refuse?"

His trousers ripped and the buttons on his shirt popped as his girth expanded, returning to his waking size. The crippling pain of gout ran through his legs. It is a dream, I will wake, I will wake now, he told himself, but consciousness did not come. There was just the pain, so intense that it forced him down to the floor, cringing at the menacing woman's feet. He knew he could reach his hand up and grasp at her skirts, he could pull her to him and force her to end this pain but he did not dare.

"You can feel the pain you feel in life in your dreams each and every night your highness, if you choose. That pain could be even more intense, if you'd like." As she spoke a spear of fiery agony flared through his legs, causing a sharp grunt to escape his lips.

"Perhaps you would also like to be visited by nightmares, afraid to sleep because each night you know you will see your beloved Maria tortured and killed, unable to save her."

"No!" There were tears welling in his eyes, tears of pain and tears of fear. It was just a dream, he reminded himself, what did it mean if he submitted to her demands in his dreams? "You will have your neutrality. England will defend your claim."

Instantly the pain was gone, he was young and fit again.

Danaan smiled a sharp, predatory smile. "A wise choice highness. I much prefer to bring pleasure rather than pain. Please remember that, when you awaken, and in a month you will dream of your Maria again, a dream so clear it will seem a memory and, like a memory, it will not fade in the light of the morning sun but stay with you.

"One final thing," she added, "Tell no one of this or me."

The sinister woman faded into nothing and, without warning, he was stood once more in the grand hall. Maria was there again, stood some way from him.

"In a month my love." She smiled, a smile of such beauty that it nearly broke his heart, and the dream vanished as consciousness returned.

George woke in a room still dark, for day had not yet come. It all seemed so ludicrous as consciousness returned, and yet. The dream was clear in his head and was not fading as a dream should. Also back was the ever-present pain in his legs, nagging at him incessantly.

He didn't give a damn about Switzerland's neutrality one way or another, not at all, but to be blackmailed by a dream. If Britain did support the claim and the pleasant dreams did not return, what then? Nothing would be lost, as far as he could see. But if there was even a chance that he could be young again, pain free again, with Maria again, he knew he should take it. Worse was the fear that the threats were true, that each and every night he would dream of Maria's torture of seeing his beloved die.

He had to get a message to Vienna straight away. He pulled the bell cord that would summon a servant. Impatience flooded him and he pulled it again and again.

He did not notice the shadowy figure of a woman who slipped through the window, out of his rooms and into the night, leaving behind no trace except the merest hint of vanilla hanging in the air.

Chapter Nine

Pompeii – 0079

Uriel awoke, his eyes suddenly snapping open, at the exact moment that the sun was supposed to set, though in truth its light had not penetrated the thick smoke from Vesuvius since the mountain had begun its angry murmuring.

Ymochel look passively at his master, not saying a word and knowing that his presence would be enough, in normal circumstances, to illicit a harsh beating at the very least.

Perhaps that would have occurred anyway, an angry scarlet glaze had passed over the ancient's eyes and his fat flesh seemed tensed as though he was preparing to strike, but before Uriel had said anything to his slave the earth trembled again.

"The world seems angry, child." Uriel seemed less than concerned but, to Ymochel's relief, the crimson glare of his master's eyes had passed and they had returned to their normal pale green hue.

"It is the mountain, Master, it throws smoke into the air and its very sides are aflame." Ymochel explained as he kept his voice low and respectful.

"I see." The ancient drew his large frame up off the bed, "And you are frightened by this. Tell me all that has occurred."

Ymochel did as his master bid; he even included the fight with Augustine, better that Uriel heard of it from his own lips then let the concubine tell it. Beyond the door to the chamber he could hear frantic pacing, the three concubines were awaiting entrance and their footfalls betrayed their anxiety. However, the earlier fight must have convinced Augustine that encroaching upon their master was not acceptable, no matter how afraid he was.

Uriel did not respond to the Nubian's story. He stood and disrobed, revealing his white, bloodless roles of fat, and then found himself a clean toga. As he stretched, to pull the robe on, his huge bulk caused his skin to tear at his arms and across his torso, rips that his vampire nature healed almost immediately, causing ribbons of red to appear and then vanish into the pale marble of his body. If the spontaneously healing wounds caused him discomfort it did not show on his face. Eventually he was dressed and it was only then that he spoke. "Come then Ymochel, let you and I survey the angry mountain."

As they left his chambers, the concubines crowded around their master clutching at the ancient's robes with desperate fingers, their voices shrill with fear and their questions running into each other to create a cacophony of incoherent babble. It seemed to Ymochel that a look of despair flashed within the ancient's tiny eyes, for just a second, as he lifted a heavy hand to silence them. He ordered the other vampires back to their rooms until he summoned them and they slunk away, whimpering as though they were dogs freshly beaten by their master.

The peristylium no longer looked like paradise. The fountains were dry and the statues fallen and broken. The smell of sulphur hung heavy in the air, creating an atmosphere of decay. Everything had been covered with a thick coating of ash blown from the cloud that spewed out of the mountain. At least the slaves are quiet now, thought Ymochel, as they entered the area. But as soon as the frightened mortals realised that someone had entered the garden their howling began afresh, wailing voices begging for release from their cells so they might escape the world's end somehow.

Uriel waddled over to the cells, his feet stirring up clouds of still warm ash. He looked at the slaves for a second, and then his voiced boomed out, "Silence!" His fierce voice was matched by the frightening changes to his features, his fangs had extended and were in clear view, his eyes had flooded with an angry scarlet. A hush fell over the terrified mortals and Ymochel could see that some, in the darkness of their captivity, held on to one another, clutching onto some human warmth within their fear.

The two vampires continued through the villa, towards the main door, Uriel leading the way and Ymochel walking a respectful distance behind. Ash had blown into the corridor from the garden, and a crack had appeared through one of the murals in the corridor, carved into the wall during one of the stronger quakes no doubt.

They emerged into the night and looked down the shore to the distant city that nestled beneath the angry mountain. The blackness of night above the mountain and the city were absolute, the cloud of ash blocking the stars and the moon. The fires on the mountainside had been paralleled within the city, hot ash and stones causing roof timbers to set alight. In the darkness the fires looked eerily beautiful. Another quake shook the earth beneath them; the mountain had undoubtedly belched another great plume of smoke out, invisible in the night.

Yet, when the noise of the mountain subsided for a moment, Ymochel was struck by the unnatural silence. The normal animal and insect noises of the night creatures were missing, as though the animals of the region had shown the good sense to make their escapes. He desperately hoped that his master would show the same good sense.

They stood in silence for a few moments more, until Uriel spoke. "I will return to my chambers now. Bring me one of the slaves and then wait for my summons. I will speak to all my children together."

Extracting the slave from the cell did not prove as easy a task as it should have, fear had caused the slaves to loose their normal subservient demeanour and, as soon as they realised that Uriel was not in sight, they tried to push their way past Ymochel in a wave of human bodies. His strength, however, was far superior to theirs and soon they were quelled. Ymochel selected the one who had appeared to be the source of their attempted escape and took him to provide for his master's pleasure.

How typical of their master, Ymochel mused. The Fledgling was sure they were in danger. The fury of the mountain had already touched the villa; escape from its reach seemed the best, and only, option. Yet the only concern the fat vampire had was the drinking blood, living up to his name of the Leech indeed.

He stood without Uriel's chamber, patiently waiting for the ancient to finish his first meal of the evening, though inside he felt anything but serene. The other vampires had slunk out of their rooms and stood close and yet he felt perceptibly separate from the concubines, who clung tightly to each other for mutual comfort, but neither sought from him nor offered him succour. What weaklings they were. He could never deny that he felt terribly afraid, but his bearing had more in common with the confidence displayed by their bloated master than with these craven fools. With a word from the ancient and, given their strength and speed, they could be easily away, yet they sobbed quietly into each others arms.

Occasionally Augustine would glance over to him, a mixture of fear and loathing burning in his eyes, but his gaze was never challenging. That was one less problem he supposed. The thought made him laugh silently to himself, though the humour refused to break upon his impassive features. How petty I am, he considered, almost as bad as the Leech. Amidst all this danger I find pleasure in knowing that the spineless fool now fears me.

A bell rang from within Uriel's chamber. The four Fledglings filed slowly into the ancient's presence.

The slave, a young man who had a Germanic look about him, lay discarded upon the floor, his body quite pallid following his forced exsanguination. The slave's throat had been brutally ripped open, Uriel took no pleasure in simply piercing the neck of a victim and drinking carefully. He liked to gorge himself. Spilt blood had doused his toga and the four vampires felt their fangs involuntarily slide out as the coppery scent of blood cut through the fetid sulphurous stench that had now invaded all the rooms of the villa.

"My children, come to me," the Leech's voice was deceptively seductive and seemed quite out of place flowing from his vast, lunar face.

The ancient held his arms out and the two females, Diana and Mercia, placed themselves within their embrace. Augustine curled at his feet, looking more like a lap dog than one of the Velvet. Ymochel stood before his master and lowered his eyes.

"You are all worried my children, you are all scared."

Ymochel's disdain at the ancient's patronising words was interrupted by Augustine. "Master, what is happening?" His words were edged with a desperation that caused Ymochel to forget how much he hated the ancient for a second as his vitriol turned itself instinctively towards the concubine.

Uriel was ill pleased with the interruption. "You will not interrupt me Augustine!" His voice cracked like a whip. "Only speak when I deem it appropriate."

The concubine's head still faced the ancient but his eyes were downcast.

"You are all scared," continued the ancient, "And there is no reason why you should not be. I doubt any of you have witnessed the phenomena occurring beyond the villa before this night.

"Some of the slaves cry out and claim that the world is ending, and I would expect little else from the livestock, but we are of the Velvet. Each of you has received my kiss. I expect more from you.

"The Greeks could tell you of this phenomenon. They would tell you that the God Hephaestus stokes the fires of his furnace. In truth I know Hephaestus, he is a Child of Undjit, a Child of the Velvet, and he does not live within the mountain, nor has he a furnace that he would stoke." Indeed, Uriel considered silently, Hephaestus has never been a practical creature, why the Greeks named their blacksmith God after him he would never understand.

"What we see may be the extent of the phenomena," continued the ancient, "Or it may be that the lifeblood of the earth will erupt from the mountain's veins. Whichever occurs, we will be safe. The villa is situated far enough from the mountain that we will be inconvenienced and no more.

"That said, I wish you to be aware that we will, in all probability, move from this place very soon. I fear that fair

Pompeii is not as auspiciously placed as our home. It may be best if we visit Rome for a while.

"Diana and Mercia, retire to your rooms, I have no need for your services this night. Ymochel will supply you with a slave each, to sate any hunger you may have.

"Ymochel, once you have seen to that, pick five prime specimens for me, and await my pleasure.

"Augustine you will remain with me."

With that they were dismissed; there would be no debate. Uriel had spoken and that is how it would be. Ymochel could not help but wonder, however, if they were as safe as the master maintained? Why had all the animals fled? His people had believed that much could be learnt from the animal cousins, if you had eyes to see.

Ymochel had brought the slaves to Mercia and Diana when he heard the bell ring from within Uriel's chamber. The reaction he had received from the two females had been cold, but not unexpected. They were obviously terrified and also jealous that Augustine had been allowed to stay with their master. They took their angst and fears out on

Ymochel, but their words meant nothing to him. He felt no love or even camaraderie for his fellow vampires.

Ymochel had not, by the time the bell rang, selected the five mortals for his master and it was with great trepidation that he answered the summons, fearing the ancient's wrath when his tardiness was revealed.

On entering the chamber he noticed Augustine led on the floor, it seemed that his head was below Uriel's toga. He had only just passed through the doorway when Uriel tossed something to the Nubian. His reactions were quick and he caught it, turning it over in his hands to inspect it. Suddenly he realised that Augustine did not have his head buried beneath his master's robe. Ymochel held the concubine's severed head, the blank eyes staring up at him still seemed terrified, though any light they might have contained had died away. Rapid decomposition took hold and the Nubian looked on with horror as the flesh crumbled into dust, sloughing from the skull as Augustine slipped from the pages of history. Then the skull itself crumbled; Augustine simply slipped through his fingers as though he was sand and within seconds it was as though the concubine had never been. During the whole grizzly event the decaying skull exuded the foul reek of corruption, the stench assailing

Ymochel's sensitive nose and overpowering the pervasive odour of sulphur.

"He irritated me." The master announced bluntly.

Ymochel said nothing, the ancient's temper was notorious, but he had never gone as far as to bestow true death in the five years that Ymochel had been of the Velvet.

"Your silence is appreciated, my Ymochel," Uriel had noted the Fledgling's purposeful silence, enjoying the fact that Ymochel was intelligent enough to remain quiet, Augustine certainly had not been.

"Unlike that one", Uriel's foot kicked the crumpled toga, which contained nothing but fine dust, "His prattling was most unappreciated." Uriel cast his eyes down at the empty clothes; Augustine had proved himself unworthy once too often. The punishment had, he mused to himself, been uncharacteristically swift, though perhaps he should have disposed of the fool five years earlier.

Ymochel's face remained impassive, but inside he trembled. This was not the ancient's customary expression of anger. Uriel seemed too composed and his eyes were almost placid, and yet Ymochel could sense the immense rage bottled up behind their calm appearance.

"You have not brought me my food." The softly spoken words were not a question, and so Ymochel did not respond. His eyes drifted subserviently to the floor, unwilling to provoke the rage he knew the ancient suppressed. "No, but then I did not give you the time did I?

"You deserve to be disciplined for entering my room without my bidding earlier, but the situation was… unusual, and your presence deterred Augustine in his efforts to wake me, and so I forgive you. Just do not think to enter here again without permission, unless…

"Ymochel, I believe us safe, but you must stand watch tomorrow. Have four strong slaves ready to bear my litter. If the situation seems to be too dangerous, as the day progresses, we will leave this place."

It seemed the ancient was more anxious then he had allowed the Fledglings to believe. Ymochel simply nodded, painfully aware that questioning his master's concern would elicit a painful response, and instead asked, "Master, the concubines?"

"The sky is blackened, if they can be roused from their stupor then bring them, if not… leave them. Concern yourself only with my safety."

"Yes Master."

"Good. Now bring me my food and see to it that I am not disturbed."

Ymochel left his Bloodfather. He was filled with loathing for the ancient vampire. If the ancient was at all concerned then they should leave now, but his master was more interested with feeding his enormous appetite, leaving Ymochel with the responsibility of guarding their safety. Ymochel the slave. Ymochel who was destined to spend eternity in servitude to the gargantuan monster. For a moment a vision filled Ymochel's mind, unbidden. His mind's eye was filled with beauteous images of Uriel's obese head viciously ripped from his body. The flesh was melting into the wind and the stench was like a fragrant perfume.

He was unsure of where the vision had come from. Such thoughts could lead him to the true death, and, if he were honest with himself, he did not possess the necessary courage to do such a thing. Yet still the vision remained, clear in his mind and hanging like a temptation he could never dare succumb to.

Chapter Ten

New York - 2000

Beatrice was emerging from her bedroom when Steve arrived.

Upon reaching her apartment she had immediately run herself a steaming hot bath, brimming with luxurious bubbles. As the water filled the large tub she stripped out of her suit, letting it fall crumpled to the beige tiles. A discarded corporate skin.

Looking in the mirror for a moment, she let out a tired sigh and then started to meticulously remove her makeup, letting out the occasional pointless curse as steam from the hot running water clouded the mirror. Once the futile cursing was concluded she would wipe the steam from the cold glass and continue removing the mask of cosmetics.

The bath had filled by the time she was finished. She turned the faucet off and sank into the scalding hot water. The heat caused her bunched muscles to immediately relax and she took a deep, contented breath, letting the light aroma fill her senses.

She lay in the water for at least half an hour, allowing the heat to work its magic. For as long as she could remember immersion in a hot bath had been the panacea to all her ills. During her parents messy divorce she had taken bath after bath, allowing the water to wash away the pain of the arguments and wrangling. Then, during her college years, she would hide in the bathtub whenever the pressure of her course became too much. Somehow the devilish problems set as course work, which seemed impossibly complicated prior to her filling her tub, became so much clearer after the bath.

After a while the realisation dawned that Steve was due to arrive very soon and so she washed and, grudgingly, got out of the water. She towelled her skin, pink from the water, and then slipped on a robe and walked through to the bedroom, enjoying the feel of the soft carpet fibres tickling her naked feet, after the cold, hard bathroom tiles.

In her room she pulled on a pair of comfortable knickers, then a sweatshirt and pants. Finally she pushed her feet into an old pair of slipper socks. Comfort clothes, the perfect remedy for an all too trying day, especially when she had been forced to curtail her bathing.

That thought caused her mind to slip back to the office and to the Jackson account, with its inherent problems. She was most definitely having trouble with Emerett Jackson's figures. No! The thought was so loud in her head that she almost audibly shouted it. I will not think about work, she admonished herself. That is work, this is home, and never shall they meet. Not entirely true, she had often taken work home, but tonight she needed to relax, to leave it all firmly behind so that she could face the problem the next day with fresh eyes.

With that she stood and left the bedroom, her hairdryer untouched and her hair still damp and tousled. By that time she was absolutely ravenous and her stomach gave a grumble of appreciation when Steve let himself in.

When he saw her he ran his fingers through his short brown hair, "Jeez girl, you look fantastic."

His sarcasm was not lost on her, nor was it appreciated. She shot him a look that clearly said, "Fuck you." Then she realised that he wasn't carrying anything. "Steve! You're supposed to have brought food."

The young man gave a shrug that somehow merged into the shedding of his thick winter overcoat. "No worries babe, I thought I'd order it from here."

"God dammit, Steve, I'm hungry." The irritation in her voice carried a dangerous undertone of anger. This was too damn typical of him.

"It'll only take an extra half hour, chill out."

She sucked in a breath of air and choked back the comment that lay tantalisingly on the tip of her tongue. Instead she turned and marched off to the kitchen, her feet hitting each step a little harder than normal.

Her hand reached out to take the Chinese menu from beneath the fridge magnet. Before her fingers reached it, Steve was behind her, his arms snaking around her waist and the hard stubble on his chin brushing her shoulder as he moved to kiss her neck.

Beatrice twisted to avoid the kiss, the twist become a sharp pull out of his arms as his hands moved up her body, attempting to cup her breasts.

"What the Hell is up with you!" Her voice was shrill.

For a moment it seemed that his eyes brimmed with regret, but that was quickly subsumed by annoyance. "Up with me! What the fuck is up with you?"

She sighed, "I'm hungry. You came here with promises of take out. I could have eaten when I got home if I thought you were going to let me down."

He laughed. It was short and without humour, but it was a laugh none the less. "We're still getting take out, aren't we?"

"Yeah, so what was all that bullshit about?"

"Bullshit," there was a genuine tone of hurt in his voice now, "I was just being close to you."

"You were trying to grab my tits."

"I was trying to hold you. You know…"

"I know only too well." She interrupted, "You're horny."

He shrugged, "So, I'm horny. I'm also here with my girlfriend. What's wrong with horny?"

"Steve I'm hungry and I'm shattered, neither of which equals horny."

His voice became a little more raised, "You're always fuckin' tired."

"What's that meant to mean?"

"Just what I said. You're always tired. Too tired to have any fun, too tired to go out, too tired to screw…"

Her indignation rose. "Oh, I am so sorry; I work damn hard and…"

He laughed, short, sarcastic and just enough to cut her off midstream. "You don't do anything but work anymore."

"Oh I am sorry," her voice wavered slightly with emotion, "I am so fucking sorry. Well if you don't like it you can… you can just fuck off."

Suddenly Steve noticed the very grim glint of determination in her eyes. "Bea. Look I'm sorry okay… let's start tonight over…"

"Just go Steve…" her voice was barely a whisper.

"What do you…"

"Steve I said go. Let me eat something and sleep. Just go."

Anger sparked within Steve again. Anger at her work and the importance she placed in it. Anger that she was dismissing him. Anger at himself, for pushing it when he should have known not to.

The fact that he was angry with himself should have diffused his emotions, but they were running too high. He turned on his heel and stormed out of the kitchen. He grabbed his coat and yelled, "Screw you!" The next thing Beatrice heard was the apartment door slamming shut.

She walked through into the lounge, slapping the light switch hard as she passed it, causing the room to fall into a soothing darkness. She sank onto a chair and, for a moment, she thought she might cry, but she was too tired to summon the tears. So she sat, her head in her hands, until her stomach growled again, single-mindedly ignoring the maelstrom of emotions and demanding food.

She moved back to the kitchen to try and find something to eat. She didn't hear the apartment door being carefully opened and closed.

Steve stood for a moment. Already doubt had entered his heart, causing him to feel a sickening lurch in his stomach. The anger faded leaving only regret.

What would he do? Shit! What would he do? The damn woman infuriated him, but fuck he loved her. He'd have to show her. He'd have to do something.

But not tonight. They both had to cool off. He pulled his coat tight around himself, warding away the cold New York breeze. He looked away from the apartment block and wandered down the street towards the subway. For a moment he thought of trying to find his buddies, they would be in a downtown bar, already drunk by now. He couldn't face it, not with the mood that now sat heavily on his shoulders; he simply wanted to go home to bed.

Danaan stood in the darkened lounge, her senses focused on Beatrice. She had let herself into the apartment when the ape of a boyfriend had stormed out. The lock had not proved an obstacle; you didn't live the best part of a thousand years without learning a thing or two about locks.

For a moment Danaan had considered going after him, contemplated punishing him for the hurt he had caused Beatrice.

She stopped herself. She had to handle the girl's seduction carefully. There could be no room for regrets, things had to be cautiously carried out if the eternity she planned was to come to pass.

The vampire watched intently as the girl picked at some ham from the refrigerator. Her instincts caused her to gently brush Beatrice's mind as she studied her. Fatigue, both physical and emotional, had stolen her appetite, despite her hunger. All the girl wanted to do was succeed and to have a little support from the person closest to her. Her boyfriend seemed incapable of offering her that support, he wanted to party and drink and screw, and responsibilities were an alien concept to him. Danaan sensed that Beatrice was secretly jealous of him, jealous of the attitude that allowed him to coast through life. She secretly yearned for excitement but her own sense of duty pushed her hard into a world were work was the all-consuming passion.

The girl's thoughts had moved onto her parents and Danaan thought she understood were this inflated sense of responsibility came from. Beatrice felt her father had let the family down and she would not allow herself to do that.

Her thoughts flashed back to Steve. He reminded her of her father. That was why he made her so angry. The father who had left his family for a young girl. The father who let his job go to Hell whilst he went out drinking, to the point that he couldn't afford child support. The father who had let them all down.

Danaan wanted to go to her, wanted to hold her and whisper that it would all be all right. She could not do it though, not yet.

Beatrice turned and left the kitchen. Unable to find the desire to eat, her desire turned to her bed instead.

Danaan sank into the deepest shadows, the blackest corner of the darkened lounge and watched as the girl walked through to the bedroom.

Careful now Danaan, thought the vampire, the seduction must be subtle. The Children of Shang-Di work through dreams.

Chapter Eleven

Castle Csejthe, Carpathian Mountains – 1580

A cold wind blew down from the mountain peaks, fingers of an icy hand that caressed each rock and crevasse until they finally reached the imposing fortress. It whistled through the windows of Castle Csejthe, causing dust to dance across the reception hall. It ruffled dresses, and encouraged the hems of robes to flow. Torches flickered in their stands casting an eerie amber glow that merged with the moonlight, which flooded spectral silver tones from high above the Carpathian peaks.

Erzsébet looked down at the man from her lofty position on the throne. His robes told an entirely different story to the tale that ran torrentially from his lips.

According to his words he was an initiate, an alchemist from the order of Hermes Trismegistus. He had served the innumerate crown princes of Europe and all had benefited from both his wise council and his magical arts. He was close, he claimed, to unlocking the lost secrets of the philosopher's stone. He certainly knew the names of the planets and had openly revealed the name of the stone that burned, but this was knowledge that even a patron such as Erzsébet knew. If words could be classed as currency then surely he would be the richest man in the world.

His robes told another story. Threadbare and patched in many places, stains muted any colour which might have been visible beneath the encrusted grime. If one looked closely, Erzsébet observed, one could notice the tell tale holes where a dagger had parted the cloth, and yet by some miracle he had escaped, probably from the hands of a disgruntled sponsor when his promises had come to naught. His stringy grey beard was also encrusted with dirt, and it was difficult to ascertain the colour of his complexion beneath the accumulated filth. The pig had neither washed nor changed, she presumed, since he ran from the hall of the last foolish noble who had been taken in by his words and promises.

Surely taking the opportunity to bathe at a nearby inn, or carrying a spare set of good quality robes would not be too much to contemplate, in order that visage matched articulation?

No, it was obviously too much. Why should he pay an innkeeper for a hot, drawn bath? Why keep fine robes rather than sell them and use the coin for food? Not when the vast majority of lesser nobles had neither the wit nor the wisdom to ignore his fine speech and look with their eyes.

But not her. No, not Erzsébet. She was of the royal Magyar line, after all, born of the family named valiant. True, she had been forced to come to this God forsaken rural nightmare of a land to seal a political gain. Forced to marry the same kind of fool who, where it not for his blind devotion to Rome, would have happily listened to the man's pretty speech. Ferenc Nadasdy had never struck her as a fine catch; indeed his social status was so low that, when they eventually married, he had hyphenated his name with hers. Unfortunately, her family had disagreed with her objections and overruled her dissent.

Now the bastard was away again. He was always away playing at war against the damned Turks.

She cast an eye around the hall. The man opened his mouth, threatening to allow his words to come tumbling out yet again, but a deftly raised hand silenced him.

The hall was desolate, she decided. Oh, there were people enough. Servants scurried through shadows which danced to the tune of the torches. Guards flanked the door, for the bastard would not leave her unguarded, not that any Turk would waste his time to come traipsing up the side of the Carpathians, even for her. There were the ones whom her wisdom had informed her were not charlatans. Astrologers, numerologists, mages and all other shades of practitioner of the occult arts. If her good Christian husband were here, if he thought to show any interest at all in his bride, his temper would explode at the thought of their kind in his hall. Reason enough, beyond her insatiable search for knowledge, to keep them in service. They also added much-needed colour to the castle, their resplendent robes, vibrant hues shimmering in the torch light, made up for the lack of decoration.

Her husband believed that to be austere in decoration was to show service to God. As such there were not the paintings and tapestries nor the statues and ornaments that adorned her family's holdings. The only hanging in the hall was the tapestry of her family crest, though that owed more to Ferenc's celebration of his good fortune than it did to keeping his wife happy.

She made up her mind that, upon the occasion of his next brief visit to the castle, she would need to discuss decoration. Surely God would want His glory reflected? Surely the Turks her husband defeated in the name of that God had treasures that could adorn their halls? Fine carpets that could be laid along the uniformly grey corridors and fine tapestries to hang from the walls, where presently only cobwebs hung. What, she wondered, was the point of his endless warfare if it brought no plunder of riches to Csejthe?

Her mind flicked back to the man. She needed to deal with his petition.

"Sir, you have said many fine words and many of your utterances, being only a woman, were lost upon me."

He smiled; the fool obviously thought he had her. "Your Grace, if there is anything you would like me to elaborate upon…"

"Yes," she cut him off, "In the endless torrent of effluent that streamed out of your mouth your name was lost."

He looked much less assured now, though his words rallied quickly, "Magus Erasmus Boch, your grace."

"Master Boch; indeed," she purposefully refused to address him as magus, a slight he certainly noticed. She turned her address to the rest of the room, "It seems to me that Master Boch is much less than his fine words would indicate. It also seems to me that Master Boch should leave the Carpathians now, leave Transylvania altogether, and never again set foot in this land."

Boch was crestfallen. The patter that had won him patronage in countless noble halls had failed him. It had failed to sway a woman. He looked furtively around the hall. The occultists already in her paid service turned their backs on him, he would gain no support from them. The guards looked all too eager to reach for their swords, and he had heard rumours about the welcome that could be found in Erzsébet Báthory's dungeon.

He may have been a charlatan, but he was certainly no fool. Bowing low, in order to maintain some shred of dignity, he retreated from the hall. It was clear to him that he would have to ply his trade further a field. Messages would flood to her family, and from them to the various noble houses, unfortunately the Báthory family held sway in much of the region.

Erzsébet caught the eye of Katrina as the noisome little man retreated. She was a minor noble, a cousin Erzsébet believed, who had recently come to Csejthe. Katrina nodded her approval to Erzsébet, her beautiful face moving slightly and a thin, but sparkling, smile creeping across her features. Erzsébet needed no such approval, and from any other would have taken umbrage. But how could she feel anger towards such a beautiful cousin?

Erzsébet felt fatigued. Why, she mused, did they always insist on petitioning at night? Perhaps they felt it made them appear more mysterious, that it would better their chances for patronage. She had been more lenient to Boch than she should have been, perhaps she should have a guard go after him and introduce him to the black depths of the castle. She would think on it, after all, he could not get far on foot, at night, in the Carpathians.

She stood and paced from the hall, her long red dress flowing gracefully across the rough granite floor. The audience had ended.

Danaan walked along the corridor, her footfalls as quiet as a mouse. She was enjoying her new life as Katrina, cousin to Erzsébet Báthory. For a moment she stopped by an arrow slit and peered through the thick wall, looking out towards the countryside. It was breathtaking; the soaring, angular mountains reaching grey into the night, their snowy peaks scraping at the rich silken skies. The silver disc of the moon emerged from behind one of those peaks and it seemed as though a person might be able to scale the mountain's heights and climb onto the lunar expanse. The moon had long been her companion, creature of the night as she was. Once she had been a young woman, her rhythm controlled by the moon, now that heavenly body was her confidant, her companion and her friend, waxing and waning into her life.

Nestled around the mountains were vast swathes of forests, a bountiful green sea, wild and untamed by mortal man. The nearby towns and farms were not in view from where she stood and it could almost be that the castle was the only bastion of humanity in the magnificent wilds. She was truly glad she had come here. In five hundred years it had to be the most breathtaking scenery she had laid her immortal eyes upon.

In the distance a wolf howled, and then the night seemed to come alive, as a second answered and then a third. The peasants feared and hated the huge, wild dogs, their calls signalling danger, especially in the winter months when food was scarce and a lone traveller might prove irresistible. Even in the summer the creatures were reviled, the peasants fearful that stray livestock might fall prey to their hunger. Danaan, however, thought their song beautiful and haunting. A hymn to the wilderness. From down below she could hear the gentle refrain of the stream that flowed behind the castle, a light melody that complemented the plaintive wails of the wolves.

She turned from the view, refusing to let it enchant her further and continued towards Erzsébet's chambers.

It had been easy enough to ingratiate herself into the castle. A little knowledge of the noble families had allowed her to construct a family lineage that had seen her accepted and was difficult to trace and disprove. With a few well-spoken words Danaan had become Katrina, distant cousin to Erzsébet and honoured guest. She had not even needed to manipulate her hostess's mind. Her grace, it seemed, longed for a more sophisticated company than this rural holding could offer. Erzsébet truly seemed to resent this land, this castle, as much as Danaan truly loved it.

Erzsébet wanted to dance at great parties, to hold court amongst the nobility. She wanted a social life that this place was unable to offer her. Danaan wanted to dance too. Her dance, however, would be a solitary dance through the trees, along the mountainsides and by the banks of rivers. Unlike the peasants she had no fear of the predators that skulked through the wild. Whilst she had no real skill when it came to controlling animals, not like certain Bloodlines of the Velvet, she had no need to fear them. Recognising a higher predator the wolves and bears would keep a respectful distance.

Perhaps tomorrow night, she told herself, she would sneak from the castle and dance the great dance of the wild. Tonight she had another urge she wished to indulge.

As she rounded a corner a serving girl almost bumped into her, the young girl letting out a brief squeal of panic when she realised who she had nearly collided with. The girl scurried past her, eyes fixed firmly to the floor and her hands clasped to her breast above her simple smock. They feared her, the servants, they feared her strange habit of sleeping through the day and feared, it seemed, any relation of their mistress. Danaan did not care for the fears of these fools, they were unimportant, merely insects who scurried around Csejthe performing an endless cycle of tasks. Something to provide material comfort and, deep in the shadows, safely hidden from prying eyes, to provide sustenance.

She reached the door to Erzsébet's chambers. She was about to knock when the door opened and a guard came from the room, his face set in a mask of grim determination. She brushed his mind and caught the name Boch, the horrid little man who had begged an audience with Erzsébet. Her 'cousin' saw her without her chamber and immediately waved the vampire in enthusiastically.

"Your Grace," Danaan's voice was filled with charm, and her smile lit up her face. "I hope that I am not disturbing you."

"Oh my dear Katrina, you could never disturb me and you must call me Erzsébet, you know that."

"Erzsébet," Danaan corrected herself, allowing a girlish giggle to escape. At the sight of Danaan displaying such womanly charms, Erzsébet reached forward and clasped the brunette gently by the back of the head. She pulled her close and they started to kiss passionately. Within seconds they were fumbling at each other's clothes,

Danaan's clumsy fingers purposeful, allowing the young mortal the illusion that she was inexperienced at such things. When she had arrived she had thought to seduce the noble, she had not even had chance to begin when Erzsébet began making overtures towards her. It had been enjoyable to be the one seduced. Erzsébet's tastes were very much Sapphic; the beautiful young noble girl who had visited her home had been a prize she was determined to gain. Danaan had held out a little, drawing the seduction out, but only a little.

As their garments fell away they moved to the elaborately carved four-poster bed. Whilst the rest of Csejthe was austere, Erzsébet had decorated her bedroom in the highest fashions from the cities.

They curled around each other, Erzsébet letting her fingers trail across the vampire's pale skin, her fingers lightly grazing a nipple, which instantly hardened.

"Your skin is so beautiful, almost porcelain in appearance," she whispered to Danaan, "Almost as perfect as mine."

Danaan had noted that Erzsébet thought much of the beauty of her own skin and complexion. Whilst it was true that she was a beautiful woman, the vampire could not see that which the woman believed. She did not tell her this however.

"Your skin is the most beautiful, the most perfect I have ever seen," she lied. Her words fanned the woman's fantasy and pandered to her ego. She began to kiss Danaan, the kisses urgent and heated.

Danaan fell onto the bed, the mortal woman above her and her veins filled with the stolen blood of a scullery girl. Could life, the vampire wondered, be any better?

Chapter Twelve

London – 1884

Thick smog clung to the streets, disguising all but the closest objects. Baal trailed after his master, the vampire Qutrub. Normally, when he was in public, Baal wore wide brimmed hats and high collars, all the better to hide his face from casual glances. He was not ashamed, but the stares that his broken face attracted were better avoided.

That was the paradox of being born into the line of Qutrub. The ancient was quite beautiful but insisted that only those of a monstrous visage were brought into his line. He gained a perverse thrill from being surrounded by the hideous and grotesque. His insistence that only the most misshapen mortals were brought into his line was absolute and it was well known, amongst his get, that if one sought permission directly from the Concilium to bring a mortal over, and that mortal did not meet Qutrub's perverted standards, then the presumptuous Sponsor would meet true death at the ancient's hand. As such none of his get would petition the Concilium directly; first they would petition the Bloodfather.

As a mortal Baal had drawn attention wherever he went. He was tall, some six foot three, and well built. It was his face, however, that drew the most attention. His nose bulbous and misshapen, his thick lips barely contained the large broken, blackened teeth. His eyes appeared small, lost within his substantial rubbery lids. Boils sprouted from his skin and his skull was malformed, the extreme lumps all too visible through the patchy, lank black hair that clung haphazardly to his malformed skull. All this had been captured eternally, a macabre tableau of the grotesque, as Qutrub's blood had fallen into the dark maw of his mouth.

Yet, whilst Qutrub demanded such in his children, he also demanded that they did not attract too much unwanted attention amongst the mortal world. As his line possessed neither Undjit's line's ability to camouflage themselves amongst mortal man, nor Shang-Di's line's ability to twist memory and befuddle mortal minds, the children of Qutrub had learnt to hide behind artificial disguise.

Here in the deep London fog, however, such artifice was unnecessary.

Baal was not happy to be in London. Qutrub had demanded they travel to the English Capitol and, even now he was immortal, Baal was not the greatest of seamen. The boat journey from Calais had been uncomfortable. It was only his vampiric nature that had prevented him from being physically sick. Quite obviously there was no food to vomit, nothing in his stomach except stolen blood, and his body, once it had taken the blood, was stubbornly unwilling to release it again.

Beyond the inconvenience of the journey was the tiresome fact that they had left the Nubian vampire Ymochel in Vienna, ostensibly to recover from his last participation in Qutrub's experiments. Baal dearly wished he had been left with the son of a bitch; he was enjoying having his sadistic way with the prisoner. It felt good to carve the beauty clean from his face. The fact that his features regenerated only increased the enjoyment, the regeneration allowed Baal to perform the mutilation again and again, allowing him to perfect his gruesome sculpture.

Within the smog sound seemed distant and muffled, even to his keen senses. The nearby rattle of a mist hidden carriage seemed otherworldly, the clatter of hooves twisted within the choking mists.

As they approached their destination, however, the sounds of mortals grew more distinct and Baal placed the large hat back on his head, sinking his head deep within his coat's turned up collar. Qutrub did not even look to ensure he had done it. In their Bloodline obedience was both expected and guaranteed.

When they entered the fair Qutrub led the way, knowing exactly where he wanted to go. He had journeyed to England for one reason only, and he would not allow them to be distracted from his goal. They reached the sideshow tent and, after the ancient handed over the correct coins, entered. Baal knew enough to realise that once his master had seen what he had travelled to see they would return directly to continental Europe. When the mood took him, as it often did, his master could be very single-minded.

Behind the curtain, Joseph waited. His occupation saddened him and yet it provided him with money and that would be in short supply otherwise.

Tom Norman, the entrepreneur who had taken Joseph under his wing, came onto the small stage.

"It's nearly time Joseph," his voice was soft and caring, he knew that the spectacle upset his prodigy.

Norman helped the man remove his robe, the deformities on his hands making disrobing by himself difficult, revealing his twisted body. The disease had run rampant through Joseph. It had twisted his torso and limbs and his head was distorted, his features virtually vanished within the growths. Despite himself Norman shuddered.

He took his leave and walked off the stage and manoeuvred himself in front of the curtain.

"My Lords, Ladies and Gentleman," he intoned, "I would ask you to prepare yourself for the cruellest joke nature has ever visited upon man. Those of you with a nervous disposition may wish to leave as I present the Elephant Man."

On cue the curtain parted, revealing Joseph to the gawping crowd.

There were gasps and cries. A woman towards the front fainted at the sight of him. No matter how often he heard these reactions it still hurt the unfortunate man, like a spear through his heart. Not that night, however. His attention was focused on the beautiful creature with light mocha skin who stared intently at him, a thin smile twisted upon his face. The smile was enigmatic, ecstatic and cruel at once.

His almond eyes were full of longing and seemed to contain a timeless wisdom and a measure of malice in equal degrees. Yet despite the malevolence that seemed to infect his perfect features it seemed to Joseph that this was an angel looking upon him.

The beautiful one leant over and whispered something to his large companion, whose features were lost within the turn of his collar and brim of his hat.

The curtain fell and Norman rushed back stage to him to help him with his robe.

"That one," Qutrub had whispered to Baal, "Would make a perfect addition to my line."

Baal nodded knowing that his master meant it, but aware that Joseph Merrick's public profile was too high for Qutrub to risk spiriting him away. In the coming months the ancient's frustration at not being able to take him would build and the full force of that frustration would be focused upon the Nubian. Baal allowed himself a distorted smile at that thought.

As they left Qutrub left an envelope for Merrick, it contained a considerable sum of money but no note. Payment for the pleasure he had given the ancient through his very existence. They made their way through the smog-shrouded streets, heading back to Vienna. The whole purpose of them being in England had taken less than a couple of minutes.

Chapter Thirteen

New York City – 2000

The wind blew cold through New York City, it swooped between skyscrapers and flowed along streets buffeting car aerials and whipping up discarded pieces of paper, then forcing them to perform solitary minarets. One such piece began a dance around Ymochel's feet, until its dance reached a crescendo and it seemed to run the length of his leg. Ymochel seemed unaware of its presence.

He was also unaware of the other vampire who stood beside him. The vampire was all too aware of Ymochel, however. He watched him intently and had done so, as often as time allowed, since the Nubian was released from the ministrations of Qutrub of the Flesh. He had no orders to follow Ymochel, the Concilium had decided that his time had been served, and no one could argue that the hundred and sixty years spent with the Flesh would have been a living Hell, after all Qutrub had kept the Nubian vampire sixty years longer than the Concilium had originally determined. The vampire who stared relentlessly at the Nubian did not agree with the Concilium judgement, however. He would never publicly voice his concern at their decision, for he was a loyal servant of the ancients, but he had taken it upon himself to watch the Nubian just in case his instincts were correct.

He looked up and down Ymochel's body. There was no doubt that he was a beautiful specimen, Uriel had always chosen beauty; not that beauty was of any concern to him. There was an inner power, however, almost physically manifesting, that he could not consolidate with the Nubian's age. Even at almost 2000 years old, a vampire should not give the impression of so much raw power.

Ymochel wore an immaculate Armani suit, classic black with a lilac silk shirt. He knew that Ymochel had found a mortal his own size and firstly stolen his life, then his possessions and money. He had no problem with that. That was how the predator lived; his concern was how that predator then lived the Velvet life.

He circled Ymochel, taking in all he could. Sometimes he wished that he had gained the gift of the children of Shang-Di, the ability to look into the Nubian's mind would have been enlightening he was sure. As he paced slowly around Ymochel, the younger vampire remained unaware of his observer.

At times like these the vampire revelled in the power of his gift, the ability to remain unseen even in the closest of proximities. It could be thrilling, standing next to his quarry, knowing that they were unaware of him. The ability to observe every detail and remain unmolested. At other times the gift disturbed him, even after so many centuries, he was dislocated from the world, not truly part of it, but the gift had been a price and he had willingly paid it. The price was one of absolute anonymity, a life of constant secrets and lies, and it had been paid for more than three thousand years. If he had to make his choice again he would gladly take the Velvet and pay the price. Debts should always be repaid and some debts were worth accumulating.

His attention slipped back to the Nubian. Ymochel had lived a flawless life since his release. He was angry with the Concilium, that much was clear, but never acted against the Velvet. Then his behaviour had suddenly changed, he became aware of her. It was clear that he was somehow obsessed with the Praetorian, and was going to great lengths to ensure she was unaware that he watched her. He had committed no crime against her or the Concilium, but something seemed wrong, the picture was slightly out of focus. The fact that Danaan was the focal point of Ymochel's obsession disturbed him more than he was willing to admit, even to himself.

Ymochel's shoulder slumped slightly, he was moving away, abandoning his vigil. He probably hungered, the vampire knew he did. He considered following the Nubian, but decided against it.

Slipping instead down an alley he came across a homeless woman. To a human she would probably be imperceptible, nothing more than a lump of rags hidden beneath sheets of fetid, damp cardboard. Even if he had not been blessed to be reborn with the acute senses of unlife, he would have seen her. He had been trained to see the invisible, both as a mortal and a Child of the Velvet.

He felt comfortable with the countless homeless in the cities of the world; they were very much like him. Hidden from the eyes of the majority they were unseen, quickly forgotten and generally ignored. It had always been like that, he recalled. There had never been a major city in his long life that had not had its unseen citizens, though in the modern age they had become an invisible plague.

As he came closer he could smell the cheap liquor that had guided her into her restless sleep. It mattered not, the alcohol in her blood was unimportant as it would not affect him unless he willed it to do so. He bent down and lifted a filthy arm enwrapped in layers of soiled clothing. He placed the wrist to his mouth and began to suckle; the woman never woke as he gently drank her blood. There was the slightest reaction as the pleasant venom expelled from his fangs caused her to moan slightly and her body to shudder. Sensual dreams came unbidden into her mind as her body reacted to the aphrodisiac effects of the bite of the line of Undjit.

Eventually her heart stopped. He didn't normally kill, though his conscience never bothered him when he did. He knew, however, that even taking a small amount would have considerably lowered her chances of survival through the bitterly cold night. Better he gained the benefit of her lifeblood than wasting it, especially when she would likely be dead before the dawn broke.

He had made a decision. The Nubian's obsession with Danaan was worrying him, nagging at him in ways long forgotten. He needed to report it and receive advice.

His first instinct was to go to Undjit, he might be a servant of the Concilium but his loyalty remained ultimately, and silently, with her. He refused to place his faith in modern communication methods, unless ordered to do so. Such communiqués could be intercepted and for one so used to being hidden he detested the tendency of such methods to leave a trail. Other vampires might even have considered more mystical methods of communication, but he lacked the necessary knowledge and skills. The only remaining option was a face to face audience, however, that demanded a trans-Atlantic flight. His Mistress was in the great caverns of the Concilium and, whilst such a flight was more than possible with careful planning, it was undesirable and time consuming.

Better, he considered, for him to go directly to the current Emperor. Jumlin had taken the mantle of Emperor that very day and was currently still in his home, a large house on the shore of Platte Lake.

He could leave now and make some headway, traveling across country to Morrison County, Minnesota.

Chapter Fourteen

Vienna – 1815

The reception was not a bore to him, though he suffered no illusions that many would have found it so. For Charles Maurice de Talleyrand-Perigord it was lifeblood itself. In the room the diplomats, who would the next day meet in the Congress of Vienna to carve out the fate of Europe, milled around in seemingly random patterns, though there was truly nothing random and each move was part of a larger, well thought out, stratagem. All across the room those with ears to hear could discern the cut and thrust of politics. Talleyrand was one such person; it was almost all he lived for despite his advancing years. The men would meander around the room, dropping acid comments into pleasantries, building and breaking alliances.

Beneath the flickering lights of the ornate candelabra the profile of Europe was shaped, the lungs of diplomats providing the bellows for the forge. He almost regretted the fact that he was going to have to sneak away, but there were some things that were more important, not many but some. He would lose no ground by leaving, he was sure. The main alliances were already in place and he was sure that he knew the positions of all the main players.

"Ah, Talleyrand, my dear chap." The Englishman's voice was deceptively pleasant, but Castlereagh was a shrewd negotiator with a razor sharp mind. Despite the unpleasantness between England and France, caused by Bonaparte, he and Castlereagh had become staunch allies. In the negotiations neither France nor England had territorial claims, thus Talleyrand believed he could trust the man, plus his source had indicated he should. It would not do to slight the man, however, and Talleyrand realised that he could not escape just yet.

"Castlereagh, it is good to see you my friend." The Frenchman gave a slight nod as he spoke. Knowing how few Englishmen spoke anything other than their own tongue he replied in English. He knew, however, that Castlereagh spoke many other languages, including French, but it was all part of the game, a subtle reminder of English ignorance.

The Englishman laughed genially at the Frenchman's reply, "But surely not unexpected, after all, where would we be but here?"

"Indeed," the Frenchman smiled, "Could there be a better place to be? The fire of politics light the night brighter than the sun ever could, no?"

"You are a strange one and no doubt. Now for myself, I desire nothing more than to be at home. Sat upon a comfortable chair before a roaring fire with a brandy in my hand and the dog at my feet." As if to illustrate his words he raised a brandy glass to his lips and sipped at the aromatic drink.

Talleyrand laughed lightly, though inside all he truly wanted was to be away from the place, a feeling that added a virtually imperceptible timbre of frustration to the laughter.

A servant came over to them and whispered to Castlereagh. The Englishman's face darkened for a second, but the cloud quickly passed. "If you will excuse me, my friend," His voice deliberately increased in volume, "It seems the Prince Regent has sent me an urgent missive."

Several of the diplomats heard that and, like them, Talleyrand was all too aware of what the words actually meant. It could well be that Prince George had decided to interfere in the diplomatic process; England's position may have shifted. He suddenly regretted his decision to leave the reception early but the answers he needed might be found elsewhere anyway.

All eyes were on the Englishman and Talleyrand used the opportunity to escape the reception, hopefully, unobserved. He slipped out of the building and pulled his cloak tightly around himself. Part of him wanted to abandon the liaison, to re-enter the building and discover what instructions the Prince Regent had sent to Castlereagh but a greater part of him wanted to visit her, and so he pressed on through the night, his progress slowed slightly by the damage he had caused his own foot when he was just four years old. The dislocated foot had caused much consternation amongst his family, though with hindsight it was the most opportune accident that could have befallen him. The injury had made him unfit for military service, the path his family had expected him to take. It was common to put the interest of the family ahead of the desires of the individual amongst France's aristocratic families, Talleyrand, even as a child, knew it to be so. As the years went by his escape from a military life was a reward not sweet enough to take the bitter pain of his father's obvious disappointment away. However, being unfit for military service had ensured that he could choose his own destiny; the accident had led him to the seminary and, eventually, politics. Within politics he found his niche, a place from where he could serve France, so much more than the military would have allowed. As the years went by, and his embroilment in domestic and European politics deepened, the spectre of his father's disappointment melted away. Because of this he always endured the nagging pain in his leg with a certain pride, even though, with the advancement of years, that nagging had become much stronger.

He kept a wary eye behind himself for he did not wish to be followed, although he still hoped that Castlereagh's announcement had allowed him to avoid unwanted attention. For one terrible moment he thought that someone did trail his path but then panic became relief as the person vanished from view. Just some late night traveller whose path had coincided with his own for a while, he realised.

He reached the tall town house, glanced around again to ensure that the cobbled street was deserted, and knocked at the door.

It was Catherine herself who answered the door. The beautiful woman had been his mistress for almost a decade and, he mused with wonder, had not seemed to age in that time. She was also a shrewd advisor and, it seemed, had an extensive web of espionage at her fingertips for she seemed to know the plans of all his rivals. Talleyrand was no fool, he might be besotted with the woman and, he told himself, who would not be, but he knew there was more to her than met the eye.

Her long brown hair was hidden at the moment beneath a fashionably large, white wig. When free, however, it was the most glorious chestnut hue, with a hint of natural curl. Its colour was all the more striking when contrasted with her porcelain complexion and sparkling blue eyes. Her lips were thin, but pouted in the sweetest of ways. The curve of her hips and the ample round of her bosom were a sight to behold. She seemed eternally thirty years old and he was glad of it.

At times he told himself he must be a fool, for whenever he thought of her womanly body he seemed to lose all curiosity as to the source of her insights into the vast arena of European politics. In truth he knew he could never delve too deeply for fear of losing her and the woman had never led him astray with either knowledge or advice. In fact she had saved his career on numerous occasions and given him the reputation he enjoyed in the process.

"Catherine, my love."

"Charles, I have missed you, you were not followed were you?" The woman, he mused, was very discreet. Sometimes doubt would rise within him however, causing him to believe that her discretion was less to do with him and more to do with her secrets. Then he would remind himself that, in fact, it was unimportant. Their concerns were both shared and served by her discretion and his, and that was the most important thing.

For a second he caught sight of himself in the mirror. He was an old man, his reflection reminded him, not to mention a Bishop as well. Despite this, his indiscretions with the bewitching creature did not prey on his conscience. He was an aristocrat who had served both the King and Bonaparte, though secretly his loyalty was forever to the King, for his true loyalty was for France herself and he honestly believed her destiny was tied with her monarchy. Leading multiple lives, assuming roles was not new to him. After all, he mused, wasn't that what the entire cut and thrust of politics was based upon. He might be a bishop but he was a libertine first. He just had to be circumspect. The final thought reminded him that she had asked him a question.

"No," he answered, hoping that she assumed his delay in answering was due to him carefully considering his journey to the house and not because of the wandering of an old man's mind.

She smiled her sweet smile and led him into the house closing the door behind them.

In actual fact he had been followed and she knew it. Her true name was Ceres, a Child of the Velvet of the bloodline of Remus and Praetorian of the Concilium. A Saxony agent had followed him from the reception, the very man Talleyrand had believed was trailing him, but another Praetorian had intercepted the spy. He would not have been harmed, Saxony would undoubtedly have blamed both Talleyrand and France if their agent had mysteriously died, but they had ensured he could not report on the diplomat's whereabouts.

She led the man straight to the boudoir. Their lovemaking was the most difficult part of this particular assignment. Not that she found Talleyrand unattractive, nor because he was mortal, but because she could hear the hot rush of his blood pumping through his veins as he lay upon her. Were she of Shang-Di's line she might have dared to take a drop, offering him pleasure beyond belief and clouding his mind to the events. Being of Remus' line it was not possible, for her bite only brought agony.

She longed for the assignment to be over, for Talleyrand to retire from the public eye. Even though the man was over sixty she could feel a distinctive warmth in his blood, radiating through his skin. She would actually swear that she could smell its unusual spice though it remained trapped in his veins. As soon as it was possible she would feed from this one, it was this vow that gave her strength each time he bedded her.

Their lovemaking was a sensual and yet languid affair. Ceres enjoyed the feel of his hard member pushed deep inside her and her orgasm, when it came, was genuine. With a hard thrust he ejaculated, they shifted positions and she lay in his arms, her face turned from him. He took her silence for exhaustion, but in truth she was trying to compose herself, to put her hunger at bay. When she had been given the assignment she had questioned the sense of it. Shang-Di's line was normally used when seduction was needed, her line was better known for being strategists and, along with Qutrub's line, extractor's of information. She was told that Danaan had already walked the man's dreams and discovered that, coincidentally, she was physically very similar to what the mortal saw as his ideal woman. As things transpired his seduction had been remarkably simple.

She finally managed to control her thirst. She turned to him and kissed his lips hard.

"You are due to discuss the position of Switzerland tomorrow, are you not my love?"

Her knowledge never failed to surprise Talleyrand; the exact agenda of the Congress had not been made public. He didn't question the knowledge, however, he simply confirmed that her information was correct.

"I suspect," she said, "That your interests would be best served by agreeing to neutrality for the country."

"Would it were that simple, France is a powerful voice, yes, but I do not believe there is much support for the proposal."

"But if two powerful voices were to support it…"

"I do not honestly know who would support it. England would be most likely, but I have no idea of what Castlereagh's position is on the proposal. In truth it did not seem the most important agenda item."

"I think it is very important. It will provide stability for the rest of Europe."

He thought on this for a moment, stability in Europe was certainly what France needed more than anything. Once again the beautiful Catherine might have a point. "As you say," he said at last, "I could always investigate Castlereagh's thoughts before the meeting."

"I believe you should," she agreed, "Though I have it on good authority that the Prince Regent is rather enthusiastic of the proposal."

He almost broke his own rule and questioned her on this. She could only be referring to the message Castlereagh had received earlier. How was it that this beautiful woman could know the content of messages from the Prince Regent of England? He caught his questions in his throat and, instead, nestled against her ample bosom and drifted to sleep.

Ceres let him sleep; there were still many hours before dawn. She would wake him later.

Chapter Fifteen

New York City – 2000

It was like lying upon a cloud. The bed was so soft, so comfortable. The silk sheets felt smooth and thrillingly cool against Beatrice's naked skin. She couldn't see anything but the bed, which seemed to glow in its own soft illumination. Beyond it was only darkness, yet the darkness was anything but frightening. It was safe, full of comfort. She was safe; she was happy; she was waiting for something, but what that was she could not remember.

Neither could she remember why she was naked, she normally wore clothes to bed… but… the memory was out of reach and somehow unimportant. It felt good, she realised, especially with the sensual feel of the silk.

She raised her head. At the bottom of the bed something was emerging from the well of darkness. At first it seemed unreal, blackness upon blackness. Then it took form and she realised it was a figure. As the person climbed onto the bed and started to crawl across it towards her she realised it was a girl, as naked as she was. Long, dark hair fell over the girl's face, obscuring her identity.

Beatrice still felt no fear, just a curiosity, a desire to know who this stranger was. The sight of her crawling ever so slowly towards her, feline movements across white silk, her face concealed but the shadowy form of naked breast visible was somehow thrilling.

The girl reached her feet and threw her head back, causing her hair to tumble down her back. Beatrice knew her... it was... it was... The knowledge lay hidden for a moment. Then she realised. It was the European girl she had bumped into on the street. But what was she doing here? Why was she on the bed with her? Perhaps if she could remember the manner of their meeting, but that memory too was out of reach. It seemed almost from another lifetime.

She gently moved Beatrice's feet apart, spreading her legs slightly. Beatrice did not resist. The woman crawled further up the bed, between her legs. Skin lightly brushed against skin and a thrill shot through Beatrice, an electric current causing the hairs on her arm to stand to attention.

The girl lowered her head; her lips touched skin just above Beatrice's pubic triangle and lay butterfly kisses upon her. The kisses moved up Beatrice's body, until they reached the soft mounds of her breasts. The lips kissed one nipple gently, sucking it into the girl's soft mouth, and then the other. Beatrice's nipples hardened instantly and she felt a warm moisture spread between her thighs. This was heavenly, she thought. Something within her suspected that she should find it very wrong, but she couldn't for a single moment think why that should be.

The girl continued up from her breasts. Her tongue drew a graceful line up Beatrice's neck, and then she kissed her lips. Soft, simple kisses. Beatrice began to squirm ecstatically, rubbing her sex against the girl's leg. She reached up and grabbed her beautiful face, both hands reaching for the Goddess. She pulled the girl hard to her and started to kiss her back. Not chaste kisses, but a long, sensual kiss, full of passion. Her tongue snaked into the girl's mouth, exploring, searching, and needing. Her senses were full of the girl, her beauty, the gentle groans of passion that escaped from her mouth, the softness of her skin, the taste of her lips and her scent, a gentle perfume of vanilla.

The fire within her exploded into life. She took the girl by the shoulders and pushed her down her body, towards her engorged sex. The girl knew what Beatrice wanted, she put her mouth against her vagina and her tongue began to probe and explore, the tongue lashing expertly in a way that Beatrice had never experienced before. All the while Beatrice ground herself into the girl's face wanting her to reach the very core of herself with her tongue.

Within moments she felt the orgasm build within her, rising to a crescendo…

Danaan looked at Beatrice from across the room. Beatrice had thrown the covers off herself and slipped her hand between her legs, where it moved back and forth urgently.

The vampire slipped from the human's mind and moved silently out of the room. The first step had been taken. As she closed the apartment door behind her the mortal's orgiastic cry pierced the night and Danaan allowed herself a slight, satisfied smile. The turmoil and upset she had felt on the Millennium Eve had evaporated like morning dew before a long forgotten sun. She was supremely confident, with the arrogance that only a vampire could possess, that she could easily seduce the mortal. Yet it was not the confidence that had caused the negative emotions to flee. She was, like all vampires, a creature that craved sensation. The hunt, for it truly was a hunt, had filled her with a much needed sense of purpose. Beatrice would be hers and, at that precise moment, the hunt was all that counted.

The orgasm woke her. She found her hand still at her own sex, her fingers slick with her own moisture. For a second she lay, panting, enjoying the feeling of the glow that ran through her body.

Then realisation. She had dreamt of being with another woman. She was repulsed by her dream, by her reaction to it and, at the same time, she was strangely thrilled and sexually fulfilled in a way she had never been before.

Unable to cope with the confusion she curled into a ball and fell back into an exhausted sleep that was, this time, dreamless.

Chapter Sixteen

Castle Csejthe, Carpathian Mountains – 1580

Danaan awoke from the stupor as soon as the sun sank beyond the horizon. She pulled the heavy drapes that surrounded her bed aside and stepped onto the cold granite, relishing the chill breeze that stole across her porcelain skin and the cold that stole from the floor into her bare feet.

One of the advantages of the affair with Erzsébet was the fact that the Countess would permit no one to know of their indiscretions. Rumour and innuendo was one thing, but if a servant actually found the castle's mistress in bed with another, woman or man... Suffice it to say that Erzsébet would find the scandal intolerable. Thus Danaan was actively encouraged to return to her own room after their trysts, thus conveniently avoiding the thorny question of why she retreated from her lover's arms before the dawn.

As she dressed she contemplated what she would do with the evening. The wild of the mountains and forests called to her still. She thought she might venture out tonight, to dance through the forests.

Hunger clawed at her entire body, sending the intimate pain, which only one of the Velvet could fully understand, coursing through her veins and her nerves like an empty fire that roared through her entire being. She had tried, in vain, to distract herself, through the sensation of cold upon her body, by planning her evening, even in the feminine intricacies of dressing but all for naught. Yet she was not surprised, the persistence of the agony that ran through every cell and burned her veins could not be ignored, she knew that. Danaan had been circumspect with regard her feeding since she had arrived and, though she had fed before she had gone to Erzsébet, the night before, it had been too little. Before she could dance through the wilds she needed to feed. Perhaps she could stave the need until she had left the castle and find herself a meal of good peasant stock, hardy blood from a resilient people. The thought pleased her, though it also caused the hunger to grow within her even more as she imagined such hot, wholesome blood filling her ever hungry mouth.

She had just finished lacing her boots when a knock at her door broke her reverie. A second knock came, more insistent this time, followed by a rattling of the door handle. The testing of the handle caused her a moment of consternation as she knew that no servant would be so presumptuous.

Danaan strode to the heavy wooden door and turned the key in the lock. A loud creak sounded as she pulled it open, the large metal hinges grating in protest. I should procure some goose fat from the kitchens for that, the vampire determined.

"Katrina, my dear cousin," Erzsébet positively glowed, a smile burning radiantly that set her delicate features alight.

"Erzsébet," Danaan's voice was filled with delight at the sight of her hostess, though inside the gnawing hunger and her desire for the wilds made the presence of the woman little more than an irritant. Five centuries had allowed Danaan to become a veritable fountain of false charm, however. "You honour me. What can I do for you?"

"You can honour me with your presence this evening," her voice dropped to a conspiratorial whisper as she leaned closer to the vampire, "I wish to show you something."

No doubt it was something one of her pet occultists had devised but Danaan felt that she could not refuse. Let this be quick she thought as her feet followed Erzsébet, whilst her heart was tugged by the majesty of the mountains and the lure of the forest. The distant cry of a wolf, plaintive and haunting, only served to cause her further consternation at the disruption of her plans

Danaan became somewhat more perturbed as Erzsébet led her down into the bowels of the castle. Like all travellers through the land she had heard tales of Báthory's dungeon, though she had assumed that it was her distant husband who made use of the place. Once established within Csejthe, Danaan had discovered that Erzsébet delighted in bringing captives into its dark jaws, though the knowledge had not disturbed her. The nobility enforced their rule with a vicious brutality and with her husband almost perpetually absent it was down to Erzsébet to ensure that the social order was maintained.

But why on earth would the woman take her into the dungeon? Perhaps as a mortal she would have been frightened, fearful that the Countess had turned her affections from her and sought to punish her for some reason, but she was secure in the knowledge that she could overpower Erzsébet and any guard she had in attendance. Unfortunately such a display of power would undoubtedly bring this most delicious chapter of her life to a premature end.

They entered an antechamber and the guard left their side, crossing the room to join a fellow. Torchlight flickered wildly in the draft that whistled down the stairway they had just descended. The room had a musty odour and, beneath that, Danaan's sensitive nose could detect the coppery hint of spilled blood, old now and without any vitality but still alluring. The smell piqued Danaan's hunger further and she could hear clearly the pounding heartbeat of her hostess and the two guards who stood either side of a door on the far wall. She felt her fangs extend slightly, an autonomic reaction; with supreme strength of will she forced them to retract.

Erzsébet had moved over to a table, her fingers tracing gently along a small hardwood box adorned with exquisite carvings of a distinctly erotic nature. "Come here darling cousin," her voice almost sang.

When Danaan had moved closer the woman flicked a silver latch on the side of the box and opened the lid.

Danaan moved closer still to get a better view of its contents. The inside of the box was lined with velvet, upon which rested a silver object of curious design. A pair of pincers, shaped somewhat like eagle talons. Erzsébet lifted them reverently from the box and held them out to Danaan. The vampire turned them around, wondering at their design. They were forged from hardened silver and appeared wickedly sharp. She had never seen their like before.

"My husband disappoints me some times, I have made no secret of this, especially to him," Erzsébet explained. "These represent all that disappoints me in him, and also those rare moments when he fills me with the utmost respect.

"When he first showed me these it was a profound moment. A moment that made me proud to be mistress of this God-forsaken castle. You see my husband created these himself, they were forged of his design. They are a device worthy of a man known as the Black Hero of Hungary.

"Imagine my disappointment when he decided that these were too cruel to use on another, even a heathen."

She motioned to the guards who retreated through the door. When they were out of earshot she continued. "I bear my heart to you tonight, my dearest Katrina. I have an aunt and she taught me two things, things I wish to share with you.

"She taught me the pleasure of Sapphic love, and this I have already instructed you in and shared with you."

Danaan suppressed a smile at that comment, the woman truly believed her an inexperienced girl. If only she knew. Erzsébet, meanwhile, had taken a whip from the wall and had attached the talons to its end.

"The second thing she taught me," Continued the Countess, "was the pleasure that can be gained through inflicting suffering.

"Ah... here we are..."

The guards had returned dragging a naked man between them. As they clasped his wrists in chains suspended on the far wall Danaan recognised him as Boch, the horrid little man from the night before. He had been treated roughly, bruises covered his dirt-encrusted skin, his manhood was shrivelled to nothing and it was clear from his red-rimmed eyes that he had been brought to tears recently.

"He did not leave your lands?"

"Sweet Katrina! He did not get the chance. I decided I had been far too lenient and had him arrested before he had got a mile from the castle. Probably just as well," she laughed, the sound sharp with an unpleasant edge, "his filthy flesh may have poisoned some innocent wolf."

She turned to the guards, "You may leave us."

The guards moved towards the stairs and Erzsébet turned her attention back to Danaan. "The secret of flagellation," she explained, "Is in the action of the wrist." Her voice dropped to a conspiratorial whisper, "Much like the secret of cunnelingus is in the action of the tongue."

She turned towards Boch and readied the whip.

"Erzsébet, is it normal to have them face you?"

"A good question cousin. I confess that if you see such punishments in the town square the whip is applied to the back. But this is for our pleasure and how much more pleasure will we gain if we can see the agony etched upon his face."

Her words ended and the whip cracked.

The silver pincer caught Boch's flesh, the talons digging deep into the tissue of his emaciated chest. As her wrist flicked back the flesh ripped, tearing chunks of tissue. Blood sprayed and crimson rivulets ran down his filthy, bruised chest. Boch's face contorted in agony and a piercing scream ripped from his throat.

"Ahhh... a screamer... good..." Erzsébet's voice had become husky. The whip lashed out again and another scream echoed around the antechamber.

The smell of blood was almost unbearable. The hunger coursed through Danaan's entire being. She dug her fingernails hard into her clenched fists, piercing the flesh in the vain hope that pain would hold the hunger back.

She could hear Erzsébet's heartbeat, a deafening drumming that exploded from her slim frame. As the blood flowed and the screams grew louder so Erzsébet became excited. Her heartbeat became faster, thundering, pushing at Danaan's every nerve. She could smell the mortal's sex, her excitement adding a musky layer to the tangy scent of fresh blood. The Countess found the flagellation sexually stimulating.

It was too much. Danaan's fangs had fully extended. The hunger was a searing pain. Her self-control was fleeing. With the last vestiges of her will Danaan forced herself to turn away and run up the stairs, somehow maintaining a mortal speed, though her legs could have carried her with a swiftness faster than a mortal could dream of emulating. She fled from the dungeon and temptation. Away from the desire to run to Boch and lick the blood from his wounds. Away from the desire to suckle the blood from Erzsébet's engorged labia.

Danaan slammed the door to her room closed, the wood rattling in the frame. On her way back she had passed a maid and forced the girl to accompany her. She had entered the mortal's mind but it was all she could do to ensure the girl overlooked the exposed fangs and the sharp desire in her eyes. Danaan had been forced to grab her wrist and drag her to her chambers; the poor girl was convinced that she had done something to offend the young noble woman, something that had caused Danaan to decide to administer a beating.

She was no more than fifteen, a plump girl, but pretty enough. Danaan raised the girl's wrist up and the vampire's control slipped for a brief second. The girl saw the extended canines as Danaan started to bite down. A scream welled in her chest but died into a contented sigh as the fangs pierced the flesh. A useful side effect of her heritage, the pleasure her bite gave caused the girl to forget the fact that the noble woman was suckling on her blood. The girl surrendered to the heady pleasures of the Bloodline of Shang-Di.

The hunger began to subside. Rationale had replaced instinct, but the maid was very weak, very close to death.

The screech of hinges came like a death wail.

"Cousin, I never thought your constitution would be so delicate..."

Danaan had neglected to lock the door.

Erzsébet's words had been spoken as she entered the bedchamber, the prelude to a longer sentence; they died in her throat as her eyes took in the scene. The maid was pale, her arm slick with blood as was Danaan's mouth. Danaan let the arm drop and the maid slumped to the floor in a faint.

Danaan, preparing to fight, dropped into an instinctive crouch; she had been exposed. Her eyes glowed with a fierce fire, her fangs were still extended. She looked for all the world like some feral beast. Desperately she entered Erzsébet's mind, hoping to limit the damage. With some she may have been able to confuse the memory, with others confuse their awareness enough to escape without resorting to violence, but not with Erzsébet. The strength of the woman was impressive; her mind was like a steel trap, though Danaan now suspected that her strength was largely lent by insanity

Erzsébet gave out a small laugh. "How interesting."

Chapter Seventeen

New York – 2000

The neon sign glowed with an eerie blue light; its letters reflected in the dark puddle of rainwater on the street, the sign crackled slightly as it burned into the night. A foot, misplaced, catching the water caused the reflected sign to dissolve into fractured light for a moment, as moisture tried to soak through the patent leather shoes.

Dark Waters was one of the most exclusive clubs in New York for devotees of life's more extreme pleasures. Entrance to the club was not easily gained, to become a member one had to be both rich and powerful. Once inside a patron could indulge their every fantasy, their every whim and, should an accident occur, the Management would take care of it. There was never an investigation by the authorities; the fact that politicians, judges and the most powerful of businessmen, and women, were members ensured that discretion was assured.

It was also a place where the Bloodline of Qutrub could come, undisturbed. There were three such clubs around the globe, the ownership of each passing through myriad holding companies and names, some real and some imagined, a veritable labyrinth of bureaucracy but all, eventually, under the control of the ancient.

When Ymochel had been released from the ancient he had been given special dispensation to indulge himself within the clubs, should he wish. The permission was unusual, Qutrub normally only allowed his own Bloodline to pass through the ornate doors of his clubs. After the one hundred and sixty years of pleasure that the fiend had extracted from Ymochel's body, it seemed the ancient had come to think of him as one of his own.

Ymochel, for his part, hated the ancient, but the clubs were ideal for picking up an easy meal. Vampires were asked to be careful not to kill within the club, though a few accidental deaths inevitably proved unavoidable over the years. However, if their meal were hospitalised, well that was all part of the game, the Management took very good care of those employees who needed medical attention.

At first he had sworn that he would not take the ancient up on his offer, but with the passing of years he had succumbed to the lure of the clubs. Once he had fallen to that temptation he had told himself that he would not indulge in the darker, more sadistic offerings available in Dark Waters. For centuries he had detested the concept that pleasure could be gained by causing suffering, it was just another abuse of power, just another reminder of his time with Uriel and the poison of his Bloodline's bite. Yet, once a member of the club, he found himself gravitating to just that form of activity. He also gained pleasure from it and was astounded to discover that such pleasure came without the bitter aftertaste of guilt. He had discovered that he enjoyed causing pain and that there were those in the world who enjoyed receiving it. Now, whenever he returned to New York he would visit the club, though he would struggle with his own conscience and desires before finally, inevitably, giving in and visiting the establishment. Since returning to New York, a few months earlier, he had managed to avoid the club, until this night.

It was clear that Qutrub knew what Ymochel did in the club, nothing occurred in Dark Waters that the ancient was not aware of. Perhaps the twisted ancient gained pleasure from Ymochel's dramatic shift in perspective, it was clear that the long years in the ancient's clutches had invoked a massive swing in the Nubian's consciousness, morality and tastes.

He had left his vigil; though that did not matter as he knew that he could easily pick up the Praetorian's trail again. At that moment he needed to feed, but more desperately he needed to vent his frustrations. Violence allowed a singular clarity of the mind that nothing else was able to offer.

He walked through the entrance, past the discreet, but very efficient, security and into the reception hall; plush velvet couches rode upon a sea of the most luxurious crimson carpet, the room amply illuminated by a crystal chandelier.

He passed through the hall, knowing exactly where he was going, and continued along the corridor that led to the various rooms of the club. An elderly mortal came out of one of the rooms, the opening of the door allowing the explosive beat of dance music to escape the excellent sound proofing and flashing strobe lights to play feverishly upon the corridor wall. Ymochel shook his head, he had no liking for modern 'music', he found it to be all noise without substance.

The cacophony ended, much to the Nubian's relief, as the door closed and the vampire continued along the corridor. Eventually he reached his intended destination; he opened the door and passed into a baroque styled room. He relaxed into a chair, sinking deeply into the plush leather of the seat. Folding his arms comfortably in his lap, Ymochel allowed the soothing music of the string quartet wash over him, as he waited for the major-domo.

He didn't have to wait long.

The major-domo was a grave looking Japanese man of about forty years of age. He wore a beautifully crafted suit of charcoal grey and his slightly long black hair was slicked back and tied in a tight ponytail. He recognised his latest customer as soon as he came into the room.

The major-domo has never met his employer and was not one to listen to gossip, especially when that gossip came from people he knew full well had never met the entrepreneur either. He knew, however, that his employer had a select group of friends all of whom were to receive preferential treatment in the club. The President of the United States could be in the room, but if one of the select group were there he would have to wait.

He was curious about this one, though he would never let his curiosity show. Curiosity would lead to unemployment… or worse. Yet he was an odd one this guest of the employer. Most of the employer's friends never gave a name, he knew that this one was called Michael; indeed he had insisted that he was not referred to as Sir. He knew no more than that, but it was more than he knew about the others who came in very rarely. This Michael was also more of a frequent visitor; he had been in the club often in previous years, though he had not patronised the club for a couple of years, which led the major-domo to believe he probably lived in New York at least some of the time. He was strikingly handsome as well, it seemed that the majority of the employer's friends were grotesquely ugly.

If he had not known better he would have thought this Michael an impostor but, when he first arrived, conformation of his status had been swift in arriving.

"Michael-san, welcome. What may Dark Waters do for you this evening?"

"Something simple," Ymochel's sonorous voice sounded like silk, "A room, a girl and a gauntlet."

"Of course Michael-san, the arrangements will be made swiftly."

The major-domo had turned to leave but Michael's voice stopped him in his tracks, "About the girl…"

The human turned back.

"She should be Caucasian, her skin pale, wearing an elegant dress I think. Long dark hair and… make sure she's strictly a dyke."

The major-domo nodded, "As you wish."

"Oh and I'd have your medical crew on standby," his own words made Ymochel laugh, the laughter booming through the room. The major-domo smiled, his time in the club had made him impervious to any requirement a customer might have. All things considered this was a very simple request.

A single spotlight fell onto the girl, making her the focal part of the room. Her hands were shackled to a chain that hung from the ceiling. Her hair had been brushed gently over her shoulder, off her back, before the beautiful two thousand dollar dress had been ripped open, exposing her back and bare buttocks.

She whimpered slightly, wondering what the man would do next. She normally serviced submissives and only ever women. When the major-domo had told her that she must service this client, however, she knew better than to argue. Besides Dark Waters always compensated their girls well. At that moment the compensation meant little, she was so scared that the man was going to push his dirty cock into her, the thought of it made her feel physically sick.

Ymochel slipped his hand into the gauntlet. He flexed the metal, smiling at its sharp ridges. He saw the tension contorting the muscles in her back. He saw the genuine fear. It was tangible, he could smell it, taste it even. This was just what he wanted.

"Fucking dyke bitch!" His hand flicked out and red lines sprouted across her skin. He had held back, there was no sense in breaking her too soon.

Her scream was beautiful, merging with and complementing the music piped into the room from the baroque room.

"That's it bitch, scream."

He lashed out again, more blood running down her back.

"Fucking dyke whore... Fucking piece of shit!"

Again and again he hit her, until his hunger could take no more. Then he was knelt behind her, licking the blood that was smeared thick across her back. He raised himself behind her and sank his fangs deep into her neck, drinking her and letting all the pain of his Bloodline flood her nerves. Her screams rang out until her throat was too hoarse to make a sound.

His hands clasped the sides of her head; give the Praetorian a Praetorian's death. It was like a whisper in his mind.

The tension in his forearms built, it was so easy. Just rip upwards and bring her the true death.

The tension suddenly left his arms and he let the girl go. She slumped forward, still suspended by the chains. He had stopped himself, it wasn't Danaan. But it would be, soon it would be.

He took off the gauntlet and let it drop to the floor. Then he turned and walked to the door. As he walked he hummed Mozart's symphony in F to himself. He felt calm and confident in the knowledge of how best he might proceed.

There was enough time to shower, he decided, before racing the dawn home.

The girl was still breathing, but barely, as the medical crew rushed in. The major-domo surveyed her wrecked body, lifting her head before allowing the medics to work their magic. The girl would probably be out of commission for some time but there could be no doubt that she had certainly earned her money.

Chapter Eighteen

Pompeii – 0079

It had been a couple of hours before dawn when Uriel fell into the stupor, forced into the deathlike sleep early due to over-consumption. Like the day before it would be impossible to wake him. Ymochel decided that the preparations needed to be made in case they had to leave the villa. During the night he had selected four slaves and removed them to cells in another part of the domicile. He ensured that they were fed and watered. All four appeared to be strong men, if a little malnourished. He had explained to them that they would be expected to carry the master of the house's litter should the mountain become even angrier. If anything they seemed relieved, they had been handed a means of escape.

Once Uriel had succumbed to the stupor he had pulled the litter into the ancient's chambers and manoeuvred the fat, insensible form of his master onto it. He made a mental note that, if they did not flee, he would have to extract him from the litter before the night came, lest his master realise that Ymochel had again entered the chambers for less than a good reason.

About an hour before dawn he opened the doors to the concubines' rooms. Mercia was already asleep in her room, the female having surrendered to the lure of the stupor early, probably in an attempt to escape her own fear. Diana, however, paced her room. When she saw Ymochel she hissed at him, disdain brimming in her eyes. The Nubian retreated, but his mind was filled with the memory of how he had drained Augustine to submissiveness. Suddenly the imagery was replaced with the sight of the male concubine's head rotting in his hands. For a second the rotten head transformed, and it was Diana's head that stared blank eyed at him. The image shattered as the door slammed shut behind him.

With no more to do he left the villa and sat upon a rock his eyes looking over to the fires still burning on the mountainside, no longer heeding the grey dust that coated the rock. His toga was already filthy with the unavoidable substance.

It was only a few minutes past dawn, a dawn that could not break through the thick clouds, when the explosion rocked the earth.

Fiery rocks exploded from the head of the mountain and red veins of molten earth began bleeding down its side.

Ymochel leapt to his feet and ran into the villa, cracks were opening up the walls and plaster fell like snow from the ceiling. Yet, despite the devastation that surrounded him within the villa, he was oblivious to the true extent of the Hell that was visited upon Pompeii.

Outside the city the sea shrank back, the water vaporising. Burning floods of vapour and ash fell upon the city, a hurricane that captured all in its path, stretching from Pompeii to Herculaneum. Yet the Gods smiled upon the vampires it seemed, the burning winds did not extend as far South as the villa.

The vapour fell onto trees and houses, onto people. The citizens of Pompeii tried in vain to escape the city, running down the streets with blankets over their heads, in a hope that they might protect them. All that the winds touched became petrified, captured as though caught in a gorgons' stare. In centuries to come men would discover the city once more and find them still, citizens running for their lives, slaves cowering in fear, the last kiss of a couple resigned to their fate. Trapped for eternity.

All the while more and more of the lifeblood of the planet oozed out of the mountain, as though it were a gapping wound in the side of the world.

Before Ymochel reached the atrium he collided with Diana. She screamed at him incoherently, simultaneously begging answers and blaming him for the ill that had befallen them.

Ymochel's hand shot out, slapping the concubine across her face, trying to calm her but was answered with painful scratches as she clawed at his face, red slashes opening up across his black skin. His anger exploded, he grabbed the hysterical vampire by her shoulders and sank his fangs deep into her neck.

Her hysteria calmed as he drained her, to the point that he knew that she would follow if he commanded. He could feel her energy, her power, washing into him, filling him. The gashes on his face healed, leaving the skin on his cheek flawless.

Suddenly, he knew what he should do. It was so clear, painted in images in his mind. His fangs left her neck and his hands slid up from the shoulders. His nails extended into talons, piercing her neck. He expected her to fight back, but she simply looked at him with meek eyes. He yanked upwards and her head came away. There was a small rush of energy from her fallen body and then decay began to take hold

He threw the rotting head to one side and ran towards Mercia's room. The power had not left him, as it had with Augustine the day before. Inside, instinctively, he realised that her power was now his. He had stolen all that she was, and her very essence was now part of Ymochel.

He threw the door open to Mercia's room. The last concubine slept. He looked at her for the briefest of moments wondering if he dared bestow Diana's fate upon her. No, he felt sleepy; he had drunk too much already. He needed to get away from this place and if he stole her essence then he knew the stupor of the daylight hours would quickly steal upon him. He would not try to wake her though; the concubines had always treated him with bitter contempt.

By the time he entered the master's chamber Mercia's decimated body already rotted, as did the sluggish pool of stolen blood that had spilled out of her open neck. She had not woken, even when he tore her head from her body. The explosion of energy as she died had been larger then it had been with Diana, her essence thrown into the ether. For a moment he had almost failed to execute the female, something instinctive within him forcing him to stay his hand. It was as though he was unable to kill her without first draining her. Then calm had descended upon him, from where he did not know, and his hands had pulled her head from her shoulders almost with their own volition.

Ymochel manhandled the litter, pulling it into the devastated peristylium. He had briefly considered whether he could visit the concubine's fate upon his master, but he was terrified that the obese vampire might awaken. Whilst the thought of spending eternity as Uriel's slave filled him was a loathing that he would never be able to put into words, his vampire nature would not allow him to wantonly commit suicide. The stupor that draining would bring could well see his death stealing upon him as he slept in the villa. More painful would be his master waking as he tried to remove his head from his huge neck. He then considered leaving the ancient to the villa's fate, but if the anger of nature failed to wash over the villa, if the ancient awoke to discover that Ymochel had abandoned him then he would be hunted and the pain visited upon him when caught, he was sure, would have him begging for death.

Instead Ymochel released the four slaves chosen as litter bearers. For a moment he feared they might bolt, but the terror that brimmed in their eyes was as much for the feral creature with blood-stained mouth that stood before them, his nature unhidden, as it was for the Hell that exploded out of the mountain.

They picked up the litter and with Ymochel leading the way they ran, ignoring the weight of their burden and the wails of the few remaining slaves, still locked in their cells.

Outside the villa fire was spreading along trees and through the grasses, racing from the doomed city and speeding down the coast towards them. Ymochel choose a path away from the fire. As they made their escape the flames reached the villa, the screams of the remaining slaves, still locked in the villa's slave pen, were lost within the roar of the inferno.

The journey was hard, wind direction pushed the flames this way and that. The slaves were exhausted. The very air was fiercely hot, burning their lungs, smoke and the stench of sulphur caused their eyes to sting and water until the humans' eyes were as red as the vampire's feral stare.

Eventually Ymochel called a halt. The twists and turns forced upon them by the flames had caused them to stray dangerously close to the mountain. A thick slick of lava had pooled nearby, it's surface ablaze, the heat almost unbearable.

Ymochel laughed, though even he could not tell if it was an insanely hysterical laugh or the relief of a moment of perfect clarity.

He turned to the slaves, "Go, I release you."

They did not need a second command. Despite their scorched lungs they ran from the litter and the beast that commanded them.

It was as though it was a vision come unbidden into his mind and he acted out the role. Ymochel pulled the slumbering ancient from the litter and dragged him closer and closer to the lava.

Fangs sank into Uriel's neck and his blood bubbled into Ymochel's mouth, slowly at first, then more quickly. The power that flooded him was like an explosion in his mind. The feeding was no longer conscious, his mouth suckled instinctively as his senses flared. A million suns exploded in his vision. His nerves were on fire.

The ancient stirred, but Ymochel held on, his mind fighting to keep control, his fingernails becoming talons that pierced the blubbery shoulders. Uriel fought back, trying to rest himself away, but it was too late, Ymochel had stolen too much of the ancient's strength. For a moment they were physically deadlocked, but the Nubian's mouth still suckled and soon he had the advantage.

Eventually Uriel slumped; Ymochel felt the stupor stealing upon him and sensed the stolen strength starting to wane as it began to flood from him, back to the ancient. He grabbed at the ancient's head and started to pull upwards. Uriel was no Fledgling vampire like Diana, however. Without warning the ancient's hands shot upwards and grabbed Ymochel's wrists, wrenching them away from his head and causing Ymochel to stumble backwards and out of his master's grip. Uriel twisted around to face the traitorous Fledgling. Beneath his toga the flesh ripped as he moved, but with his blood stolen it did not heal, thin lances of pain shot through his fat flesh.

Ymochel felt a pure panic flow through his veins, stronger even than the power he had stolen. Power that was streaming from him back to its rightful owner. He had sealed his own fate, he realised. He could not think, he simply stood paralysed, trapped in Uriel's hateful glare as crimson tears brimmed in his eyes.

Then it came to him, cold and unbidden, cutting through the panic. He rushed at the ancient and grabbed at him. With a supreme effort he picked up the mammoth vampire and threw him towards the lava.

The flames enveloped the ancient and his scream echoed through the countryside. The flames coiled around the flesh and wormed their way inside him, bursting out through his eyes and his open maw, even as the lava ate through his body with a devastating efficiency.

An explosion threw Ymochel backwards, not physical, but psychic. The ancient had found true death, and his death rushed from the decimated body like a cry echoing around the world. Then Ymochel knew, he knew that the other vampires would know that the ancient had perished, he knew that they would come to this place searching for answers.

The stupor threatened to take him. With an effort he shrugged the deep sleep away and crawled to the litter, pushing himself up on it. Gripping the wood tightly he threw it into the lava. The slaves had tripped and the litter had fallen. It was a horrible tragedy.

Every ounce of Ymochel's self wanted to surrender to the onrushing sleep, and he fell to the floor once again. He fought through the stupor and crawled to the lava, the blistering heat forcing his senses to stay alert.

There was no time to think, or he could not do it. He thrust his arm into the burning magma and screamed, an unending howl that echoed through the countryside. Agony shot through him, agony that he thought no man could ever feel, much less describe. Pain worse than that felt when Uriel had drained the mortal he had once been to the point of death. Pain worse than the beatings and punishments that Uriel regularly mete out to his get. An agony deeper than the pain of enslavement. As long as he lived he was sure that he would feel no pain as intense as this. Yet, a cold voice told him, it was a beautiful pain; it was the agony of freedom.

He fell backwards; his lower arm was gone, completely disintegrated past the elbow, what remained of the upper arm charred and useless. Agony was still rolling through his mind he crawled away from the lava. He crawled and crawled until the absolute darkness of the stupor dragged him, mercifully, from the pain.

Chapter Nineteen

New York – 2000

The dreams had come nightly.

After the first night Beatrice had felt ashamed, dirty even, and incapable of reconciling the absolute eroticism of the dream with her own, supposed, heterosexuality. She had stood, in the morning, under a blazing hot shower, trying to wash the filth away, as though the scolding waters could sear the dream and make it as though it had never been so.

She had gone to work, and cast the dream from her mind. Yet that night, alone in her sleep, the girl had come again and this time it was Beatrice who instigated, it was Beatrice taking the mystery woman to heights of passion, and gaining an orgasm herself at the very sight of the woman's climax.

Again, the next morning, she had felt wretched. Wretched at the thought that she had done that to a woman, wretched at the warm, satisfied glow that filled her body. When she got home from the office she had drunk a quart of vodka, hoping that the alcohol would chase the dreams away. It didn't. Again she dreamed, this time she and the mystery woman pleasured each other in a sixty-nine position, bringing each other to orgasm simultaneously. It was as though they fed of each other's passion.

When she awoke she didn't feel the guilt she had felt the previous two mornings, she felt wicked, yes, but not wretched. She was beginning to accept that she might have a homosexual side to her nature. That evening she did not turn to the bottle, but to the television. She rented an adult movie from the cable pay-per-view service and watched excitedly as the women in the movie pleasured each other. Eventually it became too much and she found her hand sliding down the waistband of her knickers. As the women on the screen brought each other to orgasm, Beatrice masturbated furiously, her ecstatic cries ringing through the apartment.

When she went to bed that evening she thought that the dreams might not come. Her masturbation had left her feeling sexually spent. But they came again, and again, through her dreams, she climaxed.

During those days Steve had tried to call several times. She avoided him, too busy to take his calls at work and screening her calls at home. He had tried to let himself in the flat on the second night but she had taken the keys from him and kicked him out.

She didn't know why exactly. The emotions were too tangled and complicated. She was still angry with him, that was true, and he had been with her long enough to know that when she was angry she needed time and space in which to calm down. That wasn't the only reason, however. It was partially guilt. She was guilty for cheating on him, albeit in her dreams. It was also partially shame, shame that she had become most definitely bi-curious, perhaps even bi-sexual, seemingly overnight. There was also a sense of frustration, she knew that he would want to make up, and making up for Steve involved sex. She just didn't want it, he didn't have what she wanted, he wasn't a woman. He wasn't she realised, the dream woman. The realisation shocked her, perhaps she hadn't even become bi-sexual but lesbian?

The woman had become real to her. That was a silly thing to think, of course, because she was real, Beatrice had seen her on the street the night the dreams started. Yet, in some ways, the love affair in her dreams had become real, or, at least, the emotions had.

It was all too confusing, perhaps if Steve were more sensitive she could talk to him about her confused feelings and sexuality. If only he didn't always think through his dick.

The day after she had rented the adult movie things became worse. She was noticing women and no longer as rivals but as potential conquests. She had needed to travel up to the eighteenth floor at work and when she entered the elevator she had found herself alone with Vicky from Human Resources. She had known the girl for a couple of years and had even been out for drinks with her once or twice, yet she had never seen her with the eyes she used in the elevator. As the car went slowly upwards she couldn't help but notice the curve of Vicky's breast and the way that the buttons of her blouse had conspired to part the fabric slightly. She couldn't tear her eyes away from the lace of the bra, and how it revealed the soft mound of flesh. She noticed how the nipples poked through the satin fabric of the blouse, and suddenly wanted to take those nipples into her mouth, to suckle on them and nibble at them. She actually started to feel wet at the thought and then embarrassed, convinced that Vicky might realise what she was thinking.

She noticed the perfume Vicky was wearing, and it began to make her feel light-headed. Suddenly she had the desire to pounce on the woman, to pin her against the lift wall and take her. The lift announced that they were on the seventeenth floor, the door opened and, mercifully, Vicky exited. It was then that Beatrice realised that she was going to have to do something about her newfound obsession. Her mind drifted back to the movie the night before and the situations it had portrayed.

So it was that Beatrice found herself leaving her apartment that evening. Beneath the black dress she was wearing her nicest thong and bra set and a pair of hold-up stockings.

As she walked onto the street she failed to notice Steve standing on the other side of the road, obscured by the shadows of the doorway he hid in.

Steve saw Beatrice leave the apartment building. She was wearing her best little black dress. Something was going on, this just wasn't like Beatrice. Not the ignoring him and taking her key back, she was prone to mood swings; he had come to accept that. But dressed up, going out. That wasn't like her at all.

For a second he actually thought that maybe she'd found a new man, but dismissed the thought as quickly as it came. Beatrice had no time for romantic trysts, it would distract her from her all consuming work. He started to follow her; he'd remain at a discreet distance and discover exactly what was happening. He stepped onto the sidewalk, emerging from the shadows. The night was crisp and clear, following the rains that day and the lights from the occasional passing car reflected on the slick, wet roads. He failed to notice the man approaching him from behind.

A hand fell firmly onto his shoulder and Steve's anger flashed. Without thinking he spun around, his hand clenched into a fist, which he swung at the unseen assailant. A large black hand caught his fist, stopping the punch with such force that it jarred his shoulder.

The man holding his fist in his hand was huge, at least six foot four compared to Steve's five foot ten and, beneath the very fine suit, obviously muscular.

"What the Hell…"

"My name is Michael," said the stranger, his voice soft and friendly, "We need to talk about your woman."

"Beatrice… what about her… who the Hell do you think you are?"

"Come with me," said the man, "and we will talk."

"Where?" Steve was obviously confused. Who was this strange man? What did he want with him and Beatrice? He looked the stranger straight in the eyes, but there were no answers there, just unfathomable mysteries. He rubbed his aching shoulder through his thick coat.

"There is a bar a block from here, we can sit and talk. Come with me now." It was a command, not a request.

Against all his better judgments Steve followed Michael to the bar. His eyes flashed down the road, trying to catch a glimpse of Beatrice but she had vanished into the night.

Chapter Twenty

West Yorkshire, England – 1347

The campfire had just, grudgingly, flickered into life; the damp sticks producing as much smoke as they did light. The woman, a nun, knelt on the floor warming her hands whilst the two guards stood nearby grumbling to each other.

"Dame Startin," the taller of the two guards addressed the woman, "begging yer pardon, but I'd ask you to reconsider. This forest ain't safe."

The woman shook her head and, silently, asked God for strength before replying. "Master Warder, I have left the title of Dame behind. I am the Prioress of Kirklees now."

"As you say ma'm, but I'd still ask you to reconsider." There seemed to be a small edge of panic or anxiety in the grizzled man's voice.

"Master Warder, for better or for worse I fear that we are stuck in the forest until day breaks. I will not risk the horses by stumbling blind through the undergrowth."

"But the inn is only two hours ride and 'tis a lot safer than this 'ere forest." He insisted.

"The inn may as well be a hundred leagues distant if one of our mounts breaks a leg, and we have no need to fear the forest. The outlaws in Sherwood are centred around Nottingham and we are in Yorkshire. I doubt they will travel all this way to rob a penniless nun. Now will they?"

"Ma'm, the notorious brigands are to be found round Nottingham way, I grant you, but the forest is still thick with thieves, none-the-less."

For a moment her voice carried the edge of her previous station in life. "Sir, I will broke no more discussion on the matter, we make camp here." Her voice softened slightly before she added, "How long until we reach the priory if we ride at daybreak?"

Jack Warder groaned inaudibly, if she wanted to make good time to the priory they would not be stopping at the inn to break fast. "God willin', we'll be there by sunset tomorrow ma'm."

Startin's voice dropped into a mumble as she turned her attention back to the fire, "Good... good..." The discussion was over.

The guards moved out of earshot to confer.

"What do you make of it James?"

"It's a rum 'un, I'll give you that," replied the second guard, "But I can un'erstand it. A trip will lame a horse an' that'll slow us down on the morrow."

"Not as much as 'avin' our throats cut." Warder ran a dirt-encrusted finger menacingly across his throat to illustrate his point.

"Aye, you 'ave a good point Jack lad, we'll just 'ave to keep a good watch." James shrugged and then added, "As it is I 'ave to make water, you make sure her ladyship don't stray from the fire now."

Neither guard noticed the shadow slipping through the trees, outside the light from the campfire.

James Goldborough watched his companion return to the campfire and then headed into the trees; he wanted to make sure he was out of sight of the camp. It wouldn't do him any good to allow a lady of God to see him making water.

His friend's concerns were well founded; the forest had become notorious in recent years. That said the Prioress was also right, most of the trouble was out round Nottingham. Thieves were not a localised problem though and caution was always needed. That was why Lord Grafton had insisted an armed guard escort the Prioress to her new position. Warder had been irritable through the entire journey, however, probably down to the fact that they'd had to take horses; he'd never been much of a horseman. If the truth was told neither of them were comfortable around the Prioress. She was a devout woman, of that there could be little doubt, but that also meant that when they stopped for the night, on the nights when they had stopped at inns, there had been no chance to play dice or get drunk or whore. Plenty of time for that on the way home though, James grinned to himself.

Once out of sight of the camp James lifted his padded aketon and dropped his hose. A relieved sigh escaped his mouth as the hot stream of urine splashed against the side of the oak.

He never saw the shadow creeping behind him, never knew it was there until two icy cold hands gripped his head.

He managed a startled grunt before the hands twisted, snapping his neck and killing him instantly.

His body dropped softly to the floor, his own urine running back from the tree and pooling around his corpse, and the shadow slipped back into the night.

Jack Warder took off his kettle hat, placing it gently onto the floor so as not to disturb the Prioress, and then removed the padded coif that sat beneath it and scratched. The damned coif made his head itch. Probably full of lice, he thought, as he scratched furiously at his sweat-dampened hair.

The sooner they were out of the damn forest the better. He believed all he had said about outlaws true enough, but then there was the other thing. He hadn't had the courage to mention it to the Prioress, she'd never believe him, nor to James for that matter, the younger guard would have laughed until he pissed himself. Jack knew better though, Jack knew the forest was haunted.

His cousin Ben had told him the stories. The tale of the White Lady who haunted the forest. Some said it was the ghost of a Saxon lady restless after the Normans had taken her husband's lands and then raped and killed her a few hundred years back. Others said it was the presence of Saint Modwenna punishing those who broke the Commandments, though Jack couldn't say why a Saint would attack those out in the forest. Worse thing was, he thought to himself, if it was the Blessed Saint then he was doomed if she found him. He had never been one for observing the Commandments.

Thing was, this White Lady was real enough, Ben had sworn it, and he'd never known the boy lie.

He scratched at his head again. The prioress seemed lost in her own thoughts and the horses, tied to a nearby tree, were quiet enough. James was taking his own sweet time though.

"Jack come 'ere."

He looked at the Prioress but she hadn't reacted. The other guard's voice had seemed odd, no more than a whisper. He might have seen something in the trees, something that had forced him to lower his voice. Maybe he had caught sight of brigands in the woods. Warder picked up his rough handled knife and moved to the edge of the clearing.

"James, James Goldborough, where are you?" He hissed.

The shadow touched his mind again and whispered "Over 'ere Jack." To Warder it sounded like Goldborough, though he wasn't to know that his friend lay dead amongst the trees.

Warder moved further into the forest, away from the light of the fire, fear gripping his stomach. Damn the boy, he thought, what sort of game was he playing? Tree branches caught at his clothing, tugging at him in the dark, and scraped across his rough face. A sound made him whirl around, cracking his head on a low branch. He swore lightly, it had been an owl. As he rubbed his sore skull he realised that he had left his helm at the camp.

"Goldborough?" His voice was stretched, barely audible above the frantic pounding of his own heart.

James Goldborough did not reply.

"What the hell…" He thought he saw a shadow flitting through the undergrowth, but then rationalised that it was just the thin moonlight moving through the swaying branches. Even so his hand gripped the knife tightly, his knuckles white.

"To Hell with you Goldborough, enough of your games." He said almost too loudly. He turned to move back to the camp.

He glimpsed her for just a second before the talon like fingernails ripped his throat. Enough time for him to recognise the White Lady. Enough time for his feverish mind to realise that he had been right to believe Ben and for a stream of urine to soil his dirty grey hose.

He fell to the floor, clutching the gapping hole in his throat, blood spraying through his fingers and spilling onto the forest floor. Unable to make a sound. Unable to warn his charge.

The shadow flitted towards the clearing.

At the edge of the clearing, outside the light flickering from the fire, she watched the Prioress. The older woman was praying, her fingers flickering over a set of ornate rosary beads.

The shadow circled around until it stood behind the Prioress, head still bent in prayer. She edged closer and closer until she stood directly above the nun. Her white fingers, stained red with Jack Warder's blood, reached out slowly and then gently pulled back the wimple.

The Prioress' eyes shot open; she twisted around to see a young girl, beautiful and yet so pale of skin. She was about to ask the girl her name when the girl's mouth opened and she saw the fangs and the luminescent flash of red in the girl's eyes.

She lifted the rosary, holding the tiny crucifix up to the devil, for devil it surely must have been. "God preserve me... I beg of you Lord, preserve your servant."

The vampire laughed, the woman was absolutely sincere in her prayer, sincere in both her will to live and her belief that her God would protect her. She took the rosary from the Prioress' hand and looked at it for a moment before throwing it to one side. "Which God would that be?" She asked the trembling nun, and then she struck, her fangs burying deep into the older woman's neck.

For a moment the Prioress felt the touch of paradise. She sank into the vampire's embrace willingly, offering up her life.

The horses panicked, neighing and whinnying franticly, pulling back at the ropes that tied them and kicking back into the night, kicking naught but air, or each other.

One of them managed to break its head collar and ran into the night, neighing furiously.

The vampire ignored the horses and fed.

Two nights later the new Prioress of Kirklees arrived at her post, her habit stained from her travels, her ornate rosary clutched in her hands.

Her appearance took the nuns aback at first. She was so much younger than they had expected and she was also a day late. They asked her where her escorts had gone, concerned that she should have travelled the roads alone. Her escorts had been forced to return to their Lord with all haste after ensuring she was safe, she explained. Surely the nuns had seen the horsemen galloping off down the road. One remembered that she had and then another. Foolish men, thought one, always rushing here and there. They should have come in for the night, rested and returned to their Lord on the morrow.

Within hours Danaan had settled into the Prioress' room, leaving explicit orders that she was extremely fatigued and was not to be disturbed the following day.

Chapter Twenty One

New York City – 2000

Steve sat in a booth, the strange man blocking his exit. A glass of whiskey on the rocks placed before him. The bar itself was pleasant enough, a few drinkers sat along the counter and one or two booths were filled. The presence of other people made Steve feel a little more at ease. A TV set was suspended above the corner of the bar, just in the periphery of Steve's vision, playing MTV, the music piped around the room.

He didn't know why he had gone to the bar with the stranger; for the life of him he couldn't see how this Michael would know Beatrice. All he knew was that she was acting strangely and he had to find out why. If, somehow, this guy could tell him then it was worth coming. It was at least worth trying.

Ymochel looked at the human before him. He was about twenty-five, the vampire guessed, and had a temper. His rashness would have to be controlled, but he might prove useful. The Praetorian had taken a very definite interest in the mortal girl. She had visited her every night and yet, he believed, she had not revealed herself to the girl. He didn't understand why, he had no way of knowing what it was she did every night. The Praetorian's gifts were alien to him. He instinctively knew that the mortal girl was important, perhaps the key to his revenge. Yes, this boy might prove useful.

"You said you wanted to talk..." Steve picked up the glass and absently rolled the whiskey around the inside of the tumbler causing the ice to chink musically.

"Something is happening with your woman, your ... Beatrice." It was a statement.

"If you know what's going on..."

"I can't be sure, but... there is a woman, a pretty girl with long dark hair."

"That's not Beatrice." Steve had known that this would prove futile. He stood to leave but Michael's commanding voice stopped him and forced him to sink back down to the seat.

"I never said it was. Has Beatrice ever mentioned her?"

Steve shook his head, this was useless. He should have followed Beatrice rather than coming here.

"No, I don't think they've actually met yet, but she is showing a great deal of interest in your woman."

"I don't understand… Look, I've got to go." Steve stood again and started edging out of the booth, intending to barge past the stranger if necessary.

"Sit down!" The command boomed and suddenly Steve felt very afraid, Ymochel could see it in his eyes, yet he remained standing. Good, that showed courage or, perhaps, stupidity, either could be used. "Sit down," the tone was more pleasant now, "and let me explain."

Steve slumped back into the chair and took a sip of the whiskey.

"I do not know what this woman calls herself now, but she has taken an interest in your Beatrice. The interest she shows is enough to make Beatrice act… strangely."

"You aren't making any sense."

Time to let the proverbial cat out of the bag, "This woman I describe to you, she is a vampire."

Steve laughed, though he really couldn't see the humour. This Michael looked totally sincere, but… a vampire. The conversation had shifted from simply bizarre to a bad movie script.

"You do not believe me?"

Steve choked back the laughter, "Believe you! Jesus, have you heard yourself?"

"I know these things…"

"Why? Are you some sort of vampire hunter?" He laughed again, but the laugh was humourless and inside he simply wanted to get away from the crazy son of a bitch. New York was full of madmen and it seemed he had agreed to go to a bar with one of them.

"I was once a man but, against my will, I was forced to become one of them. I wish to stop it happening. I wish to stop their killing; I don't want others to share my fate." His voice was low, full of melancholy.

"So… you're a vampire too?" Steve laughed again, though there was only anxiety in the sound. His apparent sincerity suddenly made Steve very afraid, not because he believed that this strange man was a vampire, but because Steve realised that Michael believed it.

Ymochel opened his mouth, his fangs were fully extended. Steve's laughter died in his throat. But… They were prosthetics, they had to be. There was no such thing as vampires. Something primordial within him began to panic, despite his rationale, that part of the human psyche that recognises the predator screamed a timeless warning, and yet somehow he managed to keep his cool.

"Nice fangs, they must have cost a bit."

Ymochel allowed his fangs to retract. Steve's numb fingers let the glass slip between them; it landed on the table with a bang, somehow staying upright. Yet, though he had seen it, he could not believe his own eyes. He had seen TV shows with street magicians doing the seemingly impossible in full view, it must be something like that, he told himself. Steve's gaze ricocheted around the room to see if anyone else had noticed the spectacle that had occurred before him, yet the patrons and barman continued to go about their business.

Ymochel shook his head slightly; five hundred years ago he would have found a crucifix pushed into his face. "You do not believe me, come I will show you."

For a moment they sat in silence. Steve stared firstly at his drink and then at the vampire, if vampire he was. Despite the fangs Steve could do nothing but disbelieve and yet something within him, some kernel of instinct told him to accept the fantastical. If the man truly were a vampire, the last thing Steve should do was go with him, he knew that, and yet if Beatrice were in trouble…

For his part Ymochel casually glanced around the bar. All about him he could see slaves, as surely as if he were in ancient Rome. The barfly who was a slave to the amber liquid placed before him, the bartender who was a slave to his wage. For so long he had fought against the condition, there had even been times when he had attempted to help mortals escape their oppression, but the world seemed geared towards power, those who gained it wielding it mercilessly against the helpless. Now all that consumed him was the need to be free from the tyranny of the Concilium, that and the need for revenge, to exact vengeance for one hundred and sixty years of Hell and the death of a Fledgling he had truly loved, in his own way. This mortal would help him, he would be a part of Ymochel's scheme, or he would die.

Suddenly Ymochel stood and headed towards the door. Steve picked up the glass and drained it; savouring the acrid burn of the alcohol, in that moment it seemed to be the only thing that was real. Then, against all his better judgement, he followed. He didn't know why and, truthfully, neither did Ymochel.

They exited onto the street; a light rain had started falling coating the street in a thin film of water that reflected the lights of New York in a shimmer of colour. Ymochel sniffed the air, trying to catch a hint of the Praetorian. There... The slightest suggestion of her presence, but enough to track her. He was trusting to luck now, trusting that he could show the mortal something to set him upon the path he had in mind.

"This way." He pointed down the road.

The human and the vampire set off together.

Chapter Twenty Two

Castle Csejthe, Carpathian Mountains – 1580

Danaan sat in her room.

It had been a week since she had accidentally revealed herself to Erzsébet and since then she had been a prisoner. Not a prisoner of Erzsébet, though she knew that the Countess would disagree on that point, but more a prisoner of her own self-doubt.

To a degree it was amusing the lengths to which Erzsébet had gone to hold her there. The shutters on the window were bolted shut and the door locked from without. Both had crucifixes nailed to them to prevent her egress. Garlic also hung over the shutters, and the juice of the pungent bulb had been rubbed against the edge of the door.

All these things had been done with the certain peasant knowledge that a strigoï could not pass such holy artefacts and was repulsed by the overpowering aroma of the bulbs. It was a pity that the folklore was no more than uneducated superstition. Danaan could grasp the crucifix with ease, after all she had posed as a Prioress once, though the Countess could not know that, and she had always quite liked garlic as a mortal, and though she now no longer partook of mortal food the smell reminded her of simpler times.

Of course she had not revealed to the Countess that these measures were inconsequential and yet still she remained.

Each night Erzsébet came to her. She brought her a servant to feed upon. Danaan ensured that she drank the smallest possible amount and was secretly amused by her captor's disappointment that none of the girls were drained unto death. Danaan also believed that Erzsébet wanted the girls to suffer, but she brought them the most pleasant of sensations and ensured that their minds were sufficiently fogged so no memory of her feeding would haunt them.

The girl would be removed and then the questions would come. Some she answered, though not always with the truth. When asked if she were indeed strigoï she gladly confirmed this, though the folklore of the restless dead was nothing like the truth of the Velvet. When asked how old she was her answer was purposefully vague. She couldn't remember, she would falsely confess. Danaan had hoped this would throw the Countess off track but her stratagem had failed, Erzsébet had decided that she was actually far older than she was.

Erzsébet would ask many questions that strayed too close to the heart of the Concilium. To these the vampire confessed that she couldn't answer, and whilst the Countess was obviously disappointed by the reply, Danaan did not lie. If she revealed too much about the truth of her kind she was sure that her unlife would be forfeit.

Erzsébet would flatter, threaten, cajole and try to seduce. All her tactics failed. Danaan was tempted more than once to surrender to the seduction. Not that she had any intention of revealing anything through it, but because Erzsébet was a very good lover, and the vampire had needs beyond blood. It would, of course, have been a folly, but the temptation was there none the less.

She had not yet been taken to Erzsébet's dungeon, though she feared that this might occur soon. Feared it because she had been full of doubt as to her next move and such a threat would have forced her hand.

The doubt, however, was lifting. Her next course of action was becoming clear in her mind.

Finally, each night, Erzsébet would ask the same question, "Will you make me like you?" Each night Danaan would truthfully answer, "I cannot." Erzsébet would become angry and then petulant in turns, though Danaan wondered how strong the woman's reaction would be if she added, "And I wouldn't want to even if I could."

Then, as though the tide had turned, the Countess' mood would improve, she would lean over to the vampire and kiss her cheek gently and whisper, "We will continue our discussion tomorrow evening."

Danaan paced back and forth, the Countess had not yet arrived, but the course of action was now crystal clear. Danaan would leave this place tonight; she would present herself to the Concilium and confess that a mortal had stumbled onto her secret.

They would want to know why she had not simply dispatched the mortal and she would have to confess that the mortal was a person of no small standing in the world. She would have to admit that Erzsébet's death would have brought more questions than solutions and would have directed the eyes of the European monarchy in their direction.

This had been the nub of her problem, one she felt she could not win. Kill Erzsébet and be accused of placing the Children of the Velvet in harms way, let her live and be accused of the same.

Oh Ariadnne, she thought, if only you could see me now. What would you say? That this situation was typical of me; that I was a disgrace to the blood you gave me, to the Velvet Kiss you bestowed. She would say that I have been characteristically rash, Danaan mused darkly, or, more probably, she would continue to say nothing at all.

Tonight she would leave this place, but not before Erzsébet was provided with the 'show' she so desperately craved.

Her long, slender fingers traced the ornate cross that was placed across the old wooden shutters. It was worth more than the average peasant would earn in their lifetime. Encrusted in jewels and exquisitely engraved it was really quite beautiful.

The key turned in the door, Danaan pulled her hand back quickly and moved over to her bed. When Erzsébet entered the room the vampire was sat quite demurely on the edge of the bed.

The maid who was with the Countess that evening was the same maid with whom Danaan had been caught. The girl looked apprehensive, wondering why she had been brought here. The servants had been talking amongst themselves, speculations abounded as to what sin had caused their mistress to lock the Lady Katrina in her room and puzzling over the strange duties they were required to perform each evening. Strange in that none of them could remember precisely what they had been asked to do; Danaan had been very thorough when it came to keeping their memories of the events indistinct.

The poor girl, thought Danaan as the Countess directed her towards the bed. This was no time to become sentimental, however. The girl sat and Danaan touched her mind, trying to make it all seem like the most pleasant dream. When the bite came she focused hard, pouring life's pleasures into the girl, but when the time came to break away, as she had done every other night, Danaan continued to feed. Yes, Erzsébet would get her 'show', she would see a vampire drain a victim completely.

Danaan had contemplated her escape and there were two possibilities, both would require her full strength. She could exit through the castle but she had dismissed the notion. That would be a blood bath and a guard might get lucky, one errant swing to her neck with one of their wicked swords and it could all be over.

Her other option…

She let the girl's body drop to the floor and, in a moment almost comical in its absurdity, took a handkerchief from her sleeve and dabbed the blood from her mouth.

Erzsébet squealed with joy and rushed over to the girl, examining the marks on her neck and looking into her glazed, dead eyes. She didn't notice the vampire moving to the window until she had reached it.

"This cross is quite beautiful," Danaan's tone was light and conversational.

"Indeed and it was blessed by the Bishop of Warsaw himself. Does it fill you with dread?"

Danaan reached out and grasped the artefact, smashing a myth in the process. "Not really Erzsébet, should it?"

"No! That is wrong. It should burn you… Strigoï cannot stand the touch of holy relics." The Countess voice was shrill, filled with a mixture of surprise and anger.

"Really, now who could have told you that?"

Erzsébet stood, her face turning scarlet with rage.

"I really should thank you for your hospitality my dear, darling Erzsébet, but now I must take my leave of you."

Danaan leapt at the shutters, throwing herself at them with all her vampire strength, smashing through the wood and tumbling out of the window. A shower of splinters surrounded her from the obliterated shutters. As she fell into the night she twisted her body, managing to catch a glimpse of Erzsébet's head, as the mortal peered from the castle, probably searching for a bat or other such nonsense, then the cry for the guards rang out.

Danaan crashed to the earth, an arm and leg smashing in the process sending pain searing through her body. The fall had been enormous; a mortal probably would not have survived it. She could feel the freshly stolen blood slowly working its magic. Normally a broken limb might take days to heal, for one of her age, but she did not have days. She willed the blood to heal her, willing the limbs to straighten and the bone to knit in a matter of seconds.

Such rapid healing was agony and she let out a furious scream. It also caused her unnatural body to consume the majority of the blood she had stolen, in turn triggering the relentless pounding of the hunger. She knew she should feed again, soon, but she needed to get away from Castle Csejthe before the guards had chance to catch her. She scooped up the ornate cross and with it under her arm ran into the night, direction was unimportant, escape was all that mattered. Her legs carried her with all of her preternatural speed and yet her run seemed almost graceful, rather than frantic.

As the tall trees of the forest surrounded her she began to feel safer. The terrain was tough going at the best of times, but the pale moonlight piercing the trees was so weak that fast travel through the woodlands would be difficult to say the least for her mortal pursuers. Not for Danaan, however, her senses were alive in the night. She weaved around branches and leapt gracefully over the thick undergrowth.

Suddenly she heard dogs barking in the distance. Damn it, she had forgotten about the dogs. She might be able to move through the forest faster but they could certainly track her and the dogs and guards had one distinct advantage over her, they could continue their pursuit when the sun rose.

She couldn't allow herself to panic. She couldn't afford to make a mistake.

She stopped and reached out into the night with her mind, she might not have control over animals as legend might suggest but there were certain things she could do. The dogs were too distant, she couldn't touch their minds, but she felt a pack of wolves nearby. She turned her attention to them.

Danaan brought a mental image of Csejthe's dogs to mind and then projected that image to the pack leader. Then she showed the great wolf images of the dogs tearing at wolf pups and stealing the best winter food. She tried her best to project a feeling of great anger, though whether the wolf would understand that or not was beyond her ken, it was a human emotion after all. A howl rang out and was answered by another and then another. The pack moved towards the castle and the approaching dogs. She had bought herself time.

She resumed her race through the forest. It was lucky that Erzsébet came so soon after sunset. Danaan had almost the entire night to put as much distance between herself and danger as possible. Come the dawn she would dig a shallow grave and bury herself until the night fell again, trusting that the wolves would have dealt with the dogs or, at least, sown enough confusion so that the dogs would not find her during the daytime stupor.

Come the next nightfall she would get her bearings and fathom the best way to get to the Alps and the Concilium. She had to confess to the ancients all that had happened.

Chapter Twenty Three

New York City – 2000

In the movie it had seemed so glamorous. In reality it seemed sordid and, despite that, strangely thrilling.

Unable to ignore her blossoming Sapphic urges Beatrice had ventured out into the night of New York City to search for a prostitute, a woman she could pay to fulfil her fantasies.

She had walked down the street awhile and then caught a cab to Brooklyn. It did not take long to find the areas where the prostitutes plied their trade. She searched around and found what she was looking for, a youngish woman, pale skinned and long dark hair, she wasn't as pretty as the woman who haunted her dreams, but she was a close enough match. They had talked for a little while and Beatrice had discovered she was called Tracy. The girl had been wary at first, thinking she was a rival whore, then a cop and then a Christian do-gooder. Eventually Beatrice had gotten some money from her pocket book and waved it in Tracy's face.

That loosened the girl up. Yes she was a whore and yes she would do a woman, one hundred dollars and there was a room around the corner.

The entrance to the hotel stank, refuse collected in heaps around the door, its fetid odour blending with the distinct fragrance of urine. The movie had suggested much, but it was a Californian fantasy. In New York things were real, gritty. The carpet on the stairwell was threadbare and all the colours had long faded from its fibres. Beatrice noticed the cracks in the plastered walls and the occasional stains that she thought better of examining too closely. She looked over at the elevator and, before Tracy could tell her that it no longer worked, had decided against using it.

As Beatrice entered the room she had a moment of self-doubt. What the Hell was she doing? Living the fantasy, she told herself, living it in the easiest and most convenient manner. For a moment she could almost hear the voice of a million advertisements. "Hey, it's the American dream, money can get'cha what you need." She considered running, she actually felt sick to her stomach.

"I'll 'ave the hun'red in advance, doll." Tracy's voice had a slight Italian twang to it, which was incongruous to the blanched paleness of her skin. Beatrice fumbled the money to her. "Now normally I'd tell a client no touchin', no kissin', but that's gonna be a bit hard wit' a woman, now ain't it doll."

The money had been given, but she could still run. Sure she'd be a hundred down, and possibly a hundred wiser. But payment had been made and the whore was there, and hers. Her short skirt and high heels showed the length of her leg to its best advantage. The little Lycra top was cropped framing her mid-riff and displaying her cleavage. The soft, round rise of her breast rose and fell with her breathing. Her long hair fell over her shoulders and her deep red lips looked so full.

Beatrice's carnal hunger took over. She approached the woman and ripped at her top. "Hey doll, go easy."

"I'll give you money for the clothes."

Another hundred-dollar bill materialised, more than the entire outfit was worth but Beatrice didn't mind. The top was off and she was at a nipple, sucking it into her mouth, delighting as it hardened in response to the circular movement of her tongue.

Beatrice noticed yellowed bruises on the whore's ribs, she guessed that a previous client or the prostitute's pimp had been overly rough with the girl. She refused to allow herself to be repulsed and kissed the marks, revelling in the sleaze of the situation, allowing that to build into her fantasy rather than destroying it.

The sex was rough and animalistic, as they fucked each other oblivion. There was no other term to describe it. It was no act of lovemaking; it was pure primal sex that both Beatrice and the whore enjoyed to the full. By the end they lay on the bed, drenched in sweat and exhausted the only sounds that of their exhausted panting and the droning hum of the naked light bulb that hung from the ceiling.

Beatrice rose first. She knew that deep inside herself dwelt a kernel of guilt and that guilt would grow. Not with the act itself, the sex had been magnificent and the door, which had opened through her dreams, had been well and truly stepped through. She no longer doubted her bisexuality; in fact the way she felt at that moment she might actually be a full lesbian. The guilt came because of the squalidness of paying for sex. Yet, in many respects, more than one fantasy had been fulfilled that night.

She dressed, and as she did the whore stroked her hand along her side. "Hey doll, anytime you want more, you come and find me, you hear me."

Beatrice said she would, and part of her meant it, whilst another part desperately wanted to find another way to fulfil her sexual needs and a still greater part craved only the woman from her dreams. With the dream woman she knew it would be more than sex, she knew it would be erotic and passionate and beautifully emotional.

She left the room, not disappointed to leave the squalid hotel behind. Beatrice walked out onto the main street, paused for a moment and then hailed a cab.

Danaan had been at home when the answer came.

In ages past a request to the Concilium Sanguinarius had necessitated a trip to the Alps; a messenger was likely to be mortal and thus could not be trusted. She was not sure about the other Bloodlines, but her Bloodfather had embraced the burgeoning technology that accelerated out of control in the modern world. Shang-Di owned servers in numerous countries, allowing his Bloodline to use electronic mail safely. All the mails were encoded, of course. Indeed the software on Danaan's home computer was illegal in the States, the encoding software so powerful that the Federal Government would classify it as military grade.

As an added layer of security all E-mails were written in one of a half dozen archaic languages, just in case.

She'd expected the answer to come by return mail, so it had shocked her, as she was preparing to leave for the night and return to Beatrice's apartment, when the psychic response had come. The voice of her Bloodfather rang clear in her head.

"The Concilium agree. You may Sponsor the Fledgling." As she heard the words she thought she could see the grand hall of the Concilium, a vision superimposed over her New York home.

She didn't bother going to the apartment building, she knew that Beatrice wasn't at home. The nights of dream contact had left Danaan very sensitive to the mortal, she would have been able to pinpoint her anywhere in the city.

By the time Danaan reached the hotel, Beatrice was in the throws of orgasm. It didn't take long to work out what had occurred. In some respects Danaan was pleased, the door of the mortal girl's sexuality had been passed through. In some respects she should thank the whore.

That did not change the deeper, uglier feelings Danaan felt. The whore had taken something that she felt was hers. She felt... she was… jealous. It snaked through her heart and her soul, burrowing through her reason.

Beatrice left the hotel first. Danaan watched her leave, longing to go to her but knowing it wasn't quite time. They must meet accidentally, as they had the first time; it would be as though fate played its hand. That was for tomorrow; the vampire knew that she had other business to attend to that evening.

A few minutes later the whore emerged from the building, her ripped top barely covering her breasts, and started down a nearby alley. Danaan touched her mind. The prostitute thought of going home and changing her clothes before heading back onto the streets.

The vampire flitted through the shadows, into the alley, following the whore.

Chapter Twenty Four

New York City – 2000

From the flat rooftop New York seemed like something out of a fairytale. Even in this desolate part of Brooklyn, overlooking some sleazy hotel and a refuse-strewn alley that was only partially lit by the light from the hotel windows, it was easy to ignore the bad and concentrate on the beauty painted across the skyline in electric lights. Even when the moment was shared with some crazy guy who believed he was a vampire.

Steve shivered, the cold was biting up here, the wind stronger on the rooftops than it was down in the city streets, but it wasn't the cold that made him shiver, rather it was the man next to him, this Michael. Neurosis and delusion aside he still seemed dangerous. Tall, athletic and, if his suit was anything to go by, rich; yet almost predatory in the way he moved. Well, Steve admitted to himself, if he were a vampire, he would be predatory.

How Steve would have felt if they had arrived just a couple of minutes earlier, if he had witnessed Beatrice leaving the hotel, was anyone's guess.

"What now?" He asked, though deep down he dreaded the answer.

"Be patient, she is near."

She. The mysterious woman that Michael claimed was not only obsessed with Beatrice but also a vampire. That most rational part of Steve's brain asked himself again, what the Hell am I doing here?

A woman left the hotel, obviously a whore. Despite himself, and the bizarre situation he had found himself in, Steve's interest piqued. Her last client must have been some sort of animal; her top was ripped open revealing much of the shape of her breasts. The sound of her heels clicking on the floor echoed through the alley, sharper than the constant drone of air conditioner compressors.

A chilling thought stabbed through his consciousness. He turned to Ymochel and let the thought drip like ice from his tongue. "So, is that her?"

"No, wait… there she is."

The woman he pointed to was undoubtedly quite beautiful, yet there was something not quite right about her. Steve tried to put his finger on what it was and then he suddenly realised that there was no sound, her footsteps were absolutely silent and, if it were not for the fact that he could see her, he would have assumed there was only the whore in the alley. Her movements were lithe and animalistic, and as she stalked down the alley towards the whore it seemed to him, almost, that she glided. Her entire poise was both graceful and attractive, and yet unnatural and somehow disturbing.

There was muffled cry of surprise as the woman grabbed the hooker from behind, roughly pulling her head to one side and exposing her neck, and then quite clearly... Oh my God, Steve's frantic mind tried to refuse the sight below him, but it was all too real. She had bitten into the whore's neck. The whore had succumbed to the brunette's embrace and it appeared for all the world that she was being fed upon.

"We have to help her," Steve frantically looked around the rooftop for some quick way down to the alley.

An impossibly strong hand pressed hard onto his shoulder, holding him in place. "No, wait. You must see this."

Ymochel assumed that the Praetorian would follow her normal feeding pattern, taking a little and then releasing the whore. He had concocted a drama about the vampire's feeding, how she would take a little every day, slowly drawing the victim towards death. How she would do this to the woman Beatrice. He didn't know of the jealousy that burned through Danaan's soul and so what she actually did was beyond his wildest expectations.

Steve saw the brunette release the whore, then watched in horror as her hand sliced across the woman's neck. They were up too high to clearly see the talon like nails, but he did see the whore grasp at her neck, he did see the blood spilling through her fingers, darkness upon pale white skin. The whore crumpled to the alley floor and then the brunette was gone, vanishing into the dark shadows of the alley as though she were a ghost.

Part of him refused to accept what he had seen. He could accept that he was a witness to murder, there was no escaping that, but that he had witnessed a vampire feeding…

There had to be another explanation, his mind desperately grasping for a real world that seemed to drift out of reach. Then the irrational and terrified part of him would remember the movement of the woman as she approached the whore, her unnatural grace and bearing. The sinking of her teeth into her neck...

Steve turned aside and retched, the whiskey he had recently drunk burning the back of his throat as it climbed back up his oesophagus. When he turned back to the other man his voice was shaky, "We've got... got to go to the... cops."

"And say what exactly?" Asked Ymochel, barely able to contain the dark humour that the suggestion had invoked within him.

"A woman has been murdered for God's sake!" There was a slight edge of hysteria to Steve's voice.

"Indeed, and if you go to the police and tell them that she has been murdered, they will ask you by whom. You will tell them it was a vampire that drank her blood and then slit her throat and, if they don't arrest you, they will certainly have you locked away for your own safety."

Steve shook his head, trying to deny the words but they made sense, even so they had to do something.

Ymochel's voice dropped to a conspiratorial whisper, "If you want to end this, if you want to save your Beatrice from this monster, you must do exactly what I say."

Steve looked at him for a moment, suspicion in his voice, "What's in this for you?"

"I never asked to be this way." Steve could hear the pain in the man's voice. "I was turned into one of these things against my will. Unlike the creature you just saw, I do not arbitrarily kill, nor do I take pleasure in stalking a victim like she does with your Beatrice. I have made it my mission to rid the world of these creatures."

"How do I..."

"Know that I'm telling the truth?" Ymochel finished his sentence for him. "Think about it, if I was like that thing we just watched together, you would already be dead. I am sorry that you had to witness that woman's untimely demise, I am sorry she had to die. It's just that I need your help and in order to believe it you had to see it for yourself.

"Will you help me?"

Steve let the words sink in and then nodded.

"Good. Do nothing for now, tomorrow night we shall speak again and I will tell you how we might kill these creatures." He pressed a piece of paper into Steve's hand.

"Why can't you tell me now?"

"Because you need the enormity of what you have seen to sink in. This is no game Steve. We fight for your woman, and every other person their kind would corrupt and kill with their touch."

For a second it seemed as though the black man's eyes had flashed a vivid crimson causing Steve to turn away, frightened of what was before him. He looked over the edge of the roof trying to spy the whore, the dark shadows of the alley had conspired to hide her corpse for a moment but then he noticed movement. A stray dog had found the body and was lapping at the spilled blood. He watched the macabre scene for minutes, unable to tear his eyes away. When, eventually, he turned around, the vampire had vanished into the night.

Steve looked at the piece of paper; on it were the details of where he should meet the vampire the following evening.

He slumped down with his knees tucked against his chest, ignorant of the damp coldness that soaked through the seat of his pants, and started to weep.

Chapter Twenty Five

Concilium Sanguinarius – 0080

The moon shone clear and high in the sky casting its gaze over the mountain peaks. The stars were bright, drawing pictures in the rich blackness of the night sky. Snow covered the rocks and clung up the imposing peaks, reaching to their summits.

Ymochel did not mind the snow or the cold wind that whistled over the mountains. He sat before the cave entrance to the halls of the Concilium, looking out across the majestic vista that was utterly different to the land of his mortal birth, and relished the temperature.

It had been a year since Pompeii and still, occasionally, he imagined he felt the burning lava devouring the flesh of his arm, a phantom pain that was an agony all of its own. The cold was a welcome friend now.

It was hard to believe that he was here, sat amongst these peaks that had witnessed, a few hundred years earlier, the miraculous sight of Hannibal and his elephants, a military masterstroke still discussed within the Empire. Hard to believe that his grievous crime had gone unnoticed and unpunished. Hard to believe that he was still alive, or blessed with unlife at least.

He was unsure how long he had lain, out in the open, injured. It had been a combination of sheer luck and instinct that had enabled him to crawl from immediate danger. During the daylight hours he was trapped in the stupor, the thick clouds of smoke and ash from the mountain protecting him from the deadly rays of the sun. At night he drifted in and out of consciousness, the pain of his arm almost too much to bear. He felt his sluggish blood trying to repair the damage but, despite his new stolen power, the healing process was severely hampered by the lack of fresh blood. Thus he hungered. He was no stranger to the hunger, Uriel had ensured, when first born to the Velvet, that he understood exactly what starvation felt like to a vampire. This time, however, the pain of the hunger was inconsequential compared to the agony of his decimated limb.

Then they came, vampires. Though he didn't know it at the time they were Praetorians, sent to discover what had befallen the ancient.

At first they tried to question him, but his words were an incoherent babble of whispers. Then they brought him a mortal slave and allowed him to feed. The blood worked at his limb, and that in itself was a new agony, but he maintained enough composure to explain that Uriel had been caught within the lava.

They took him with them, back to the Concilium. As they travelled they brought him food, but the healing process was slow and there was little Improvement to his arm by the time they had completed their slow trek to the Alps. When he was finally laid upon a bed in the heart of the Concilium a little of the charring of his upper arm had healed, but there was no sign of the lower limb regenerating.

A vampire came to him that first night, he discovered later that it was Remus the eldest Bloodson of Uriel, and again he was asked what had happened to Uriel and to the concubines.

He explained how the mountain had become angry and how Uriel had told them not to be concerned. He detailed the slaying of Augustine and the laying of plans to make an escape should the need arise.

He explained that the mountain had exploded and that he had escaped from the villa with Uriel on a litter. He claimed that he had been unable to wake the two remaining concubines from their stupor and, as ordered by the Bloodfather, he had left them.

Remus asked how it had come to pass that he had not fallen into the stupor and Ymochel revealed how Uriel would have him feed so that he could walk in the daylight. Remus did not appear shocked by the knowledge but simply shook his head resignedly as Ymochel spoke. Remus then asked if either of the concubines might have survived. Ymochel did not know, but he had seen fire spreading towards the villa as they escaped.

Continuing with his tale, Ymochel told how the slaves had stumbled with the litter, of how the ancient had fallen and tumbled towards the lava, still trapped in his daylight sleep. He then said that he had tried to reach the ancient and lifted his devastated limb. As he spoke his voice shook and to Remus it appeared that grief had overcome the Fledgling, though in truth it was the memory of the agony that caused his whole limbs to shake and his chest to heave. The solitary crimson tear was easy to produce, the pain of his arm constantly pushed him to the verge of tears.

As the vampire left it seemed to Ymochel that he had succeeded, that Uriel's murder would be believed to be nothing more than an unfortunate accident. Then he over heard the Praetorians outside his door whispering, heard them say that he would be questioned again by one they called the Morning Star, as he eavesdropped he discovered that the Morning Star had the ability to tell truth from lie.

It seemed so unfair, he thought as he looked around the spacious room he had been given for his recuperation. He had survived the fury of mother Earth and had sacrificed his limb to freedom. Now he was in a luxurious cavern room, richly decorated with furniture and wall hangings from the east. Each day freshly washed and perfumed mortals were brought to him in order to quench his hunger and aid his healing. Sometimes one of the Velvet skilled in music would come to entertain him, though they never spoke to him, and whether this was out of fear or reverence he neither knew nor cared. All this would be lost, dashed away when the truth teller spoke to him.

When he was questioned again he truly felt fear, but some inner instinct took over. Each lie he told came with an exertion of will, a desire to make lie appear truth. He had no idea if it would work, and later he discovered that no other

Child seemed to have this gift. Each lie took an enormous effort to cover and by the end of the questioning he was exhausted. As he mused upon the enigma, over the subsequent centuries, he guessed that the gift of lies must have come from the power he had stolen from the ancient. At the time all that truly mattered was that the Morning Star was satisfied and Ymochel had escaped his fate.

His arm took months to heal. No Child of the Velvet had ever before had such a close brush with the lifeblood of the planet and survived. How his healing would progress, and the time it would take, was a mystery to even the most ancient within the halls of the Concilium.

During those months Remus came to see him often. Eventually Ymochel discovered that the vampire was, as the eldest of their Bloodline, to become the new Bloodfather of their line and take Uriel's place on the Concilium Sanguinarius. The Nubian then began to fear that Remus' interest was that of a master with a new slave. He couldn't allow that, he had escaped slavery once and he would not allow himself to be fettered again. Soon, however, it became obvious that was not the case and that Remus considered Ymochel a free man, though it was also apparent that Remus expected the Nubian to show a loyalty to his Bloodline that he could not feel.

Often Remus despaired at Ymochel's lack of knowledge of the heritage and laws of the Velvet. He educated Ymochel in their ways. It seemed that Ymochel's bravery, in attempting to save the ancient, was to be rewarded. With only five years passed since being born to the Velvet a new Sponsor should be found for Ymochel, but he was to receive the petition of growth. As far as he could understand that meant he would be a citizen in his own right, yet he quickly grew to believe that the rules of the Concilium were nothing more than fetters to hold the Children of the Velvet in thrall to the ancients. It seemed Remus had noticed the pained look of distaste etched onto his handsome features, when this understanding came to him, but the new Bloodfather took it to be a symptom of the long and painful healing process.

One night, as they spoke, Ymochel asked how their food was so readily available here in the high peaks where so few humans would venture. Remus explained about the pens in the heart of the mountain where humans were reared simply as livestock.

He had gone to the pens a few nights later and seen the slaves for himself, but these were less than slaves. Dirty and living in their own filth, they had no language and no spark of human spirit in their eyes. They were truly cattle. Ymochel realised that one of the Velvet must have washed and perfumed the slaves that were brought to him nightly, an attempt no doubt to make the squalid creatures more palatable.

A Praetorian saw him watching and laughed. They were a necessary evil up here in the mountains, he explained, but so dull. The Praetorian confided that he preferred a good hunt.

Ymochel had visited the pens for a reason, he had wanted to look on these humans, these slaves, not when they were brought to him and the hunger was upon him. He had wondered whether the plight of the slaves would spark a feeling of outrage within him or, even, illicit concern for their situation. He felt nothing for them, he realised. They were nothing to him, these dull and listless creatures who were less than human. He was free, and it seemed that was all that mattered.

Ymochel's reminiscence was interrupted by the sound of footfalls behind him.

"It is a beautiful night my friend," exclaimed Remus.

"It is Bloodfather."

"Oh Ymochel please, I have said often enough that you should call me Remus."

"My apologies, Remus."

"How is the arm?"

Ymochel held his arm up, showing the unblemished skin. "Sometimes I still feel the touch of molten stone, as though it was still upon me, eating through flesh and bone."

Remus sat on a stone by the Nubian, "You performed an act of supreme courage and it seems unfair, to me at least, that you should still suffer.

"I could talk to Shang-Di if you like. His Bloodline can walk in men's minds and control the dreams of mortals. Whilst our kind does not dream perhaps there might be a way that he could dull the memory."

The last thing Ymochel wanted was a damn mentalist walking around his mind, "I prefer to remember."

Remus nodded as though he understood. They sat in silence for a moment; the only sound was that of the wind whistling through the mountains.

It was Remus who spoke first, "You have seemed restless these past few weeks."

"I think I may leave this place."

"Where would you go?"

"Rome, Eshu has said he can provide me with the papers of a free man." Eshu was the Concilium's archivist. He had taken quite an interest in Ymochel trying to coax out of him detail of the events at Pompeii, wanting to know all he could so that the archives were as complete as possible. To Ymochel's mind such detail as the strength of the stench of sulphur seemed an irrelevance but he had indulged the archivist, as far as he could.

"I would tread warily in Rome; the Empire may crumble over the coming centuries."

Ymochel looked quizzically at the other vampire.

"Qutrub of the Flesh has taken an interest in the place since our Bloodfather perished," explained Remus. Qutrub's interests had become known as soon as the death of Uriel had been discovered. Remus had spent five fruitless years of searching for the ancient's complicity in the Judean cult, and suddenly all the Flesh's interests in the cult, and Rome herself, were revealed. Remus had tried to maintain the control of the region that Uriel had been afforded, arguing that Rome belonged to his Bloodline, but his standing amongst the ancients was too tenuous and the vote had gone against him. It was a refusal that still stung at his heart, though he had publicly accepted the rule of the majority with good grace.

"He also nurtures a sect that seems to be taking hold in the desert regions of the Empire." Remus continued, "If I know Qutrub at all he will use this cult to plant seeds of chaos through the world. He likes nothing more than seeing mortals at each other's throats. He gains much pleasure from war and misery."

"I will be careful." Ymochel looked at the other vampire with sincere eyes. In his heart he knew he must go to Rome, he knew he must walk in a place where he had once been called slave as a free man. He needed the taste of that liberty on his tongue more than he needed the coppery essence of blood.

Remus nodded slowly. "You know, my friend, there is much you could perform for our Bloodline. A man of your integrity and loyalty could further our interests in many ways."

Ymochel shrugged, "Perhaps, but I need to walk alone for a while…"

Remus laid a hand on Ymochel's shoulder, "You showed much devotion to our Bloodfather. The wound you received was most grievous. I would feel secure in my place here if I could be confident that men such as yourself possessed the same loyalty to me as Uriel knew."

So that was what he wanted, Ymochel realised, he wanted to chain the newly freed slave with bonds of allegiance. It was another way of limiting his hard earned liberty, another insidious form of control.

"I swear," Ymochel intoned, his voice earnest, "That all I did for Uriel I would do for you, Bloodfather." For a moment he pictured the gargantuan ancient burning in lava. In his mind he could see the ancient screaming, though in his mind the agonised shrieks were both silent and eternal. Then, suddenly, it was Remus who was consumed by the flame, Remus whose mouth gaped in a silent scream.

Remus smiled, content it seemed with the Nubian's response, and his hand squeezed Ymochel's shoulder gently, "That is good to know my friend. I wish you would reconsider staying and serving the Bloodline but your wounds need to heal, I understand that, and if travelling will help those wounds heal…" His voice trailed off for a moment and then he continued, "Well, wherever you choose to go, walk with the blessing of the Concilium and of our Bloodline."

Remus stood and walked back towards the mountain entrance. Ymochel remained sitting. As he looked out over the mountainside, he considered how pathetically easy it would have been to toss Remus over the edge. For a moment he considered that he might chase after the new Bloodfather and do just that but his mind was suddenly flooded with images of a broken Remus, lying at the foot of the mountain as his undead flesh clung tenaciously to life. He could picture the Bloodfather clawing his way up the mountainside eager to reveal the Nubian's treachery.

One day, he thought, it would be done, but it would be done properly.

After awhile Ymochel began to laugh, a deep booming laugh that echoed through the mountains, uncaring of who might hear it.

Chapter Twenty Six

Castle Csejthe, the Carpathians – 1608

It had been almost thirty years since the stregoïca who called herself Katrina had fled the castle. The escape had been both a shock and something of a revelation. The shock had come because she could not understand why the stregoïca had wanted to flee. Was she not protected? Was she not well fed? Despite the fact that a dead thing had masqueraded as a member of her family Erzsébet had even been willing to continue a carnal affair with her.

The revelation came in the things the escape had revealed. Stregoïca, despite the legends, had no aversion to holy relics and, as she had jumped through a window wreathed in garlic, no aversion to the pungent bulbs either. They were incredibly hardy, whilst the jump could not have killed that which was already dead, it should have at least slowed her. It also showed the control they had over animals, when the dogs had been released a pack of wolves had descended upon the well trained hounds, ripping them to shreds.

For years Erzsébet had searched for her. Her spies watched out for a dark haired woman called Katrina at social functions through the kingdoms. Her astrologers tried to find her, but with no apparent date of birth or death the heavens were silent. Her scryers tried to see her in visions and crystals, but she was obscured from their view. The stregoïca had, essentially, vanished.

She did try to learn all she could about these creatures, but the folklore was flawed. Much was said about their hatred of all things holy, for example, and that would cause her to disregard that piece of folklore.

Then, in the spring of 1604 Ferenc died. She did not mourn, he had been nothing but a disappointment to her. Sexually she preferred a woman to fill her bed. She had never managed to persuade him to end the austere décor of the castle and that had continued to raise her ire. He had also still been intent on making war, leaving her without his presence in the castle for long periods of time, returning only to ensure she was with child and later to see their children. It had not come as a shock to hear that his apparently pious nature was a lie. Ferenc, she discovered, had died in Bucharest, the whore he had just rutted with had stabbed him when he refused payment. Ever the political animals, the Báthory family ensured that the official news of his death stated he had died of an unknown illness.

Her thoughts turned to re-marriage immediately. By a quirk of dynastic lineage Erzsébet had become the next in line to become King of Poland, but as a woman she had no power. A husband was needed, but one that would please her sensibilities this time and over whom she could wield full control. Therein lay the rub, for when she looked in the mirror she no longer saw the beautiful girl with the perfect complexion. Time had taken its toll. She was old, and she looked it. Could an old widow hope to find such a suitor? The only interest she had received were from terrible old bores with political hunger.

Then the miracle had happened. She had been in her room at the time. The serving girl was going about her business, unnoticed by Erzsébet. She only had eyes for the mirror, for the face that time had ravaged. She noticed the girl when the foolish little slut had bumped into her. Erzsébet had turned on the girl, anger welling up in her breast. She struck out and her nails raked across the girl's cheek, ripping the flesh. Blood splashed across her hand.

The girl ran from the room in tears and Erzsébet had taken a handkerchief to wipe the blood away. The skin seemed so much smoother, younger. She had gone straight to Master Bennier, the alchemist currently in her employ. He looked at her skin and agreed, it was rejuvenated. The alchemist looked through his tomes of lore and, after some time, he claimed to have found the answer. There had been cases, he said, where ladies of the highest breeding could take on the appearance of a woman much younger by bathing in a maiden's blood. It was clear, he informed her, that the correct constitution, as owned by the better class of person, would allow the juvenescent effects of blood to come to the fore.

Erzsébet was sure that was correct, but then her mind went back to the stregoïca and she realised that the alchemist perhaps was not entirely on the right path. It was then she comprehended what had happened. Katrina had done something to her, she had given Erzsébet a gift. It had probably occurred during their lovemaking, something passed from the girl's dead mouth when it was fastened hard to her cunny.

That was why Katrina had insisted over and over again that she could not make Erzsébet like her, she had already done so. A new path had opened to her, one she had been following ever since.

Her trusted friend Dorotta entered the room, breaking her from her memories.

"My Lady, all is prepared."

They left the room together, arm in arm.

Since she had discovered the secret of an eternally youthful visage, Erzsébet's moods had visibly improved. Laughter filled the halls of Csejthe once more. She loved her life again and, almost perversely, she had come to love the castle. It was a beautiful building really. The transformation had been achieved by simply adding the decoration that Ferenc had refused for so long.

"What can I expect today my dear?"

Dorotta smiled, "Your bath is being filled my lady, as always, but I have found you an exceptional one from the academy."

The academy for young ladies had been Dorotta's idea, a means to attract the best and brightest young ladies of good breeding to Castle Csejthe.

They descended the stairs and passed through the antechamber, where the charlatan Boch had tempted Katrina so much with his blood, and into the recently constructed bathhouse.

The bath itself was large and ornate, especially commissioned for the room. It was filled with blood, still warm.

Above the bath was a cage in which several girls had been placed. They had all been bled in a variety of ways, needles stuck in the flesh and cuts made in their bodies in order to fill the bath. The room was filled with their whimpering cries, a finer symphony than any she had heard in the concert halls of the cities.

Around the bath stood several women, all wearing robes of black. They were Erzsébet's witches, trusted women to help her with her great work. One came over and helped the Countess out of her ornate bathrobe, crimson in colour with the Báthory coat of arms intricately stitched in gold thread. A golden dragon rearing from the deep red of her breast.

Erzsébet walked to the bath and the witch took her arm helping her into the pool of blood. The rejuvenating liquid sloshed against her legs, leaving crimson stains were the viscous fluid touched, blood showered from the girls above, splattering her face and hair.

"Where is the exceptional one?"

The girl was brought forward. She was naked, her hands chained behind her back. The two witches who led her by the arms forced her to stand on the edge of the bath before the Countess. The girl was shivering, silent tears running down her face. Her mother had sent her to the academy, she had not wanted to come, she had not wanted to leave her home behind. Her mother had told her not to be so silly, she had explained that time spent with Erzsébet Báthory could only improve her social status.

All the girl had really wanted was to stay at home with her family, to attend the society balls and find a fine husband. Her mother had decided that the prospects of a fine match would be greatly improved if her manners were enhanced. She had told her that it would be a grand adventure, one in which she would meet her equals and make friendships that would last a lifetime and develop her standing in polite society even further.

For a moment her mind flashed to the gardens in the family estate and she could hear once more the sound of laughter as her brothers and sisters ran around the large hedge maze. Sometimes it scared her, the tall labyrinth of greenery. It was so easy to become lost and so easy to imagine that monsters lurked within the twists and turns.

She had confessed her fears to her mother who had told her, in the most gentle of terms, not to be so silly. Mother had held her close and told her that there were no such things as monsters, that such creatures were no more than the uneducated fantasies of the peasant classes.

Mother had been wrong, however, there most certainly were monsters. She stood naked and helpless before one; Erzsébet Báthory stripped and splattered with gore was more horrifying than any fiend she might have summoned into her childhood imaginings.

The memory of her familial gardens shattered and was replaced by the certain knowledge that she was going to die, she was to be the next victim of the monster and no one would save her.

Her gaze darted around the chamber of horrors, desperately searching for anything that might offer a glimmer of hope, but there was no hope to be found.

She began to sob heavily.

"There, there dear," said Erzsébet, her voice soothingly soft, "You are part of a great work, a great, great work." She ran her hand across the smooth, milky skin of the girl's stomach, her fingertips lingering amongst the downy pubic hair.

"Jesus Christ and all the Saints save me." The words were little more than sobs. Erzsébet laughed and it was a harsh, bitter sound; Katrina had shown her the folly of the way of the cross. There was only one truth, a truth that was actually hinted at in the bible, though its meaning had been ignored and perverted. Blood was the only truth.

One of the witches brought a knife up, between the girl's legs, whilst two more held her steady and upright. The razor edge of the knife bit into the flesh, causing the girl to screech, the sound filling Erzsébet with delight. The blade cut deep, severing the femoral artery and blood spurted furiously out of the wound, dousing the Countess.

She laughed, the sound a girlish giggle, and then pushed her mouth against the wound, drinking deeply from the warm fount as the girl died. The hot spill of life almost choked the Countess but she fought the desire to gag, knowing that the ingestion of the blood would help its miraculous alchemies.

In her mind she said a silent thank you to Katrina, for the stregoïca had shown her the way. She was beautiful again, eternally beautiful.

Chapter Twenty Seven

New York City – 2000

The hour hand of the clock moved slowly, laboriously making its circuit of the off-white face as though each numeral conspired to slow its progress. The day seemed to drag in an endless cycle of frustration punctuated only by brief flashes of anger.

The frustration came from a need to further explore her sexuality, a desire to get out of the sterile white cubicle and prowl the city. In the past she would have been able to throw herself into work. What had become of the woman who had been so dedicated to her career that she had worked on New Years Day? She knew she should be working and yet all she could do was push paper around her desk and watch the slow marching clock.

The events of the night before had solidified something within her. It was as though for the first time ever she had been sexually fulfilled and she wanted, no she needed, to explore that feeling.

At times her elation would crash, just for a second, and she would feel sordid. Not because she had slept with a woman, but because she had slept with a whore. The first time this had happened she logged onto the internet. Within a few minutes she had a list of gay clubs she would try. She intended to explore this new side of her but she would do it the old fashioned way. She would enter the dating scene, she would go to a bar or a club and try to pick up or be picked up.

The momentary flashes of feeling sordid were not the source of her anger, however. That had one name, Steve. He had tried to call her several times through the day and she had slammed the phone down and eventually had his calls blocked.

He had then tried to get into the building to see her, but she had already notified security, just in case, and he was unceremoniously thrown out of the office complex.

She was angry with him, but she was also angry with herself. She was treating him deplorably and she knew it. In truth she owed him an explanation but what would she say. "It's not you, it's me. I'm going through some things at the moment." That sounded so trite, despite the fact it was true.

She could imagine his reaction if she added to that, "Oh, by the way, I think I'm gay. No offence but you're packing the wrong genitalia."

Eventually the clock reached its goal and it was time for home. She would shower, change and then check out some of the clubs. Part of her hoped she would bump into her dream woman, but that was, she realised, a slim hope. Strange that a chance meeting, a meeting of a few seconds and no communication, had opened such a door within her.

Her hope was fuelled by the dream she had enjoyed the night before. Perhaps it was the physical act of love with another woman that had tempered her nighttime visions, but rather than a deeply erotic dream that had found her waking to her own orgasm, the dream had been romantic. She had dreamed of the woman again, but in the dream they had simply held each other, revelling in each other's presence. It was as though by acting out her nocturnal fantasy she had obeyed her mind's message and her subconscious was telling her this.

It was chance that made her look out of the window, down onto the street. The sun was setting, and New York was lighting itself. It might have been breathtaking if she hadn't spotted Steve, standing on the stairs to the building, waiting for her. She stumbled into an empty cubicle and fell into a chair, her head sinking into her hands. The son of a bitch. She was going to have to face him, she realised, but she couldn't, not yet.

She kept going to the window, peering down at him, fearful that he would see her from down below. Fear turned to a simmering fury. She was going to have to get a restraining order; she was going to have to do something. Talk to him, the rational part of her mind cried, but the advice was swallowed in a churning sea of resentment.

It went on for an hour, an hour that seemed to drag on longer than the rest of the day had. Then, as she peered out of the window for what seemed like the hundredth time he suddenly turned and paced off down the street. Perhaps he had gotten bored or, more likely he believed he had missed her. Either way it didn't matter, it was her chance to escape. All her plans for the evening had dissolved, her fantasy that she might meet the dream woman vanished. She simply wanted to get home. She wanted to hide.

Danaan stood in the shadows watching the entrance and watching Steve. She knew that Beatrice was still in the building, she could sense her though the mortal was too far to be able to brush her mind. Instead she tried to touch Steve's.

His mind was a veritable maelstrom of emotion; frustration, terror and panic buffeting anything that seemed like a coherent thought and made him, for all intents and purposes, unreadable.

She had considered trying to calm his mind but had decided against it. He simply did not interest her. After an hour she relented, she would calm him and then try to direct him to leave his vigil. With some clever manipulation it might be possible, he was a man after all; mental images of food would probably have him searching for a restaurant in seconds. Then, suddenly, he had started down the road, she had touched his mind quickly but the maelstrom still raged. The only clear thought she gained was a name, not even a face to go with it, Michael.

A few minutes later Beatrice left the building. She looked around, frantically checking that Steve had truly left, and then turned quickly to head towards home. They bumped into each other, much like they had that first night.

Beatrice stopped dead in her tracks as she realised that it was the woman from her dreams. She wanted to say something, anything. Her heart was leaping and a thousand butterflies had seen fit to make a home in her stomach. She became aware that a smile had broken out across her face. God, I must look like some kind of imbecile, she thought and blushed.

It was Danaan who spoke, "Would you care to join me for a drink?"

Beatrice nodded yes.

Chapter Twenty Eight

West Yorkshire, England – 1347

It had not taken long to alter Kirklees Priory to her liking. The nuns were so easy to manipulate, their emotions were festering pools of sexual frustration. She had begun the very first night, entering their dreams and pushing them towards erotic fantasies. It was all too easy to influence the good sisters.

At first one or two had begun to masturbate in secret, their shame painted across their faces the next day. Then one nun would visit another at night, as Danaan began to introduce fantasies of their fellows into the dreams. Each clandestine meeting was intercepted, the disgraced sisters caught in the act by their new Prioress, who was so understanding, so sympathetic, quick to teach them that they committed no sin in her eyes, but just as quick to explain what would happen if outsiders were to hear of their activities.

In those earliest of days the most difficult aspect of the transformation of the Priory was explaining her need to sleep during the day, but eventually it didn't matter.

Within a month the priory was an orgiastic den of sin, each nun desperate to please the Prioress and her sisters, whilst during the day the good sisters made much play of the Priory being a house of God, should a visitor arrive. Strict instruction had been left that such visitors must be gone by dusk.

Danaan was most pleased with her work. She had shelter, plus sex and food at her fingertips. It seemed, for the first time since Ariadnne had abandoned her, that she had found a place she could call home and be happy. Sometimes she considered trying to get a message to Ariadnne, to invite her to the pleasure palace she had built in her honour, but she feared the response. Terrified that she would be denied, that her fragile heart would be broken anew. So she ignored her heart and indulged her baser instincts, revelling in passion so she would not have to face her inner self.

Danaan had managed to control her more violent urges to quite an impressive degree. There had only been one near fatality, when the sweet taste of orgasm-enriched blood had made her loose control, but the girl had survived, though she had been very weak for some time.

Whenever Danaan got the urge to gorge on a victim she had taken to leaving the Priory, flitting out across the night and finding a lone traveller. The presence of the great forest allowed her to take such victims and dispose of the bodies in a way that, should they ever be discovered, they would be unrecognisable. Conveniently the creatures living within the forest quickly devoured discarded corpses, eradicating any evidence of her endless hunger.

She never considered that the outside world might encroach on her new home, that events could occur outside her control.

The Prioress' room was entombed in darkness. On the very first night Danaan had been careful to cover all the windows so that she could sleep on the bed, rather than hide beneath it as had often been her habit. Instinct had caused her to wake, the instinct that told each of the Velvet when the sun had fallen behind the horizon.

She stretched languidly, manipulating the muscles in her naked body. She looked relaxed and yet the hunger throbbed within her as always, an incessant drum beat pushing her ever on, propelling her through the countless years.

There was a knock at the door.

She opened it and discovered Sister Bridget waiting for her. Just a few weeks ago the sight of her Prioress naked would have caused the girl abject embarrassment, now it simply sparked a hunger in her soft green eyes. Yet behind the desire was something else, a pensive nervousness.

"What is it Bridget?"

"There are two men here, Prioress."

Danaan grew angry. "I have made it clear that all visitors are to leave before the sun sets."

The girl stammered, "For... forgive m... me, but I thought..."

"Spit it out girl!" There was venom in her voice.

"One of the men is gravely wounded, Prioress. It is your cousin."

"My cousin?" This was a complication; she hadn't considered the family ties that the real Dame Startin may have had, much less envisaged that one of the dead Prioress' relatives might come to Kirklees.

"Robert of Wakefield, Prioress."

Danaan nodded, as though the name meant something. "And the other man?"

"His companion, a giant of a man who calls himself John. We asked him to leave but he refused to abandon your cousin. We thought it best, given his relationship to you and his wound, to allow your cousin to stay. He is in desperate need of your healing skills, Prioress. We have housed him within the guest quarters and his companion stands guard by his door. This John seems troubled; he will not allow any of the sisters to attend your cousin and insists upon your presence"

The intrusion was unwelcome, but obviously demanded her attention. "I will dress and be there directly, tell the sisters to be... discreet whilst we have guests."

Sister Bridget nodded and left the room.

Danaan cursed under her breath as she pulled the habit on. She chose a wimple that hid her face as fully as possible and strode purposefully towards the guest quarters.

The man Bridget had identified as John stood outside a door. As he saw her approaching he bowed slightly and said "Good evening Prioress, 'tis a pity you could not come

earlier, your cousin is gravely ill. The wound in his side…"
His voice trailed off.

Danaan brushed his mind.

In his thoughts she saw a panorama of images. She witnessed them as they lay in wait amongst the green of the forest, a gang of men awaiting the Norman Lord, prior intelligence having informed them that he travelled with gold. They moved out of the camouflage of the vegetation, bows drawn. It was an easy matter to take the gold from him; there was food and ale aplenty in the coin that they stole from the rich fool.

She saw the approach of the guards, creeping through the forest; she quickly became aware that this was John's presumption, that none of those in the camp had detected the approach, that in all likelihood the guards had slit the throats of those on watch.

She saw their raid of the camp. She witnessed the men die at the point of the sword, blood and viscera falling to the moss and leaf of the floor. She became all too aware of the panic that had spread through the camp, the fleeing into the night.

She felt the genuine pain as John saw the sword passing through Robert's side and she heard Robert's scream piercing the canopy of the trees. Then she felt the anger as John rushed the guard, the sickening delight as he broke the bastard's neck. The fear as he carried his friend away from the slaughter, picking his way through the night, heading towards Kirklees and Robert's cousin, towards the one person he believed Robert would trust to tend his wounds.

Danaan knew then, she knew that the Prioress' cousin and his giant friend were outlaws, that they had been discovered and attacked in the night. That John had brought him to a place he believed could be trusted and had the skills necessary to heal the wounded outlaw. She understood.

Danaan looked at John, both his full beard and hair were encrusted with filth. His dark green hose and padded jacket were almost brown with forest dirt. He would have seemed a beggar, were it not for his eyes, which brimmed with selflessness. His soft brown eyes were filled both a fierce loyalty and a deep concern for Robert of Wakefield.

"John is it… Robert may well be my cousin, but the work of Our Lord does not end because a relation is hurt."

She hoped that the admonishment would cover her earlier absence and, indeed, the outlaw seemed regretful of his words.

Her mind continued to brush his as she spoke, there was no indication that he was aware she was not Dame Startin, that was a beginning at least.

"Come," she added, "Let us see my cuz."

With that she opened the door and entered the guest quarters.

Robert of Wakefield wore much the same clothes as his friend, though the side of his jacket was black with dried blood from his wound. His stubbled, middle-aged face was a deathly white and his head moved from side to side, following the rhythm of his pain. His lips moved constantly, mumbling unspoken words. Danaan brushed his mind but only found a world of fire devoid of coherent thought.

Within the confines of her wimple she sniffed the air, the aroma of blood was strong, yet barely hidden beyond it was the stench of death. The man was mortally wounded.

"He needs bleeding urgently," she explained to John who nodded as though he understood.

"With bleeding he will live?"

"Let us hope so. I must work and also pray for him, please leave us."

John nodded his ascent and left the room, pulling the door shut behind him, leaving Danaan with the dying man. His blood was rich; the scent of it conveyed that.

She knelt beside him, lifted his wrist to her mouth and bit down. The blood flowed into her eager mouth; despite the weakness flowing from his wound it was the best she had tasted in some time.

She became lost within the feed, drunk upon the vibrancy of the outlaw's precious fluids.

Chapter Twenty Nine

New York City – 2000

The sun had set by the time Steve walked away from Beatrice's office building.

After the revelations the evening before he had been unable to sleep, fear induced insomnia clutching at his brain, like fingernails scraping along a blackboard. Several times he lifted the receiver of his phone off its cradle and had looked long and hard at the buttons until they swam in his vision. All the time he thought about calling Beatrice but had no idea at all what he could say to her.

Prospective sentences swam in his head, "Hi babe, sorry to wake you but you are in terrible trouble, you see you're being stalked by a vampire."

The words sounded ridiculous, even after what he had witnessed, and he would start to doubt his sanity and the validity of the events which had occurred. Then the memory would return and he would see the whore in the alley, the beautiful dead thing latched onto her neck. He would see the hand flash out, and her throat open. Sometimes it seemed as though he was stood right next to them, silent and petrified as the thing drank from the poor woman's neck.

He would slam the receiver back onto its cradle then, cursing himself because he could not find the words or the courage to make the call.

Eventually the sun rose, casting a fiery orange light, tinged with roseate, through his window. He had hoped that the rising of the sun would chase away both the memory and the fears but they remained with him, steadfast companions.

He had started the day by trying to research vampires. It had been the first time in such a long while that he had set foot in a library, but he had managed to find a variety of texts on the creatures. More than he would have imagined were available.

Back home he had become increasingly worried by what he read so, ignoring his own common sense, he had tried to contact Beatrice. Again he slammed the phone down, unable to piece together a sentence that did not sound utterly insane. With a frustrated snarl he turned on the television, hoping that the mundane images would calm his fevered mind.

Flipping through the channels he came across the start of the old black and white movie of Dracula, Universal studios opus from the thirties. He settled on the channel with a frustrated resignation, half watching and half unable to concentrate through worry. Suddenly he paid attention, the words of the on screen Van Helsing resonating within him, "The strength of the vampire is people do not believe in him." Steve believed, as wholly implausible as it might be he had seen the creature with his own two eyes.

Perhaps, he thought, if she understands how sincere I am… To Hell with it, he decided, I don't care how mad I sound I have to warn her.

She had answered his first call, but had slammed the phone down on him before he could say anything. Steve had sat with the receiver cradled by his ear, listening to the drone of the disconnected tone, for some time silently weeping because he could not think what else he might do. He had tried and tried again, but to no avail. Eventually he had gone to her building.

The security guards ejected him from the building and, by that time, he had become quite frantic.

He knew what time she left work and stood at the foot of the stone steps, waiting and waiting. The longer he waited the more concerned he became, his thoughts becoming more and more frantic as his stomach churned ice water. He began to believe he was being watched, but could see no one. Little did he know that Beatrice was looking down on him from the building and the vampire scrutinised him from the deep shadows of a doorway close by.

His panic grew and grew and then his phone began to vibrate in his pocket, the alarm set to go off and remind him to meet with Michael. He reluctantly turned, realising that he could do more good working with the reluctant vampire than he was doing at present.

The meeting place was a good thirty minutes walk away. The closer he got the less people milled around. By the time he reached the place scribbled on the vampire's note the streets were deserted. He became more and more nervous. A gust of wind caught a bag, causing it to dance along the street, the rustling noise made Steve jump. His heart hammered in his chest, threatening to burst through flesh and bone. A trickle of sweat rolled along his cheek.

He continued along the street. Somewhere in the distance a dog barked, causing him to look around frantically. It felt as though the streetlights were dimming, that the eternally illuminated night of New York was fading, threatening to swamp him in darkness.

Ymochel melted out of the shadows, impeccably dressed in a suave light grey suit.

Steve gave a little choked cry of shock. He reached into a pocket in his coat and pulled out a crucifix, holding it out before him, shielding himself from the creature.

With an effort Ymochel prevented himself from laughing, instead he threw his hands up before himself, mocking the countless vampire movies pumped out by the relentless Hollywood machine. Let the fool cling to his superstitions. "Put that damn thing away, "he hissed.

"How do I know I can trust you?" It was almost a shout, bolstered by a courage born out of the effect the crucifix had on the creature.

"How can you not? You need me to save your Beatrice."

Steve faltered slightly and his arm dropped a little.

"If you do not want my help then say so, but only you can save her." The vampire continued.

"How?"

"By killing the vampire." There was a grave look in the vampire's eyes.

"Why can't you do it?"

"Put that damn thing away, we'll go to a bar and talk."

Steve reluctantly slipped the crucifix back into his pocket. He noticed that the vampire visibly relaxed when he did so and so he left his hand in his pocket, his fingers curled around the cross. Ymochel observed this and inwardly smiled, he believes that he has an advantage, good.

The vampire turned and walked down the street, his movements too fluid, leading the way to a nearby bar.

Steve sat, his leg vibrating nervously, a habit from his childhood. It was a habit that had annoyed Beatrice, he remembered, she was always telling him to keep his leg still. His hand was still thrust deep in his jacket pocket; the feel of the metal effigy of Christ brushing against his fingertips gave him a small feeling of comfort.

When the vampire placed a large glass of whiskey in front of him, however, he had to remove his hand in order to drink, holding the glass in his left hand did not feel natural.

The vampire pushed a packet of cigarettes over to him, "Smoke?"

Steve shook his head, not only in refusal but also in denial of the apparent banality of a situation that was anything but mundane. "I don't."

Ymochel's mouth curved into a half smile, "Very sensible."

"I suppose you don't have to worry about smoking, the health effects I mean," he couldn't believe he had said that, he was talking casually to a living fucking corpse.

"No I don't, but it's not something I've ever tried either." Ymochel noticed that the mortal had visibly calmed down a little; that was good.

They spoke for a while, awkward small talk on Steve's part, and a carefully planned stratagem on Ymochel's. He needed the human to trust him and so carefully drew a façade of banality around himself.

It was Steve who eventually brought the conversation back to the matter at hand.

"You said that you needed me, earlier, on the street. Why? Why can't you just kill this..." the next work choked in his throat, to say it was almost to confirm its reality. If he didn't say it, he thought wildly, perhaps it will all be nothing but a dream, a twisted and terrifying dream, but he spat the word out anyway. "... This vampire yourself?"

"I could," Ymochel admitted, "but I think I told you last night that I do not want anyone else to suffer my fate..."

Suddenly the text of the borrowed library books came to him and Steve believed he understood and the enormity of what he was being told hit him like a rock. His fingers became numb and the glass slipped from his hand, bouncing on the table and spilling its contents. "You mean..."

"You saw the vampire last night, she does not toy with her food, " Ymochel's terminology made Steve go even paler, "I can think of only one reason why she would stalk a mortal as she does with your Beatrice, she means to turn her." After seeing Danaan slaughter the whore Ymochel had decided to tell Steve this, unaware that it was actually the truth.

"Wh… why?"

"Why do these beasts do anything? It amuses them."
Ymochel again barely contained his humour, he knew he
was being melodramatic, laying it on as thick as he could,
but the mortal seemed to respond to this.

Steve was frantic. "We have to do something!"

Ymochel reached into his pocket and pulled out a
handkerchief, he draped it across the spilled liquor, allowing
the cotton to soak up the liquid before it ran off the table
onto Steve's leg. This done he spoke again. "And we will,
but this is why I cannot kill the creature."

"I don't understand."

"To prevent the change or, if we are too late, reverse
it, the vampire must be killed by a mortal."

"You mean if you…"

"If I killed the vampire then we will have condemned
your Beatrice."

"How do I do it, a stake through the heart?"

"No," Ymochel had to dissuade that particular myth,
Steve was no use if he got himself killed, and even with a
stake in her heart the Praetorian would be deadly, plus it

would only take a few seconds to pull the damn thing out, "Remove her head. One blow and clean off, fail to completely remove it and she will be upon you."

The horror of what the vampire was revealing had begun to sink in, and each word was like a sliver of ice in Steve's veins, freezing him inside. He was suggesting that Steve hew the head off the creature, a creature that for all the world looked human. His hands started to shake and he felt bile rising, burning his throat.

Ymochel watched the mortal. Over two thousand years he had learnt how to read people and could see that he was faltering.

"She's not alive my friend."

"I know but…"

"If you don't do it then your Beatrice is condemned."

"But…"

"Steve, have another drink, it will help you calm your nerves and then we shall go to your Beatrice's home and wait."

"Why there?"

Ymochel had already extended his sensitive awareness outwards but could not sense the Praetorian. He had no desire to cruise around the city in order to try and pick up her scent. He knew the bitch's habits; he supposed she would return to the mortal girl's apartment. "Because it is the best place to find the creature, and to keep a watch." He explained.

"We have to warn Beatrice," Steve's voice was strained with desperation.

"No. Trust me, if you try and tell your Beatrice of this she will not believe you. The fiend has bewitched her. All that your words, your good intentions, will do is warn the vampire that we know of her. Even if you could show her she would be unable to see." Or, he thought to himself, the Praetorian will pick up my involvement from your woman's mind and I cannot allow that to happen.

"For now we are the hunters," he continued, "You do not want to be the hunted. Believe me." There was a deadly finality to his words.

Steve dropped his head to his chest, dizziness assailing his senses, his hands grabbing the edge of the wooden table as though that might steady the roller coaster he had found himself on, and, despite himself, he began to quietly weep again. The terrible nature of it all was too much, he was stuck in a nightmare that was spiralling out of control and his only lifeline was a vampire, a murderous creature who could not possibly exist. To save the woman he loved, and in his heart he realised that he truly loved Beatrice more than he had ever believed possible, he had to kill. The thing was a killer, he had witnessed that himself, and was determined to damn Beatrice for eternity, but to actually kill it himself.

With all that had happened over the last few days he had begun to believe, for a horrible moment, that their relationship was truly over, that they had reached a point from which nothing could be salvaged. Now he knew that it could be saved and, in his heart, he wanted that more than anything. He wanted his Beatrice back and he wanted to support her work and understand her needs. He wanted, he finally comprehended, to be with her forever, for them to grow old together. How could that be, he asked himself, with all this happening? For a moment, in his mind's eye, he pictured Beatrice in a wedding gown, her hair up, her face glowing with happiness and the dress awash with blood.

White satin stained with her own blood if he did not act and with the blood of the creature that haunted her if he did.

Beyond the doubts, the fear and the tears, however, a grim determination was growing. The vision of Beatrice shifted, she was still wearing a wedding dress but she was in the alley now and it was she, not the vampire, feeding upon the whore. The vision steeled his determination. Perhaps he could do it. Perhaps...

Ymochel stood and strode to the bar to buy the mortal the promised drink. Let him wrestle with his conscience for now, he silently prayed to Gods long forgotten, but let him strike fast and true when the time comes. Anything less would be the end of the mortal and the ruin of the vampire's planned vengeance.

Steve caught his arm. There was something he wanted to know, though he didn't truthfully know why. A borrowed library book had brought the questions to mind and, now he had fallen into the rabbit hole, he wanted to know just how deep it went.

"If you exist..." The words trailed away.

"If I exist?" The Nubian prompted.

"Then... what else... ghosts... werewolves?" He felt silly asking and yet the words had been spoken, the question posed.

"I have never seen a werewolf," The Nubian answered, "As for ghosts, I do not know. I have never seen one but I have heard that certain mages control spirits... Who knows?"

It was true; he had never seen a werewolf or a ghost. He had seen men, barbarians, who would build themselves into a frenzy as they went into battle until the man was gone and all that remained was a vicious beast. He suspected that these berserkers had fuelled the myth of werewolves, snarling into battle with their fur cloaks streaked in the accumulated gore of combat. He knew, however, that they did not change physically into beasts, they sprouted no hair nor fangs nor claws.

As for spirits, he had never seen one though he believed it when he had been told that the ancient Undjit could summon and control spirits. Younger Velvet, born under the shadow of Qutrub's Christ, named those spirits demons. Whilst they could be summoned by sorcerers, however, Ymochel did not know whether they could just be seen, he had not witnessed the spectres of the departed in two thousand years and, though he had killed many times, he had never been haunted by any of his victims.

His reverie was broken as Steven added, "I just thought…"

"Thought what?"

"Well just thought you would know."

"Why should I know any more than you?"

Steven opened his mouth to answer, but an answer was not forthcoming and he shut his mouth again, his shoulders slumped slightly and he became lost in his silence. As he did so, his thoughts returned to Beatrice, and the thing that stalked her, and his hands began to tremble almost imperceptibly.

Ymochel was about to leave the booth again when the mortal spoke once more. "What…" Steve's throat was dry and his voice little more than a whisper. "What is it like?"

Ymochel looked at him for a moment before replying, instinctively knowing exactly what the youth had asked. "Terrible," he lied, "Nothing but cold emptiness and an agony deep inside that drives you forward through the years."

Steve nodded; he seemed to have made up his mind.

Chapter Thirty

Geneva – 1919

One hundred years was an inconceivable amount of time for a mortal, most mortals did not live that long. One hundred years of torture was something that no mortal could ever understand, much less bear. Ymochel was no mortal however. Ymochel who had suffered the ignominy of being sold into slavery by his father. Ymochel who had been forced into the Velvet and made to serve Uriel the Leech. Ymochel who had suffered the kiss of lava upon his flesh in order to gain his freedom.

Despite all this, the hundred years he had suffered with Qutrub were almost intolerable. The Flesh had manipulated his body beyond a mortal's understanding of pain, so great that it almost rivalled the remembered agony of the deadly kiss of Vesuvius' fires. The fact that Ymochel had not been driven utterly insane was a miracle in itself, though perhaps he had been and he just did not realise it himself.

There had been moments of relief, small oases within the agony. Moments designed to let his body heal to the point that he could be tortured again. Mysterious trips that Qutrub took allowed a few days of relief. Sometimes the ancient seemed pleased by whatever had occurred on his expedition and the relief lasted a few days longer. Other times the journey had obviously not gone to plan and his anger made Ymochel's agony reach dazzling new crescendos. Just a few short years before there had been the brief relief of moving, when war broke out the entire household had moved from Vienna to Geneva. Ymochel was aware that war ravaged Europe, and that Qutrub had manipulated the mortal nations to the brink of war, through conversations he overheard. He was not aware of just how much of the world was ravaged within the conflict. Being kept ignorant of the events beyond Qutrub's lair was another part of the torture.

If asked, Qutrub would have claimed that his art was of the highest order of science. Through his various tortures he had, over millennia, amassed the finest knowledge of human physiology, be it mortal or vampire. There were, he had noted, subtle differences between the two other then the obvious difference that the Velvet were dead things.

Vampires, for instance, developed glands in their skulls unknown to mortal physiology and, quite simply, they produced the anti-coagulant the vampire used in the feed.

As he investigated, however, he had discovered subtle differences between the Bloodlines. The line of Huginn produced only the anti-coagulant, but the line of Remus produced both this and a liberal amount of lactic acid. He had discovered that the gland, in the line of Shang-Di, produced endorphins and his own line's gland produced adrenaline. He was sure that the fabled blissful bite of Shang-Di's children had as much to do with the supernatural as it did the enzyme, indeed he was sure that all the effects of the various bites of the Velvet were as much mystical as physical, be that the pain delivered by the line of Remus or the fear produced by his own line's bite. He dearly wanted to entertain one of Jumlin's Bloodline, it was said that their bite could bring visions and Qutrub suspected that some form of alkaloid was probably involved.

Once he and Undjit had come together, each delivering True Death to one of the other's line, they sought to take the gifts of the other line into themselves but the experiment had failed, they had stolen the unfortunate Fledglings' strength, but not the unique powers of the other's Bloodline. In truth it was an experiment doomed to failure, for both of the ancients were veterans of the Bloodwar, both had fought and fed upon other bloodlines and never had their unique powers been transferred across the lines. Then, of course, they had been younger. Qutrub had hoped that the millennia had caused a shift within them that would allow such a theft. Also, during the Bloodwar, they had not had the benefit of Undjit's ritual, designed to facilitate the merging of their lines. It became quickly clear that the strengths of the Bloodline's could not be merged.

During his experiments Qutrub had discovered that it was the connection between the most primitive part of the brain and the spinal column that was vital for the Velvet; hence the removal of the head would bring True Death. Furthermore, he knew that the majority of bodily organs could be removed without ill effect, though the pain could be quite terrible; indeed they would re-grow rapidly so long as blood was available. It was the heart that was important, though he again suspected that this was more for paranormal and not physical reasons. It was clear that the vampire fed orally, not intravenously, thus it could not pump the stolen blood as such. He had begun to suspect that the heart was a manifest piece of subconscious symbolism. When Qutrub had actually written that phrase in his journal he had been unable to contain a self-effacing laugh. It was clear to see that the papers of the Swiss psychiatrist, which Undjit had insisted he read, had affected him more than he cared to admit, he had told his fellow ancient that this Jung fellow was all well and good, but he preferred the simplicity of Freud's sexual theorems.

Physically, the heart often featured in his manipulation of Velvet flesh. He could maintain the agony of his tortures by pushing a stake, or similar object, through the heart and thus preventing the vampire's uncanny healing abilities.

And yet, though he prided himself on being a scientist, he knew that he gained immeasurable pleasure from causing pain, so much so that the screams of his victims would arouse him sexually. So strong was his arousal, sometimes, that he caught himself stroking the bulge in his trousers. In the dark recesses of his lair he would casually caress his quickly exposed manhood, all pretence of the casual quickly falling away as his movements became more and more intense, unable to stop until he had brought himself to orgasm, sometimes spilling his dead seed across the living eviscerated flesh of his victim. At those times it seemed that he fed as greatly on the serenade of ghastly wails emanating from his guests and the smell of opened bodies as he did on the physical imbibing of the blood. How much greater it was, on those too often rare occasions, when the victims sexual arousal mirrored his own, especially if their arousal caused them shame and embarrassment augmented their agonies.

To the ancient there was one more aspect to his experiments, beyond science and beyond sexual gratification there was the art of it all. To be able to slowly strip away flesh and tissues to isolate a nerve, to leave a body open in such a way that the organs became a landscape upon a living canvas. The ancient's tastes were rarefied, but he knew himself well, be it the manipulation of flesh, or the manipulation of nations, he did what he did in order to cross the boundless centuries and stave the ever threatening boredom.

Qutrub was entirely enamoured with the grotesque, this was why he insisted that all born to his line were physically deformed, monstrous looking mortals. The more horrific his Children the more pleasure he found in them, capturing their hideousness for eternity, or until such time as he grew bored with them. In this respect he utterly differed from Uriel, whom he had detested with a singular passion, and as lovely as Uriel's Bloodline had to be so his Bloodline was the polar opposite.

It pleased him to have one of Uriel's get in his clutches for many reasons. The chance to bring horror into the Nubian's life was a pleasure in itself but the extended period of his incarceration had allowed his experiments to continue apace. The trouble, he had often mused, with investigating the flesh of the Velvet was the way any removed tissue would quickly corrupt. An hour removed from the body and flesh, blood, hair or skin would quickly crumble to fine dust. With Ymochel he could simply take the necessary flesh again and again, day after day, year after year.

Qutrub had ensured that the Nubian was aware of the passage of time during his incarceration. At first it had been a torture, allowing him to know just how long he had still to suffer, and Ymochel was surprised that, over the past few years, the Flesh had continued the practice. His imminent release was like a beacon of hope.

Ymochel heard voices in the dark and raised his groggy head from his chest. It was an effort, Qutrub had been almost gentle over the last few weeks, at least the various parts of his anatomy had been left in place if not intact, but the ancient had also chosen to starve him. With the constant damage to his body all his limited blood wanted to do was restore his damaged flesh and there was never enough blood for that to truly occur. The hunger of starvation had become more of a torture than the damage to his body.

"One hundred years have now passed." Ymochel recognised the voice, it belonged to Remus. The Bloodfather himself had come to deliver him from Qutrub. For the first time he almost felt kinship with him. He certainly felt gratitude. Never before had Ymochel ever felt close to his Bloodline.

"Time," said Qutrub lightly, "Certainly does fly by when one is having fun."

"Do you refer to your activities with him," Remus pointed towards the captive vampire, "or to the little war you manufactured."

Qutrub laughed, "Now Remus you know that I had nothing to do with the war, mortals are volatile - that is all."

"Don't insult me, I'm not some Fledgling, we can all see your hand in the conflict."

Qutrub simply shrugged, his slim shoulders moving sensually.

For a moment Remus seemed flustered but then continued. "Obviously I have come about Ymochel."

"I will be sorry to see him go," Qutrub confided, "He is a most remarkable specimen."

"How so?"

"When I test prospective Praetorians the outcome is always tediously predictable, within days they have tried to break their bonds and, by the end of their week with me, the majority are willing to sell their Bloodfather to me so long as the pain can be taken away.

"This one has neither attempted escape nor begged for mercy. If it was not for his screams I'd have thought him mute."

Qutrub's words were true. Ymochel had tensed against the Flesh's specially designed bonds when he was first incarcerated and had gauged them difficult, if not impossible, to escape from. Then he had considered the consequence of escape, even if he could manage it. The pain if he were caught, he imagined, would be even worse than the agony that loomed over the long decades. Beyond that, his life would be forfeit. He was not ready to die.

Nor had he begged for mercy. To beg for mercy would be to admit that he was in bondage, to have surrendered to that bondage and acknowledge Qutrub as the one who held the keys to his liberty. He had fought for his freedom, despite the chains the Concilium tried to place on all their kind, so instead he faced his imprisonment with a hollow pride.

"He is also remarkably resilient," Qutrub continued, "If I did not know better I would place him as much older than he is. I've never known one of so few years hold out so well."

Remus' eyebrows furrowed at the words. "What do you say?"

"I say that Uriel created a fine specimen, and understand that to give that bastard such a complement hurts me dearly."

From his darkened corner Ymochel thought, for a second, that he saw Remus' eyes flash red.

"I am sure that he contains secrets within him," continued Qutrub, "and I would dearly love to discover what they are."

"Secrets?"

"Sometimes I feel that there is a mystery within the creature, though that could be just an old man's fancy."

Ymochel started at that, for he knew what the mystery was. In his darkest moments he had almost cried out his hard held secrets. Not for mercy, but out of agony and fury. Countless times he had faced the temptation of revealing that he had destroyed Uriel and that he would do the same to Qutrub and to all the Concilium. Often he had bitten back the damning truth as it hovered dangerously on the tip of his tongue, but it was always on his mind. It was what kept him going. He would destroy the Concilium, the ancients and the damn Praetorian who had stolen Radu's life. She played in his mind often, she was a slave and, though she did not understand this, she actively helped ensure that the chains of the Concilium remained wrapped around the throats of all vampires. Her crimes, though they might have been born of ignorance, were worse than those who ruled.

"You wish to keep him longer, a plaything perhaps; I can see it in your eye Qutrub."

The ancient smiled his most charming smile, "Am I so easy to read Remus?" Inside, however, he laughed. This pretender to being ancient could never discern the plans and desires of the Flesh unless he openly revealed them. "No matter, the rule of the Concilium was plain, one hundred years."

Remus nodded and then added, "No less than one hundred years."

Qutrub laughed at that. "Of course, I had quite forgotten," he lied.

Ymochel began to tremble, could it be that what he perceived to be happening was, in truth, happening?

Remus walked over to the bound vampire and studied him for a moment. Then he leaned close to the Nubian and spoke softly. "Our Bloodfather named you Ymochel. Have you ever wondered why?"

Ymochel shook his head weakly.

"All our father's Children were named for Rome, all except you. Your name came from the bastard language of the Celts. Did this not strike you as strange?"

Ymochel said nothing. Qutrub came over, watching the exchange with a delighted glow to his eyes.

"You were named in the style of the Celts to remind you of your place. You were a slave of Uriel, never anything more. He named you Ymochel to remind you of your place, you did not warrant a name born of Rome.

"When the Bloodfather died I extended the hand of friendship, I wanted to draw you into the Bloodline, a magnanimous gesture on my part.

"Yet you always kept yourself apart. You have never bent knee to me in loyalty. You have flaunted the rules of the Concilium.

"I once said to the Bloodfather that we must never allow slaves to aspire above their station. I broke that rule with you and have lived to regret it. Your Fledgling embarrassed my entire Bloodline, thus you, in your pride, embarrassed my Bloodline.

"You are in no way superior to the Bloodline of Remus or the Concilium. You have the name of a slave and were drawn from a race of slaves. I believe it is time that you were reminded of that."

Remus turned to Qutrub, "Keep him."

The beautiful ancient clapped his hands with glee, "For how long?"

"Indefinitely."

Ymochel screamed then, but it was a scream of rage not pain. Fury burned brighter through him than any stolen blood ever could. Oh, he would destroy Qutrub and the Concilium and the bitch Praetorian. More so he would destroy Remus, he would enjoy drawing every last drop of blood from his veins and then ripping his head from his shoulders. It was no longer simply a question of freedom; it was a question of revenge.

It was his pledge, his prayer and his curse.

It was his only hope, when all dreams of survival faded.

He would ensure it would be so.

Chapter Thirty One

West Yorkshire, England – 1347

The blood welled from the exposed wrist, bubbling into Danaan's hungry mouth.

Robert of Wakefield may have been weak due to the mortal wound, but his blood was strong, full of life and vitality. It was the finest blood that Danaan had tasted in centuries. She felt it exploding through her system, filling her dead limbs with strength. She suckled harder determined to get the best of it before the man expired.

The room vanished from her consciousness, all that existed was the thick crimson river and her need for it. Gone was the straw pallet the man laid upon, gone was the small table with the earthenware jug of water. Gone was the plain wooden cross that hung above the pallet. Gone was the man's bow and quiver of arrows laid at the foot of the pallet. Gone was the man himself, except for the wound in the wrist spraying life into her hungry mouth. Nothing existed but the blood.

Robert of Wakefield was close to death, his heartbeat growing slower and slower, his breath was shallow. Still she fed.

She never heard the door open, never heard the cry of alarm, all sounds lost within the rushing stream of blood. The first she knew of the intruder was when she was pulled from her prey, rough calloused hands grabbing her shoulders and jerking her away from the meal, throwing her forcefully backwards. Her arm smashed into the small table, knocking it to the side. The earthenware jug fell and shattered, water spilling across the floor.

"What in Heaven have you done woman! Robert… Robert…"

Robert of Wakefield breathed his last.

John looked at the Prioress; she was curled on the floor staring at him with her wimple pulled back from her face. Her eyes were almost predatory and it seemed that scarlet flecks glowed within the brown irises. The blood of his friend was smeared over her pretty mouth. A trickle ran from the corner of her lips and, involuntarily, her tongue flicked out and licked it. As her mouth opened it seemed to John that he saw long extended fangs.

"Fiend!" He cried and launched himself at her, his arms grasping her shoulders.

Danaan gripped the sleeves of his dirty tunic and brushed his mind. She desperately tried to implant calming imagery, trying to halt his anger and his attack, but his mind was single-mindedly concentrated on destroying the Hell bitch before him. She put all her strength into pushing him back from her, but he merely stumbled, keeping a tight grip on her. His strength was impressive for a mortal.

She opened her mouth and hissed at him, the sound animalistic, almost primal. Her fangs were at full extension and her nails lengthened and sharpened. She managed to claw at his arms, ripping the tunic and tearing into the flesh, causing him to yell in pain and loosen his grip. It was enough, she twisted out of his hold and threw herself backwards, landing squat on all fours.

She circled him, ready to launch. She would bury her fangs into his neck. She would drain the immense outlaw dry. How dare he lay his dirty hands upon her? How dare he presume to touch a Child of the Velvet? Part of her was dimly aware of a commotion downstairs, which she ignored in favour of the creature before her.

She leapt but, for a large man, he was surprisingly agile. He twisted and caught her in mid-air. She clawed at him, her long talons raking his face, blood pouring into his beard.

He tossed her then, towards the window, which shattered as her body impacted the thick lead glass causing it to splinter and fall with her towards the ground, a shower of crystal rain.

The guards ran into the guest room. They had guessed that one of the outlaws had been injured and suspected it was Robert himself. They had assumed they would try and find aid at Kirklees, they had known that Robert's cousin was now Prioress.

A sword was levelled calmly at John.

"He's dead!" Cried the giant outlaw, his voice raw with emotion, "Murdered by a succubus."

The guard looked at him, puzzled.

"Succubus you say," The Captain of the Guard had heard his cry as he strode into the room.

"Aye, she drank his blood, for the sake of all that's holy go after her."

The captain walked over to the window and looked down to the ground below. The moon was bright and he saw the Prioress crumpled on the floor. He'll hang for that, thought the Captain, if for nothing else he'll hang for murdering the Prioress. Then she moved.

For a second he could not believe his own eyes. She stood and ripped at the habit, tearing it away. The naked figure ran towards the forest, her movements too smooth, unreal.

"You," He pointed at one of the guards, "Take some of the men and go after her?"

"Who m'lord?"

"This one's succubus," He motioned to the outlaw, "The woman who has just run naked into Sherwood."

The guard looked at him expecting laughter, then the realisation dawned that the Captain was being perfectly serious. He scurried out of the room.

"Well John, you led us a merry dance and no mistake." The outlaw was bleeding profusely, but there was something in his bearing, something defeated. He wouldn't run again the Captain realised, "Let me call one of the good Sisters to bind and tend your wounds."

"No, they will not touch me!" There was terror painted in his eyes.

The Captain nodded thoughtfully, "Then let us sit and you can tell me of all that has occurred here."

Chapter Thirty Two

New York City – 2000

A light breeze from the air conditioner blew across her body, soothing the heat radiating from her skin. She looked at the beautiful woman led next to her, as naked as she was, her eyes devouring her lover's beautiful body, her pale skin. In the air was the faint perfume of vanilla.

It had been a wonderful evening, she thought, and the greatest night of her life.

The woman had taken her to an exclusive cocktail bar. Beatrice protested, she couldn't afford to drink in such places, but the woman told her not to be silly. The drinks were on her.

They sat with drinks before them. Beatrice had opted for a margarita, the woman a bloody Mary. In the corner of the room a pianist played a torch song, his voice soft through the microphone. The music washed over them, unobtrusive but adding a rich ambiance to the softly lit bar.

They spoke for what seemed like eternity, learning about each other. She was called Danaan, this mystery woman. When Beatrice asked, Danaan explained that the name was Gaelic. She had been born in Normandy and then her parents had moved to England but she had spent a lot of time travelling, mainly around Europe. That, Beatrice guessed, explained the accent, European but so mysterious, so difficult to place.

The bar served meals and Danaan suggested that Beatrice eat something. She ordered a Caesar salad; Danaan ordered nothing, explaining that she had already eaten.

Beatrice felt very self conscious as she ate her food, knowing that the beautiful woman was watching her, worried that she might spill some food down herself and all too aware that the sight of someone eating was unattractive. As a result she picked at the food, unaware the Danaan adored watching mortals eat, an oral pleasure she was now denied.

She pushed the plate aside, the salad only barely touched, but she felt better for the fact that she eaten at least a little. They talked some more, the conversation light and yet very comfortable. They conversed about books and poetry, music and films. Beatrice was both astounded and thrilled that Danaan knew so much about those films and books she loved. She wasn't to know that the brunette had both taken the time to search through her possessions and also used her vampire skills to brush the girl's mind and pick up on her thoughts as they talked.

On Danaan's part she was careful, she did not want to make the beautiful mortal uneasy by seeming to know her mind too well, but skilfully steered the conversation in a way she knew delighted her companion.

Eventually Danaan suggested they go dancing and Beatrice quickly agreed, she certainly didn't want the night to end. Beatrice tried to pay something towards the bill but Danaan would not hear of it. Secretly the girl was relieved, as she had feared the bar had proven to be exorbitantly expensive.

As they left the bar she hadn't noticed that her new friend had not so much as sipped her drink.

Electronic music pulsed, so different to the music in the earlier bar. Heavy and pounding, sensual in the dry ice air. Blocking out even the possibility of conversation.

They danced for hours, dancing together, their dancing more and more intimate. They danced and their bodies communicated to each other as they could not use words, explaining through the drama of their movements their secret desires.

Eventually Beatrice collapsed exhaustedly to a seat, vibrations rose through the cushioned fabric as the heavy based pounded and she felt a smile burn across her lips. All the frustration, the anger, the guilt and the fear that had been generated through the day was gone, melted by the time spent with Danaan, dissipated by the exertion of their dance. She was happy, truly happy.

"Would you like to see my home?"

Danaan's words, shouted into Beatrice's ear so as to rise above the loud dance track, sent a thrill through the girl. A small flush crept up her cheeks as she nodded her agreement.

They walked to Danaan's car. The sight of the black Mercedes did not shock her. She had guessed that the woman was rich, Danaan's insistence that she pay for their drinks and the entrance charge for the club had indicated that much. Some sort of society heiress, Beatrice guessed.

When they had reached Danaan's home the brunette had quickly whispered something to one of the security guards and then, talking Beatrice by the hand, led her through the house. She gave the mortal a whistle stop tour that took Beatrice's breath away. The house was filled with so many beautiful things, a veritable Aladdin's cave of antique furniture and gorgeous works of art. The tour eventually reached Danaan's bedroom.

No more needed to be said. They fell into each other's arms and it seemed the most natural thing in the world. They slowly stripped each other's clothes and then took their time exploring one another, their bodies becoming more and more entwined as the pleasure built higher and higher within them. This was more thrilling then the movie Beatrice had watched, more exciting than her night with the whore and more breathtaking than her dreams, it was all she could ever have hoped for.

Finally Beatrice lay there, enjoying the cool play of air from the air conditioner. She gazed at the most beautiful person she had ever chanced to meet, knowing that she loved Danaan with her whole heart. Her dreams not only fulfilled but also surpassed. Both her body and her soul were satisfied for the first time in her life.

There was a knock at the door.

Danaan turned over, propping herself up on one elbow, "At last." She exclaimed, her voice light, "Darling I want you to trust me now."

Beatrice felt a flutter of panic in her heart. What was this? The door opened and a most beautiful woman with fiery red hair walked into the room. For a second it seemed that the newcomer was about to speak but then she sighed softly and simply stood there.

Danaan had arranged this with her security as she had reached the house. She had intended to wait, to allow a relationship with Beatrice to develop before exposing her true nature, but despite her long years already lived and the expanse of years that lay out before her she had become impatient. One of the guards had been sent to find a high-class whore.

Beatrice had pulled a silk cover over her naked body; her face had flushed scarlet. Her mind was trying to take in exactly what was happening.

"Please, don't be frightened," Danaan was speaking to Beatrice, not the whore who merely stood there whilst her mind was assailed by beautiful visions, "I need you to know all, my darling. What you see may seem strange, terrifying even, but please allow me to show you this and then permit me a chance to explain."

Beatrice pushed herself against the head of the bed, her legs curled to her chest and her arms encircling her knees. The presence of the woman had been strange, but Danaan's words were somehow frightening. She watched the brunette walk over to the redhead, she watched her lift the woman's wrist. Then she saw... but how could she... she saw Danaan's canines elongate. She saw the bite, and watched her lover drinking the red rivers that sprang from the woman's wrist.

Tears filled Beatrice's eyes. She didn't understand. It was all too much. She wanted to run and yet did not dare. Then Danaan was stood over her, the red smear around her mouth was not lipstick. Beatrice's eyes darted around the room, as though she were an animal trapped in the headlights of a car, unable to move and yet searching for a means to escape. Danaan held out a hand to the shivering girl.

"Don't touch me!" Her voice shook with fear.

"Beatrice, look at her," Danaan moved to one side. "She is unharmed."

Through tear filled eyes Beatrice saw the woman. She still stood; her face filled with ecstasy, the wound on her wrist no longer bleeding. Danaan walked over to the whore and slipped ten crisp one hundred dollar bills into her hand. "Go now," she whispered, "The men will take you home."

The whore left the room, closing the door quietly behind her.

"Know," said Danaan as she moved back to the bed, "That I could never hurt you."

Beatrice edged away from her new lover, pressing herself as hard against the wall as possible. "What the fuck are you?" The words shouted, her voice piercing.

"I am a vampire." The answer was so simple, spoken so matter-of-factly.

"You're going to kill me…" Beatrice's voice had fallen to a frightened whisper.

"Never my love." Danaan's hand stroked the girl's face, running across the tear slick cheek. Beatrice flinched but did not pull away. "I love you, I have since I first saw you and I think you love me."

"I never... not before..." The words were incoherent but Danaan saw the questions within her mind.

"I did not make you love me, nor did I make you attracted to women. That was always within you. I will admit I opened the door, but it was you who walked through it."

Beatrice stared for a moment, confused by the fact that the beautiful creature before her had seemed to answer questions she had not spoken. After a moment her confused mind found her voice again, "What are you going to do to me? What do you want?"

"I want to be with you, I want to be your lover."

"I don't... understand."

"I want you to be like me, I want us to be together through time."

It was almost too much to take in. "If I refuse you will kill me."

"No. I could not do that, I could not hurt you." As she spoke the words the enormity of what she had put in motion finally hit Danaan. Some vampires brought a Fledgling into the Velvet against their will. There was no intention of doing that with Beatrice; she would have to agree of her own will. How else could the girl love her? Yet rejection would be almost too much for her to bear.

A single crimson tear ran down her cheek.

"So, if I refuse you will let me walk away?"

"Yes," the word almost choked in her throat but it was sincere.

Beatrice looked at the vampire; she saw the pain etched across her features and the tear of blood running down her cheek. The sight of her anguish almost broke her heart. Her beautiful eyes seemed ageless and yet filled with such terrible grief and loneliness. It was too much to think about, too much to be rational about. There could be no thought, only instinct, trust and love.

She held her arm towards Danaan, offering her wrist.

Chapter Thirty Three

Vienna – 1935

The room was more reminiscent of a laboratory than a dungeon, various scientific paraphernalia such as test tubes and beakers were in plain sight, but it was a dungeon none the less.

A man came down the stairs, his feet echoing on the stone slabs, and approached the young man who pottered around the murky darkness. He had orders to visit the young gentleman, told that he should learn all he could but he didn't see how such a young person could teach him anything. The young man was quite beautiful, his face almost hermaphroditic. His skin was a light mocha, far from the Aryan ideal, and his vividly red lips were pursed in a cupid's bow. A mop of long curled hair fell over his vividly blue eyes. The younger man was making notes in a journal. The older visitor tried to discern what was being written but the long, elegant script was in a language he was not familiar with.

As he drew closer he cleared his throat, "Herr Qutrub?"

Qutrub turned and looked his visitor up and down. The man wore a stern suit cut in a dark material. His short hair was neatly brushed and side parted. His mouth was a tight thin line drawn across his square face. The mortal did not offer his hand. He thinks himself superior to me; the ancient found the thought amusing.

"Ah, Herr Mueller, I trust you had no trouble finding my home," Qutrub spoke in flawless German, yet his voice was soft and ethereal and his accent was unusual. Mueller was unable to place its origin.

"Not at all, the Führer sends his deepest regards." Heinrich Mueller wondered again why the Führer would send him to this exotic, but terribly young creature. What could this thing possible teach him?

"Ah yes, I do appreciate the Führer's philosophy, it is so… invigorating."

Mueller narrowed his eyes, unsure as to whether the younger man was insulting the Führer or was being genuine. In truth Qutrub believed every word he said, the dictator was providing him with much entertainment. Only the year before the ancient had been forced to visit Germany when Hitler began the Night of the Long Knives, the eradication of his political enemies. The sense of fear that the melodrama, as Qutrub saw it, produced had made his feeding sweet, his Bloodline enjoyed blood so much more when spiced with the taste of fear. He had ghosted into the homes of those slain, feeding upon the blood of their families.

Now the German leader intended to consolidate his absolute rule with the Gestapo and training leading lights such as Mueller was an essential part of the plan. Qutrub was more than happy to lend his help to the man he had manipulated towards the leadership of Germany.

"You see," Qutrub continued, "That is why he sent you to me. I have an unrivalled knowledge of anatomy and, more specifically, the way the human body can be manipulated in order to provide the greatest levels of pain. You have been sent to learn from the master so that you might take the knowledge I impart to you and use it to further your Führer's cause, the fulfillment of his philosophy."

Mueller felt like snorting but he had been ordered to treat Herr Qutrub with the greatest of respect. The younger man must have seen something of his derision in his face, however, for something terrible flashed across his eyes. Instantly Mueller was terrified, though he could not say why. It was as though Qutrub's eyes contained a singular malice far beyond anything the German had ever experienced before, something primal and horrifying. Then, as suddenly, the look was gone and the eyes again sparkled with a youthful enthusiasm.

"Come now Heinrich, I can call you Heinrich can't I, let us see where we might begin."

The vampire turned on his heel and walked purposefully to the back of the room. Mueller followed though he now felt some trepidation.

The back of the room was shrouded in darkness. Qutrub clapped his hands and lights sprang into life, switched on by an unseen assistant.

The illumination revealed a black man, strapped to a cross like piece of equipment. Unusually the man was not simply bound at the feet and the ankles, but metal bands held the limbs at various strategic positions. Mueller could not help but wonder why. Rather than ask, however, he simply stated, "He is a Negro."

Qutrub smiled, he particularly liked the Nazi concept of racial purity, he was sure it was going to provide him with much entertainment. Racial purity, religious purity, all such concepts led to such chaos, fear and murder in the ancient's experience. He had introduced most of those concepts into the world, after all, relishing not only the entertainment but, with groups such as the Nazis, the irony that he had manipulated a philosophy that he was, by mortal race, the antithesis of.

"Indeed he is," the ancient answered his guest, "but trust me, this one is a hardy specimen. He will serve well for a subject to practice upon."

Ymochel lifted his head and looked at the two with hateful eyes. He had wondered at his treatment over the last week. Qutrub had ensured he was fed well and his torture had been stopped for a while.

He knew why now. The son of a whore was going to let a damned mortal torture him. He was going to teach his techniques to a mortal and let him practice upon one of the Velvet.

Qutrub had picked up a set of large needles. "Now, let us start by running through the main nerve receptors."

Within minutes Heinrich Mueller understood why he had been sent to meet Herr Qutrub.

Chapter Thirty Four

Walachia – 1473

A grey light shone through the small window, catching the bars that in turn cast shadows onto the dirty floor of the cell. The smell of his own waste assailed his nose from the pail in the corner of the small room.

He had been here at least a month, his once well-groomed moustache was wild and an unkempt beard had grown. The clothes on his back seemed like rags, but had once been expensive finery, in the time before it had all gone terribly wrong. There was no mirror in the room but he imagined it would reflect a vision far removed from the man they once called Radu the beautiful.

It was his beauty that had captured the imagination and the heart of the Sultan. He had only been a child when their father had sent him and his brother Vlad to Adianople, hard to believe that it was twenty-nine years ago. Their father insisted they were to be fostered, but in truth who sent their children to the Turks to be fostered? Even though his years were few Radu had known that he and his brother were hostages, political pawns in a grander game than his child's mind could understand.

Despite the fact that he was a prisoner, he had fallen in love with the place; the well-crafted gardens in the palace were a source of constant amazement to him. Whilst Vlad rebelled constantly, making life as difficult for their captors as he could, Radu had been co-operative; he laughed to himself and corrected his last thought, very co-operative. The Sultan was pleased with the boy's accommodating nature, and his beauty if the truth were told. He would often take him to the secret places in the palace and teach him the arts of love. As a boy he had not known that there was anything wrong with such acts, though in later years he had flogged men who acted in such ways, with boys so young, to within an inch of their lives.

They had been there four years when they were finally released, allowed to return to Walachia. Vlad had taken his leave with all speed, but Radu elected to stay in Turkey, most specifically in the palace. He was taught other lessons then. He was taught tactics and politics and, as time passed, he realised he was being groomed for power. He might have been younger than Vlad, but the Sultan wanted to ensure that someone friendly to the Empire took the Walachian throne.

So he had, just a few short years ago, wresting it from his brother, deposing his kin. Vlad had found that support from King Matthius of Hungary had been withdrawn; it was probable that he had been incarcerated in this very cell. But Matthius was a Corvinus through and through, and all knew that they were notoriously fickle. The eye of the Turkish Empire had turned away from him, concerned with other games, leaving him without the support he needed to maintain power. Corvinus had switched his support back to Vlad, probably at the insistence of Rome, though possibly because the mood had taken him to do so. Now Vlad was on the throne once more and Radu had been left to rot, locked away and forgotten.

He knew that Vlad would be waging war against the Empire, and Vlad was known for employing barbaric tactics of terror. Given that the Empire had abandoned him Radu sincerely hoped that they suffered. He had always been a pawn, he realised bitterly, and now sat waiting until another of the great players wished to employ him in their grand games.

Ymochel stalked the stairs of the tower. He had watched the machinations of the Ottoman Empire and the Church of Rome with interest. Remus had been correct all those centuries before, when he said that the Judean cult was going to sow seeds of chaos throughout the world. He had later discovered that Qutrub had, indeed, been involved in their development.

As he watched, his eye had fallen upon Radu Tepes. He had first seen the man when he was only a child, held by the Turks. The mortal had been a paradox even then, both fiercely bold and sublimely compliant at once. He seemed to be just what the vampire had been searching for.

When Radu lost the throne, Ymochel had petitioned the Concilium. He had expected an argument. Whilst he had been the darling of the Concilium over a thousand years before, he had shunned the great halls, refusing to be held by their invisible cage. Vampires, however, had long memories. He had been welcomed back with enthusiasm and the petition had passed without issue, despite the fact that Radu Tepes was a mortal of standing in the affairs of the world. Defiantly he suggested that he would allow the mortal to keep his own name and, amazingly, the Concilium had agreed.

Now all he needed to assure was that Radu's boldness could be directed correctly and his compliance would be given unreservedly to Ymochel. If the Nubian could be sure of that then a new Child of the Velvet would be born. If not the mortal would die, killed in a foolhardy attempt to escape captivity.

Screams pierced the door to the cell. Radu stared at the thick wood intently, trying to guess what occurred. He was the only resident of the tower as far as he knew; there should be no one else to torture. Could it be? He dared to hope that he might be rescued, that the screams came from guards slaughtered by men loyal to Radu.

The door burst inwards, wood splintered as though it were nothing but a thin veneer rather than the thick, heavy wood that had bared his exit. Framed in the doorway was a giant of a man, his features lost in silhouette. As he moved into the cell Radu glimpsed the carnage in the guardroom beyond. In the flickering torchlight he saw men ripped apart. Limbs were smashed, twisted and ripped. Torsos had been torn apart, heads had been crushed. The guardroom was awash with blood and viscera the scene of carnage more reminiscent of the rabid fury of an animal than the act of a man.

He looked at the creature that was the source of the carnage. Dressed in the long robes of the Turks, the fine silks blackened by blood, it could almost be that he was a man, his skin a rich black. But his hands sported long vicious talons, flesh still dripping from their sharp points. His wide opened mouth contained long ivory fangs and his eyes, red, hateful and filled with power and fire. Radu stumbled away from the creature, his back impacting hard with the rough stone of the cell wall.

The creature looked at him, but made no move. Radu eventually found his voice, though it was timid and filled with fear.

"You… you are a djinn?"

What else could the creature be? He had heard tales of such creatures whilst living in the Palace. Devils from the wastelands, they were known to be creatures of magic, fire and blood. The holy book of Islam named them fiery spirits whilst the people of the deep deserts referred to them as the people of the empty spaces. He had always thought them to be superstitious nonsense, stories told to scare small children. Now, however, it seemed that one stood before him.

The creature's appearance metamorphosed before his astounded eyes, the fangs sliding upwards into his gums, the talons vanishing, leaving bloodstained nails. His eyes lost the red fire, turning to a rich brown, though they still brimmed with inner power.

"I am no djinn, Radu Tepes," His voice rich, his accent evocative of the mysteries of the East, "I am your salvation."

Radu looked at the creature, his mouth open wide.

"Radu," the vampire continued, "You have been abandoned by the Turks, deposed by your kin and left to rot by Corvinus, but I have the power to raise you above them. I offer you a taste of true dominance over man."

"And what do I give for this power, what is the price I must pay?"

Ymochel heard the words but in the mortal's eyes he saw the hunger he wanted, the desire he could use and build upon. "Come to me in obedience and love and it will be yours, we will play a game that will outlast their so called Empires."

Radu stepped forward, in his heart he knew what he must do. The creature's beauty overwhelmed him and his words dripping with promises of power seduced his heart. There was no question in his mind for he could feel the power the creature offered, radiating from his very body.

He knelt before the creature and opened the gore splattered robes. His hand gripped Ymochel's large phallus, already beginning to harden in his hand and drew it into his mouth. Radu's head moved up and down, his teeth scraping Ymochel's length. The huge penis filled his mouth, brushing hard against the back of his throat and threatening to cause him to gag despite his experience in such techniques.

Fortunately Radu had learnt his lessons well, he knew how to please, the Sultan had seen to that. Within minutes the vampire orgasm came, his dead fluids spraying into the man's eager mouth.

He lifted Radu's head, making him look up at him, red tinted sperm dribbling from the side of the nobleman's mouth. "Are you prepared to walk through fire to seize the gift I offer?"

Radu nodded and Ymochel guided him to his feet.

"Then taste of the pain of flame and be reborn."

The screams reverberated through the tower as Ymochel bit down hard and guided the man to the Velvet.

Chapter Thirty Five

New York City – 2000

When she awoke the next evening her naked body was spooned tight against Danaan's. The presence of her lover's naked body caused her to feel aroused until she remembered the enormity of what had occurred the night before.

Danaan's bite had been sweet. The sensation of the fangs sinking through her skin, her flesh, her vein had caused her to feel an intense pleasure and as Danaan drank she felt that she was lifted upon clouds, floating in a place of beautiful dreams. Weakness had taken her body as Danaan drank deeper and deeper, but the feeling of euphoria made her forget emotions such as fear. Part of her knew that she was dying but she could not remember why she should care.

Danaan had let her arm fall to the bed and, as the contact was lost she began to regain some composure, enough to dimly realise that the next breath would probably be her last.

She felt the pressure of Danaan's arm over her mouth, and tasted the coppery hint of blood as it dripped onto her tongue. She should have been repulsed but, at the very first taste, she wanted it. Her tongue stretched out, lapping at the jagged wound in the vampire's wrist and she felt the power the blood contained rippling through her body, wave after wave. Her strength began to return, her arms no longer felt like dead weights. Her heart beat so fiercely within her chest that she felt it might explode.

She grasped the wrist and pulled it tight to her ravenous mouth, suckling hard to draw the blood into her.

Suddenly Danaan pulled her wrist sharply away with a cry of, "Enough!"

Then came the pain, an intense burning through her body, causing her to double up and clutch at her stomach as tears poured from her eyes. The agony proving so intense that her throat was unable to produce a sound, her scream dying in her chest.

Danaan stroked her hair gently, "Your body dies and is reborn. It is a pain I would spare you if I could my love. Know now that you are of the Velvet, subject to the Concilium. I name you Celeste."

The words seemed alien and she could not understand why Danaan had called her by another name.

Eventually the pain receded. She felt more alive than she had ever felt before. Danaan held her close then.

Eventually she spoke. "Why did you call me Celeste?"

"It is our way that all new Fledglings are renamed."

"What is a Fledgling? Why are they renamed?"

"Hush my love, I will answer these questions tomorrow. For now let us sleep."

Celeste had opened her mouth to speak again but Danaan gently placed a finger over her lips. "My darling, can you not feel it. As the sun rises it steals our strength, we call this the stupor."

She did feel it, she realised, a dull sense that a fire was rising above the world and then nothing, her awareness fading as she fell deeply into the stupor, only vaguely aware of her lover pressed close.

Now she was awake. She was Celeste. She was a vampire. The sun had set; she could feel it in every fibre of her body.

Suddenly it came upon her, a craving so strong it could only be described as agony. The feeling seared through her body and she knew, instinctively, what she yearned for. She needed blood, needed it like nothing she had ever needed before. It was a fire burning through her every nerve, unquenchable unless she could drink of the crimson draft to soothe it.

"You feel it, don't you my darling? You feel the hunger, the ever present need."

Danaan had awoken and turned to face her.

"I must have it… now!" Any thought that the taking of blood was monstrous, that she may have supposed she would feel, was missing. The need was too much.

"You shall, later we will hunt. On the first awakening the feeling is powerful, difficult to master. I will help you control it for now."

She felt Danaan touch her mind and it was an intimacy like she had never felt before, Danaan soothed the hunger within her. It was still there, ever present, pulsing through the back of her mind, but it was dulled temporarily. Still touching her mind Danaan leaned over and kissed her deeply, she felt what Danaan felt and knew the truth of the vampire's love and also the depth of her loneliness, a hunger for companionship almost as strong as the need for blood. She understood the drive that had pushed her to seek out a lover, to transform Beatrice into Celeste.

Celeste pulled away and, intuitively, pushed Danaan from her mind. "I can never go back can I, that's why you gave me a new name?"

Danaan was visibly shocked. A newborn Fledgling should not be able to expel her so easily. Shock quickly transformed to pride, however. Celeste would make a worthy addition to the Velvet.

"No," She eventually answered, "Your mortal life is gone now my darling. How could it be otherwise? Friends and family will grow old and die whilst you are forever as you are now. A new name makes the transition easier, it helps you forget who you were and remember what you are now."

"Everything is gone…" The words were a whisper as images of her estranged parents, her sister, her job, even Steve flitted through her mind. She should have resented Danaan at that moment. The vampire should have explained all this before she made her choice. Her choice, she reminded herself, Danaan had offered her a choice and she had taken it. The guilt was hers, not the beautiful exotic creature led naked on the bed.

For her part Danaan understood. The feelings for one's family, those that the Velvet left behind and to whom they were dead, oscillated with time. When Ariadnne had first brought her over she missed her parents dearly. The sense of loss was dulled with blood and soon after with the absolute sense of power that had been gifted to her. Some twenty years after she had been turned Ariadnne had given her the news that her father had died. Danaan had not known that Ariadnne had kept watch on her mortal family, nor could she understand why. When her Sponsor had suggested that they visit England, and her father's grave, she had rejected the idea with little thought. Her family were nothing to her any longer. After she had escaped from Csejthe, and admitted her mistakes to the Concilium, she had been at the lowest ebb of her unlife. She had returned to England then, wanting to seek out her father's grave and sit by it in the moonlight. She had been unable to find it. Now she could not even remember their faces. It would not surprise her if Celeste did similar but, as Ariadnne had done for her, she would keep watch over the Fledgling's mortal past so that, when the time was right, she had the opportunity to sit by her parents graves and mourn. That, however, was for the future; the present had more pressing concerns such as feeding.

Celeste felt a stirring in her sex as she watched her beautiful maker rapt in her own hidden thoughts, a growing lust that made her want to possess Danaan's beautiful body. With an effort she controlled her raging libido, there was too much she needed to know. "What happens now?"

"Now my love," said Danaan, "I think we should get dressed and go to your apartment, I am sure there are things you wish to retrieve from there. On the way I shall explain all about the Concilium, the Velvet's ruling council, and the laws that govern us."

Celeste must have sighed for Danaan added, "It is necessary my love, though you might not think so, that these things are explained.

"Once we have retrieved your things we hunt. We will feed your hunger."

Just the mention of it made Celeste intensely aware of the throbbing need within her. She nodded her ascent to the plan.

Danaan walked over to her wardrobe to pick out some clothes. As she did Celeste noticed the beautifully ornate crucifix that hung above the head of the bed. She moved closer and ran her fingers along it. She thrilled at the cold metal and smooth cut stones, the sensation of the materials below her fingers were powerful and she realised that her tactile sense had expanded, causing feelings to be so much more intense. Part of her felt that she could spend the entire evening just running her fingers over the cross, discovering through the touch of her fingertips its every nuance. Yet, whilst this was true, a larger part of her wanted to explore the night, to revel in the new world that had been opened before her. One thing was certain however, the Hollywood image of the vampire trembling before the cross was no more than a myth.

She heard Danaan approach and asked, "Isn't it just a little perverse for a vampire to keep a cross above her bed?"

Danaan's voice was quiet as she replied, "I keep it there to remind me that I was once very young and very foolish."

Celeste looked up at her lover, wondering if Danaan would explain and unaware that she could have brushed

Danaan's mind and probably seen the memories she had referred to. The brunette simply turned and began to pull clothes on. The Fledgling shrugged and ran her fingers across the cross once again, shivering as the nerves in her fingers exploded with myriad sensations. Reluctantly she let her fingers drift from the cross and began to dress.

Chapter Thirty Six

Nuremberg – 1946

The trials had been ongoing for the best part of a year, the victorious allies sought to punish those within the Nazi regime for the worst of the crimes committed against the peoples of the world.

It had not taken much coercion to ensure the he could attend and Qutrub enjoyed watching the consequences of the war, so much so that he had abandoned his continuing amusements with Ymochel, leaving the Nubian to Baal's 'gentle' ministrations.

One by one he watched the allies sit in judgement over the highest in the Nazi party. Again and again he heard the plea that the defendant was only following orders fall on death ears. That amused him, he demanded absolute obedience in his get and he knew that Hitler had demanded similar. The allies believed that a moral man should have put down his arms when asked to do something utterly immoral.

Perhaps, he mused, a truly moral man would do such a thing, if one existed. Qutrub held morality in very low esteem, he believed in power and power alone.

There were two missing from the proceedings, two who Qutrub had deemed as loose ends. Hitler himself had committed suicide rather than let himself be captured, relieving Qutrub of the need to dispose of him. The other was Heinrich Mueller. The Gestapo official had fled Germany as the Allies made their approach into Berlin and managed to reach Switzerland, trying to find Herr Qutrub and sanctuary. It had been Baal who intercepted him and brought him to Qutrub's Geneva mansion. As the mortal knew Qutrub he could not be allowed to stand trial, he was a loose end that Qutrub had devoured with much relish.

The war had been one of Qutrub's greatest achievements, the Nazi party overwhelming his expectations. Couple that with the work he had put into the Communists in Russia and the entire scenario was a melting pot of hatred that had been guaranteed to make the ancient smile. In truth the ancient had not had so much fun in centuries. The fun, however, had come at a price and it was this price that had dominated his thoughts for some time and had now reached a point that it distracted him from the drama unfolding in the courtroom.

Mortal technology had developed at an astronomical pace and much of it was of value to the Children of the Velvet. The years through the war, in particular, had seen the technological advances spiral out of control, a speed of development far faster than at any time Qutrub could remember. He had not expected, however, the Americans, that brash, young country, to develop a weapon as terrifying as the atomic bomb. Jumlin really should have kept his continent in check, he mused, but the American ancient was more interested in the traditional Americas and had little time for the white settlers who had overrun the continent like a plague of locusts.

Reports from the Japanese islands had been slow in reaching the Concilium in the final days of the war. Two of the Children had lived in Hiroshima and were caught within the blast of the bomb. Susano had been the eldest of Shang-Di's get, and so the Children around the world had felt his true death. How he had died remained a mystery for a few days, until the Concilium finally received the report that America had dropped one of its atomic weapons on the city.

Qutrub knew all about radioactive materials. He had been most interested in the research that the Curies had produced into the unstable elements and Qutrub had noted the effects the material had on their health before the mortal couple ever did. He had experimented with radium and the effects it would have on the flesh of the undead, using Ymochel as his test subject. Burns from the material would heal, though perhaps more slowly than a burn gained from a flame. The cancerous effects of radioactive material did not affect vampiric flesh in any way; the blood would not allow it.

The effects of a nuclear blast, however, were as devastating to the undead as they were to the living.

The atomic bomb had changed the balance of power in the world and provided as great a threat to the Velvet as it did to the living. Qutrub needed to find a solution.

The ancient had been involved in the rise of Stalin in Russia, just as he had been with Hitler in Germany. In fact he deemed that turning the Germans against their allies the Russians had been a masterstroke in producing additional chaos during the war. If he could ensure that Russia had the technology to create nuclear weapons then perhaps he could create a military stalemate with America. It was clear that all the developed countries were eager to procure such technology. The way forward, however, was not as clear as it should have been.

The Concilium were understandably concerned about the new weapon. They would be watching its development closely. Shang-Di had originally demanded that the Children attempted to have the technology eradicated, although he was soon convinced that once something was created, removing it from the world stage would prove almost impossible. What Qutrub had to do was convince the Concilium that supplying the technology to the Communists was in their best interests. He had to persuade his associates on the Concilium that they could engineer a stand off. He was sure that the likes of the Morning Star would be certain that the spread of such weapons would more likely cause the use of them.

To put his plan into action he would have to leave Nuremberg and the thought irritated him. Yet he needed to think and the best thing for putting his mind on track, so to speak, was a little bit of physical manipulation, as he liked to call it.

He would have to return to Geneva and vent his frustrations on the Nubian, after a week of intense torture he felt sure that his plans would be in place.

It was only noon, the sun would be at its highest, but there was no sense in lingering longer, he could not concentrate on the trial with these worries nagging at him. Besides, he knew the sun would not damage him; he had fed awfully well the night before.

Chapter Thirty Seven

Castle Csejthe, the Carpathians – 1610

The woman in the mirror was no more than twenty years old; she certainly did not have the fifty years that Erzsébet concealed behind the alchemy of blood ritual. She was so absorbed in the perfection of her reflection that she did not notice the door open.

Danaan could not believe she was back at Csejthe. Only a fortnight earlier she had been happily ensconced in a modest house in Bucharest. Then she had the misfortune of visiting the nearby inn. Unfair to blame the inn, she admonished herself, he would have found me anyway.

She had taken a seat, the inn was quiet but she expected that it would soon fill with customers and that, amongst the clientele, she would find a suitable meal. In the meantime she enjoyed the aroma of rich foods being prepared in the kitchen, whilst she nursed a glass of wine.

One moment the seat before her had been empty and then, almost in a blink of an eye, she became aware that someone sat there.

She didn't exactly recognise him, more she recognised that he was singularly unrecognisable. "Fenrir."

"Danaan," his voice glided like silk across her senses, "How fortuitous that I should meet you here. I have a message for you."

She sat patiently, waiting for him to speak, knowing that he spoke with the voice of the Concilium Sanguinarius.

"Not here, the message should not be overheard," He indicated towards the innkeeper who busied himself behind the bar and the few patrons scattered around the room. "I believe you have a house nearby, perhaps we should go there."

She nodded, unwilling to speak. She was not sure how potent his ability to hide was. It was entirely possible that, whilst she could see him, the few mortals in the inn could not. It would do no good to be recognised as a crazy woman who spoke to herself. Such folk were remembered. Since the events at Csejthe she had come to the conclusion that a low profile was intensely desirable. She had even taken to hanging the cross she had obtained, when she had fled the castle, above her bed. All the better for reminding herself that discretion was the better part of valour.

Outside the inn the weather had taken a turn for the worse, rain lashed down from the dark, cloud-shrouded skies. Instinctively she pulled her cloak close around her, a mortal habit that she had not lost in almost six centuries.

Fenrir had vanished again, and she felt as though she walked the muddy street alone. Her boots splashed dirty water from puddles causing her boots to become speckled with mud. Her sensitive ears strained to hear his footsteps whilst her mind probed outwards trying to locate the smallest essence of him, but he was totally undetectable.

She reached her house and pushed the large iron key into the lock. The door swung open with a creak and she entered the house. She stood for a moment, unsure if Fenrir had entered or not and then gently pushed the door shut.

As she entered the living room the candles had begun to light themselves, or so it seemed, and she knew the Concilium agent was indeed with her. As the last candle sparked into life he became visible to her again.

"That is rather disconcerting," she said, her words sounded glib but they were true.

"I do apologise, it is a force of habit. I spend so much time not being seen that the effort is to allow myself to be seen, not to become hidden."

"It's as though you were invisible."

"But I am never invisible, just so inconsequential that the observer does not register my presence."

"That's…"

"The truth and nothing more, shall we sit?"

They faced each other across a long, rough-hewn table. Fenrir broke the silence.

"The Concilium wished me to speak to you about Csejthe."

A flash of panic gripped Danaan. When she had fled the Castle she had headed, with all speed, to the Concilium and told them all that had occurred. She had expected to be punished, especially after Kirklees, but they had been surprisingly understanding. She had not expected the spectre of that time to raise its head so soon.

"What of it?"

"You have not heard the rumours?"

Danaan shook her head. She had heard nothing of Erzsébet since she had escaped her clutches, though because of the events she had ceased moving in aristocratic circles. The danger of exposure and the concept that Erzsébet still searched for her were all too real. Indeed it had taken her a quarter of a century to return to this part of Europe.

"It seems your… friend… has been rather busy. Rumours abound of girls being sent to Csejthe in order that the Countess might educate them in the finer arts of appropriate social graces and etiquettes. Many have gone missing and now it appears that the bodies of some young girls have been found."

"What do you mean found?"

"The rumour has it that four bodies were discovered floating in the stream behind the castle, all girls. They were naked, grievously tortured by the state of the bodies and drained of blood."

"Peasant rumour, no doubt."

Fenrir smiled, "No doubt, but it seems that certain nobles are demanding that the Countess be investigated."

"Erzsébet won't like that," Danaan allowed herself to grin at the thought of the blind rage Erzsébet would enter if she thought that someone would dare question her actions, "But what has this to do with me?"

Fenrir scratched his nose for a second before answering, "The Concilium is concerned about the rumour of the bodies being drained of blood. They wish to know what is occurring within the castle."

"Why me? Surely you could simply enter the castle and find out yourself."

Fenrir shook his head, causing his lank hair to sway, "Do you realise how much effort the Concilium went into to rectify the problems you left in your wake following the Kirklees incident?"

Danaan did know. She had not gone willingly to the Concilium following her naked flight into the forest. The Concilium had summoned her.

It seemed that Robert of Wakefield was quite the folk hero amongst the peasants. The fact that he had died, and a witness claimed that he was killed by a she-devil who drank his blood, was bad enough. The fact that the witness had named Dame Startin as the killer, and that the noble woman could not be found, had galvanised her family into demanding immediate answers from the authorities. The scandal that surrounded the nuns, and their activities, had meant that Rome herself had become involved.

By the time the Concilium had summoned her they had already begun limiting the damage. Praetorians began to spread various wild rumours in the inns of England concerning the death of Robert in order to dilute the legend that grew around his demise. Some even said that Robert was not really dead, that he had been seen. Concilium diplomatic agents had started the misdirection of the investigations in England and Rome.

In many respects she had been lucky to receive a simple reprimand, but she had not felt lucky. As she left the great hall she could remember catching sight of Ariadnne. Her estranged lover had watched the whole drama unfold and, as Danaan had tried to catch her eye, hoping for a sad smile or a sympathetic look, she had turned away. Danaan still remembered the look of disgust seared across her face; it was etched forever into her aching heart.

"I know."

"It is the Concilium's judgement that Csejthe is your mess, Danaan. You must go there; you must see if there is any truth to these rumours and if any... untidiness... can be rectified."

"I shall ready myself for travel at once." She stood to leave the room.

The strange vampire looked past her for a moment and it seemed to Danaan that he debated something with himself, or perhaps he was remembering something. Eventually his watery eyes focused upon her again. "Danaan, the Concilium have made their judgement," he said, his voice soft, "but they said nothing about you travelling with a companion. I think I will journey with you, if you are agreeable."

Danaan had nodded her ascent before leaving the room.

Travelling with Fenrir actually proved to be quite pleasant; on the occasions he made his presence known. As they travelled they spoke to one another and Danaan was surprised with how at ease the other vampire made her feel. He told her of the halls of the Concilium and, though she had seen them with her own eyes, she found herself enjoying his descriptions, caught up in his obvious zeal.

She found herself wanting to see the halls with his eyes, wanting to share the emotions he obviously felt for the ancient caverns. She tried to brush his mind as he spoke but felt nothing; it was as though he was not there.

"Do not even try, child." His voice was kind, with no hint of anger at her attempted intrusion, even so she felt embarrassed.

"I'm sorry…" Her words were contrite.

"There is no need to be, you are a Child of Shang-Di, it is natural to you to try and walk my mind."

"I couldn't touch you, it is as though you are not there."

"No," He laughed and the sound was gentle, "All that I am is too well hidden. There are many secrets within me."

"It must be lonely…"

"My Bloodline cannot mind walk, I do not miss what I have never known."

Danaan shook her head, "No… I mean all of it, to be always hidden…"

They paused and he looked at her, for a moment his eyes were awash with melancholy, a sorrow so vivid she thought she might cry.

"There are some debts that must be paid."

She didn't understand his words but something in their tone and his bearing caused her to forgo pursuing their meaning. This was one of the secrets within him, she realised.

"Why did you ask to travel with me?" She asked instead.

"I thought you might enjoy the company," his words seemed off-hand.

"Not because…"

He interrupted her, his voice earnest, "It is not to spy on you."

"No. I mean, that's not what I was going to say. If you wanted to spy on me you could have walked besides me without my knowing."

"Then what?"

"Not because you enjoy the company?"

He sighed, and the weight of the world seemed contained in the sound.

"I am not used to it," he admitted, "but sometimes it is pleasant to spend time with another person, to talk.

"I spend so much of my time in silence, concealed from the world, both of mortals and the Velvet. It is a pleasure to simply converse."

She looked over at him and studied his face, though it was difficult to convince her mind to concentrate on his features and hold them, however she guessed that he had been roughly forty when he had received the Velvet Kiss.

"How long?" She asked.

He smiled gently. "Over two and a half thousand years I have been reborn, closer to three thousand."

"Where did you live? As a mortal I mean."

"I was born and lived in Mycenae, in Greece."

She nodded, "I would love to hear of it, as it was."

"Maybe I shall tell you sometime, but not tonight." His voice seemed full of emotion. Danaan believed that he would tell her, but only when he was ready to. Until then she would not enquire further. The fingers of his left hand drifted to a ring he wore on his right, Danaan noticed the movement and for a moment she caught what might have been a signet designed to look like a Greek mask. Fenrir noticed her gaze, fallen as it was on the ring, and pushed his hand beneath the folds of his cloak.

"What of you?" He asked.

For a second Danaan was confused by his question, distracted by the hidden ring, but quickly realised his meaning. "I was born in Normandy and moved to England when She was taken by William the Bastard."

He laughed.

"What amuses you?"

"You speak like a true Norman," he explained. "The English call him Conqueror, but you, his own people, call him Bastard."

She shrugged. She had forgotten much of her mortal life and it seemed odd that her words could so betray her history when her mind could not consciously remember such.

"I was taken by Ariadnne," She continued, "Seduced and turned."

"You no longer speak, you and your Sponsor." It was not a question.

"No." Her voice was full of pain and sadness. "We do not."

"Why?"

"I have been a fool, Fenrir, a spoilt fool. I took the gift of her love and threw it away." Her tone was raw and scarlet tears brimmed in her eyes.

"But what did you do?"

"It is too…" Her voice trailed away to nothing.

"Please," he implored, "Tell me."

Danaan rounded on him, furious at his relentless prying. Did he not know how much his questions hurt her? Ariadnne was a vital piece that was missing from her heart. When she looked at him, however, her anger faded. His eyes were full of sympathy and nothing else.

"I… I was reckless. I tried to defy the Concilium at every turn and tried to encourage her to do the same. I became more and more angry with her; I believed that if she loved the Concilium so completely, that she must love me less."

Her words were sharp with pain, "I was jealous. I believed that they controlled us and could not understand why she never resisted them."

He nodded his head slowly, causing his lank grey hair to fall over his eyes until he pushed it back. "And what do you think now?"

"I think that I was young and foolish. I think I now understand what the Concilium does and why. I respect their wisdom."

He paused for a moment, as though he carefully considered his words, and then said, "The ancients do have wisdom, though many times they do not show it. That is why we have the Concilium because, collectively, out of the schemes and plots of the ancients wisdom can be distilled."

She stopped walking and looked directly at him. "I still love her, Fenrir, and I do not know how I might win her back."

"That," he explained sadly, "I can not tell you. I do not know how to heal a heart so broken."

He drew her to him and held her in a strong embrace. For a moment she feared that he would try to kiss her, fearful that he wanted to take advantage of her pain. She enjoyed his company but she could never feel an attraction to him.

There was no kiss, just a hug of sincere sympathy. She surrendered to his arms, allowing her head to rest on his shoulder, and accepted his solace. She could not see the streak of crimson that ran from his eye.

Eventually their journey was over. As they approached the castle he had said his farewells, leaving her to enter on her own. She sensed reluctance within him but knew he believed this was a task she had to complete herself. He faded before her eyes and it was soon as though he had never been there.

She found that infiltrating the castle was easier than she had imagined it would be. There was a small door that the servants used and this had been carelessly left open. Once inside she had made her way through the shadows, constantly reaching out with her mind to feel the approach of anyone.

The castle was very different to the one she had left, the corridors were carpeted now, and the walls draped with rich tapestries. Large, beautifully crafted statues were impeccably placed at the most opportune positions. The decoration showed a faultless sense of sophistication. Ferenc had either finally given in to his wife's tastes or had died, Danaan assumed the later.

She was worried by the lack of servants, however, it was as though they all hid, closeted behind closed doors. The castle she remembered may have been austere but it had bustled with life.

Her mind touched upon two mortals approaching and, soon, she heard their voices. She pressed herself deep into the shadows behind a statue and watched them pass by.

They were women, both wearing a uniform that consisted of long black robes, hooded to hide their faces, almost like the habit of a monk. The dragon crest of house Báthory was elegantly embroidered onto the breast. They struggled with a burden between them.

They dragged a corpse, she realised, a young girl of no more than sixteen summers. The girl was naked and a series of wounds had been inflicted on her flesh, yet none of them seeped blood. Recognition came quickly. There was no blood left in the body.

"Has the Countess selected a replacement for this one?" The dulcet tones betrayed the macabre subject of the nearest robed woman's words.

"She has," The second woman sounded more common, drawn from peasant stock.

"'Tis a pity that the good pastor has refused to bury the waste, it becomes more and more difficult to find a place to dispose of the refuse."

"Perhaps the forest?"

"No," the other quickly replied, "the Countess has said that the forest is not to be used. Something about the wolves and debts of the past.

"I think, perhaps, the vegetable garden."

It was true then, Erzsébet was killing the young girls and, by the looks of things, using the blood for some nefarious purpose. Danaan gave the two enough opportunity to move fully away and then crept out of her hiding place. Her feet moved in remembered directions towards Erzsébet's room.

***

Suddenly there was not one face in the mirror but two. The second stood behind the first. Two young girls, if appearances were to be believed, neither having seen each other for thirty years but neither having aged a day since that time.

Erzsébet turned round to face her visitor, her voice was light and cordial, "Katrina, I hoped you might come."

Danaan allowed herself to touch the noble woman's mind, though it repulsed her to do so. If her mind had been strengthened by insanity before, then now it was completely distorted by it. Touching her psyche was akin to running a hand through fetid waters, choked with weeds and much worse. Yet she was able to hold her connection for long enough to understand exactly what it was that Erzsébet saw.

When the Countess looked into a mirror she saw the girl she had been some thirty years ago. More than that she saw the girl she assumed she had been, the image of her belief. The same young, pretty features that Danaan remembered were there, but the skin gleamed as though it were possessed of an inner light. Her complexion was flawless and she was the most beautiful girl in the world.

Yet when Danaan looked upon the woman with her own eyes a different story was told. She had aged, and time had not agreed with her. The story of her excesses was etched into the leathery texture of her face, deep lines cracked her skin and her eyes were lost within puffy lids. The rest of her face seemed drawn, as though she were malnourished, causing her to appear almost skeletal. Any beauty she had possessed had been eaten away by the passing years and the weight of her sins.

"Erzsébet," Danaan's voice was full of genuine sympathy, "What have you done?"

"Can you not see, my darling one, I discovered the gift you gave unto me."

"What gift?" Danaan was genuinely confused.

"You accepted me as a lover and made me stregoïca, like you. When you ran away I was angry at first, but then I understood why. You wanted me to discover your gift for myself. The blood, it makes us young does it not, me and you?"

Danaan began to shake her head furiously, "I gave you nothing. You are not like me."

Erzsébet laughed, a shrill lunatic sound, "Of course I am, look how young I have become."

"Erzsébet it is not true." She tried to penetrate the madness of the mortal's mind, tried to project the true image of Erzsébet's visage, but the image was lost, swallowed up by the lapping waters of insanity.

"I see," a dangerous edge had crept into the woman's voice, "You are jealous, you want to take the gift away. You appreciate that I am better than you, and you hate me for it like the peasant you truly are." Her hand slipped onto a large journal. She picked it up and waved it at Danaan. "I have them all here, all recorded. I have been very scientific about it. I mourn for them all but it is better they die so that one such as I might be."

The book slipped from her fingers and fell open upon the floor. The pages showing contained lists of names, all girls and detailed records of all Erzsébet had done to her victims.

"Erzsébet, please…."

"No! You want to kill me. I know it. You want to take from me all that I have gained."

A hammering pounded through the castle. Erzsébet ran to her window and looked through it. Looking over the Countess' shoulder Danaan could see the armed guards, torches blazed and swords were unsheathed. The door of the castle splintered. The mortal investigation of Erzsébet Báthory was about to begin.

The woman span around, a wild panic burning within her eyes. No matter the depths of her insanity she recognised danger when she was confronted by it.

"Help me!" She implored.

Danaan turned away from her.

"Katrina, you must help me! Together we can destroy them all." She had dropped down to her knees.

Danaan walked out of the room, closing the door quietly behind herself, ignoring the demented wails.

Fenrir materialised beside her. "Come, let us get you out of here."

He took her hand and she felt his essence surrounding her, a negative aura of utter insignificance.

As they walked he said to her, "You did well child."

She shook her head. "I failed. She has murdered hundreds and used their blood in a mockery of the Velvet."

"You did not fail, you did exactly what you were asked to do. You investigated matters."

"To what end. I couldn't stop her."

Fenrir gave a nasal snort, "Exactly how were you going to do that?"

"I wanted to show her what she was, but she couldn't see. Her mind was a place of chaos. Her insanity blinded her to the truth."

Fenrir nodded, in truth it hadn't taken a mind reader to realise that Báthory had utterly lost her grip on sanity. "You couldn't cure her, you know that?"

"True." Danaan admitted.

"So what do you suppose you should have done? Should you have killed her?"

"No, killing her would have posed more questions than it would have offered solutions."

Fenrir laughed, the timbre was reedy but it also sounded heartfelt, "Spoken like a true member of the Concilium."

"I don't understand."

"In your heart you do. Killing her would have been a mistake. If it wasn't for the fact that the mortal authorities were knocking down her door you would have been expected to find a way to alert them. Let the mortals deal with their own. Rule from the shadows, that is the lesson the ancients learnt centuries ago."

They fell silent as they entered the main entrance hall. Guards filled the place. Erzsébet's black robed witches were being held, watchful eyes and drawn swords prevented them from fleeing. Other guards led survivors out of the dungeons, though many of the men were pale; experienced soldiers shocked by what they had witnessed in Erzsébet's sanctum.

All were oblivious of the two vampires who walked amongst them.

Outside the castle one guard was doubled up, vomiting heavily onto the rough path.

"It was my fault," Danaan broke the silence, Fenrir's presence causing their voices to be hidden from the mortal, "I was careless, she saw me for what I was."

Fenrir squeezed her hand, "It was an accident Danaan. Her bloodthirsty activities caused you to betray yourself. You were careless, yes, but she probably would have found a similar path for herself anyway."

The vampires were swallowed by the night, leaving Csejthe behind.

Chapter Thirty Eight

New York City – 2000

The sweat beaded on his forehead and ran rivulets down Steve's face. A drop coalesced on the end of his nose before dropping and tumbling through the air to splash on the tiled floor. His palms were drenched too, that worried him more.

He didn't know why he was so nervous. He had spent the last night in vigil and Beatrice had never come home. He was scared for her, gravely concerned if the truth be known, but her absence did not make him nervous. If anything it should have relieved his frayed nerves.

Truthfully, in the depths of his heart, he did know why he was so nervous. Anyone would be tense if they sat in wait in an apartment building holding a large and very sharp machete, he told himself.

The previous night he and the vampire Michael had come to this place, once a haven of happy memories. Bitter sweet memories, he mentally corrected himself, after all his relationship with Beatrice was not exactly the most stable at the best of times, they had more than their fair share of arguments. He'd never hidden in wait with a weapon before.

He wondered what it meant that she had not come home the night before. Did it mean that the vampire had gotten to her? Probably, he admitted, which made his presence all the more important. Michael had told him that the only way to save Beatrice was for a human, or more correctly Steve McPhrenon, to kill the monster that had, for some reason, chosen her.

The large knife felt strange in his hand.

"One hit, so make it count." Michael's words haunted him. The meaning was clear, screw up and he was dead, worse Beatrice was lost. He'd never used a blade before, not in an aggressive way. He hoped he was up to the task.

His hands shook slightly and the sweat seeped out of his pores. He offered a fervent prayer that he had the strength to do what he must.

If Ymochel was nervous he didn't show it. He hid down the other end of the corridor. The plan was simple, the Praetorian would come out of the lift, and the human would rush her and with luck get his one strike. Steve had suggested that he approach her with a cross but Ymochel had talked him out of it. His reasoning was that such an approach would warn her. That he might not get his chance to strike. There was no lie in that, though he had purposefully continued to let Steve keep the misconception that vampires were repelled by holy symbols. He had learnt centuries ago that it was always wise to keep the upper hand, even with allies.

The human believed that Ymochel was also going to rush the Praetorian as Steve attacked. That he would try and grapple her and hold her for him. That was a lie. He would not risk exposing himself to the bitch. If she escaped then his life was as good as forfeit. No, it was down to the human, if he failed he would have to reconsider his current course of action.

That fact that it appeared that she had taken the human woman already did complicate matters. If the Praetorian had killed the girl then the vigil was all for naught. Despite her slaying of the whore two nights before, however, that would not follow her normal feeding pattern. Thus he felt sure that they would return here.

If they didn't then the plans would likely come to naught. He had already checked the Praetorian's home. There was too much security to use the human; Ymochel would have to go in alone. He had considered a daylight assault, the bitch would be trapped in the stupor, but he didn't know what her inner security was like. Anyone breaking into his current home during the day, be they vampire or human, would receive a very nasty shock. He assumed the Praetorian would have considered employing similar methods.

He wondered again at the course he had set himself on. It was fraught with danger and he had been so careful for almost two thousand years. Once more he considered telling the human how he could successfully incapacitate one of the Velvet but rapidly dismissed the thought. He might just decide to turn it round on me; a paranoid thought, he considered, but very healthy.

The lift chimed and Ymochel sensed two of his own kind. Suddenly he realised that she had actually turned the girl. No matter he would take care of Fledgling and mortal loose ends alike, once Steve had struck his vengeful blow.

Danaan and Celeste came out of the lift holding hands. To anyone else they would have looked like a pair of young lovers. To Steve all his worse nightmares became real in that one moment.

Ymochel grimaced. Come on. Now. Do it now.

The lovers walked down the corridor, towards the apartment, towards Ymochel's hiding place.

Steve ran, the machete in hand.

Danaan sensed something. A Child of the Velvet was nearby. She was preoccupied with this and did not notice the human running at her back. She reached out with her mind trying to brush the mystery vampire.

Celeste heard the footsteps; she wheeled round as Steve came upon Danaan and let out a guttural growl.

Ymochel pushed at the Praetorian's mind, he might not be a mentalist but, with the blood he had stolen from Uriel, he could keep his mind sacrosanct. He forced her away with all the strength of an ancient, causing the Praetorian to reel.

Steve brought the machete down in a vicious arc, all the force he could muster in the swing.

Danaan staggered at the force with which she had been expelled from the other vampire's mind.

The machete struck home, but her movement caused Steve to miss his mark. The blade bit into her shoulder and lodged in bone.

Ymochel barely contained a howl. The fool had missed. He threw himself through the door of the stairwell, barrelling down the flights of stairs.

Celeste saw the blade slice into Danaan's body. Only a deeply buried part of her recognised Steve. She barely had time to feel the thrill of her fangs extending and her nails transfiguring into deadly weapons.

In slow motion Steve realised he had lost his chance. He saw his love transformed into a deadly, feral beast, her eyes glowing scarlet. He looked down the corridor for Michael but the vampire was not there.

Danaan caught the name Michael in Steve's panicked mind, but it meant nothing to her. She tore the weapon out of her shoulder.

Celeste leapt. Her fangs sank deep into Steve's neck. She drank.

Danaan briefly considered running after the fleeing vampire. She looked down at Steve caught in Celeste's iron grip. The Fledgling did not offer him pleasure with her bite. She realised her lover intended to drain the human completely, gorging occurred quite often during the first feeds. A vampire learnt control with experience. Her shoulder burned with the wound and she knew she needed blood. She took Steve's wrist and bit down.

Steve was dying and he knew it. He tried to struggle but Beatrice held him so tightly, so very, very tightly. He expected that his life would flash before his eyes but that was not the case. All his awareness was filled with Beatrice and the monster she had become. Fear and horror filled him; he struggled harder but could not break her vice like grip. Then the other vampire took his wrist and his struggle ended as pleasure rolled through his body.

Danaan had brushed Steve's mind as she had taken his wrist, she watched as the horror of what his girlfriend had become was lost within the pleasure of her bite. His mind was filled with Celeste, memories of them together filled his awareness. Beautiful moments from their life before Danaan, images of the senior prom when they had danced all night and then made love, Celeste relinquishing her virginity to him. She realised that he had truly loved the woman, but also knew that he could never love her like she did and her love was eternal. Suddenly she became afraid for Celeste, afraid that if the Fledgling brushed his mind at that moment it would scar her emotionally. It would be traumatic, she decided, for Celeste to kill someone projecting so much love for her, to take a man's life whilst he remembered their first time. She tried to modify the memories, to make them of someone else, anyone else, but they were firmly fixed in place. Her focus changed and she brushed Celeste's mind, and relief flooded her as she realised that the Fledgling was not intruding on her victim's mind, she was lost within the absolute pleasure of the blood, so intense the first time the Velvet fed. Danaan kept her focus fixed on Celeste, riding her thoughts and revelling within the feeling that she had not experienced in almost a thousand years.

Ymochel burst through the door at the bottom of the stairway and rushed into the lobby of the apartment building. He didn't know, he just didn't know. Had the bitch recognised him in the brief second when she had touched his mind?

Chapter Thirty Nine

Vienna – 1979

Too bright, the city was far too bright. Streetlights and windows threw light into the night like the dimly remembered sun. No, the sun was brighter and could burn, he remembered, but it was still too bright. Why hadn't they warned him, these two lurking sentinels that dogged his every step? They had, he recalled, but he had not listened, not truly. The sound of stolen blood rushing through his veins had deafened him to their words. Still, he marvelled at the power that must be needed to produce such hideously bright illumination.

There were mortals everywhere; their clothing was strange, sleeker and more colourful than the clothing of the past. Strange metal carriages rushed past at impossible speeds, belching noisome gases into the air and flooding the roads with bright light from powerful lanterns. He had seen a horseless carriage before, in Paris during the spring of 1770, but that had been powered by steam and quite incapable of the speeds these things achieved. Whatever powered these vehicles stank and assailed his sensitive nose. The noise from them was horrendous, a shocking growl accompanied occasionally by a resonant horn sound that mimicked the frustration in his heart.

Buildings, once tall town houses, now had crackling neon signs placed above doorways. Inside mortals gathered, drinking alcohol, laughing and talking. Music blared out of small boxes, or what obviously passed for music. Gone was the majesty of the orchestra and in its place a cacophony of rhythm and inane lyrics. Cigarettes tinged the air with an acrid aroma that mingled with the greasy stench of cooking foods. It all assailed his senses.

He wandered, glassy eyed, unable to know if he could cope. Ymochel was free from Qutrub's lair, but utterly lost in the modern world.

His freedom had arrived in the form of Huggin Morning Star. The wizened African had paced purposefully into Qutrub's laboratory. Ymochel started as he became dimly aware of the ancient's arrival. A terror clutched at his heart. He was fearful that the secret had had kept locked within him might be discerned by the truth teller, he had not consumed enough blood to fool the ancient. He had not consumed enough blood in many, many years.

"Morning Star, this is unexpected." Qutrub's voice had seemed calm as always.

"I have come to free Ymochel."

"Direct as ever, on whose authority do you come?"

"The Concilium's."

Qutrub had become angry then, "I am of the Concilium, or have you forgotten!" He quickly regained his normal composure, "I do not recall us agreeing the Nubian's release."

"It is not a Concilium edict… yet. All the Bloodlines have agreed, however. We thought it best to act informally."

"Did we, my opinion has not been sought I see," there was acid in his voice, "And what of Remus, he gave me the Nubian."

"Remus has been convinced of the sense of the Fledgling's release." Huggin's voice was soft, like water gently bubbling in a stream.

"Then perhaps you would care to share this… wisdom… with me."

"Ymochel was sentenced to one hundred years in your care."

Qutrub's eyes narrowed. "Not less than one hundred years," he reminded the other ancient.

"And we have taken that into account. If his punishment appears to surpass the Concilium's judgment excessively it may cause derision amongst the Velvet. Some might seek to question our wisdom."

Qutrub thought on this for a while. There was a degree of truth in the Morning Star's words and if the other six ancients had agreed…

It would, he concluded, be embarrassing to force their consensus to a formal judgement. He would loose face with the others when defeated publicly. He suspected that one of the ancients was trying to manoeuvre him, but which one?

"I grow bored of him anyway, take him." Qutrub turned his back on the other ancient and his erstwhile guest, busying himself at his desk.

At that, two Praetorians came down the stairs and released Ymochel from his bonds, he fell into their arms, too weak from Qutrub's latest ministrations to stand.

They carried him up into the main house between them and put him in a room. A low light played and there was a bed, the sheets black silk. Ymochel collapsed upon the bed, the hunger screaming inside him, but he was too weak to respond to its hunting call. Though it was night he wanted to surrender to the stupor, to be enfolded in the soft, cool sheets and the endless blackness of a vampire's sleep.

The door opened and a mortal entered. She reeked of cheap perfume, and her face was plastered in ill applied make-up. Above the stench of her perfume was the scent of her blood, permeating through her skin and calling to him. The hunger forced his muscles into action.

"What'll it be then? Blow job or full sex?"

He leapt from the bed, ignoring the pain and fatigue that assailed his body, snarling like an animal. His claws embedded in her shoulders and she managed a stifled scream before his fangs sank into her neck. He pushed all his anger, his agony and his frustration into that bite and the pain that seared the whore's body was of such intensity that she immediately lost consciousness. He devoured her completely, her blood rushing through his injured body, healing organs, flesh, muscle and skin. He dropped her emptied body to the floor, discarded and forgotten. He needed more.

Two more whores were devoured before he began to feel anything resembling normal. A set of clothes in his size had been left on a chair. He pulled on the sweater, wondering at the fabric, it was like nothing he had known in his previous life. A pair of black trousers and some leather boots later and he opened the door, determined to escape the mansion before the decision to release him was reversed.

As he stalked through the richly decorated corridors the two Praetorians fell in beside him. They spoke to him but he did not listen, their words about the modern world ignored. One of them pushed papers into his hands, identification and currency that he would need in the modern world. He thrust the papers into his trouser pockets, not even bothering to look at them.

He eventually found the exit and Baal approached him.

"My master bids you farewell and, as a reward for the pleasure you have given him, he wishes you to know that you are always welcome in Dark Waters…"

Ymochel pushed the repulsive vampire out of his way and set off into the night, the Praetorians keeping pace with him.

All that seemed a lifetime ago, before the modern world had made its unwelcome assault on his senses. As he walked he heard a familiar piece of music coming from one of the converted houses. Instead of the brash modern music he had been hearing he heard the beautiful strains of Mozart's symphony in F. The music came from one of the boxes he had seen in other such bars. He walked in still accompanied by the Praetorians.

The bar was empty of patrons. One of the Praetorians ordered three glasses of red wine and the other directed the glowering Nubian to a corner table. When the bar's owner was looking away the Praetorians deftly emptied the wine from the glasses and filled them with blood from a flask.

Eventually Ymochel spoke, "Why are you here?" There was no anger in his voice, just a cold hatred of these symbols of the Concilium. If they heard it, however, they ignored it.

"We have orders to ensure your safety, until you adjust." The first Praetorian was a tall Caucasian whose accent had maintained a hint of his Gaelic origin.

"The world has changed much," added the second Praetorian, a man of Chinese origin. "Plus your time with the Flesh will have been trying. Believe me, we know."

Ymochel looked at him closely and slowly recognition came. Qutrub had tested the Praetorian during Ymochel's incarceration. "You know nothing. I remember you; you were there during my… stay. Within a week you wept like a mortal and begged for release." He looked towards the other, "You, what year is it?"

"Nineteen seventy-nine…" spluttered the other Praetorian.

Ymochel nodded, Qutrub had forgone keeping Ymochel informed of the passage of time over recent decades, "One hundred and sixty years." His voice rumbled with a hint of emotion, "That is how long the Flesh held me…

"You have no idea Praetorian."

If Ymochel had expected anger or argument he was disappointed, both Praetorians simply nodded. Their time with the Flesh had been the most horrific of their lives, alive or undead, neither of them could truly conceive of what such a prolonged time with the Flesh would be like, of what it might do to a person.

"Morning Star suggested that you travel to the Alps, to return to the Concilium and recover." The Gaelic Praetorian said, trying to change the subject.

"No." There was an unarguable finality to the word. The last thing Ymochel wanted was to be near the Concilium. He needed to get away from them, and their damned rules. He needed time to heal. He needed time to think.

"Where will you go?"

Ymochel had heard much about the Americas before his incarceration, but had never visited them. He knew that they were ruled by the Concilium and that an ancient resided there, but they were so distant. Perhaps there he would be able to breathe and recover.

"The Americas, how long would passage on a ship take?"

The two Praetorians cast looks at each other before the Chinese Praetorian answered, "Why not fly?"

"Do I look like a bird?" His voice was a dangerous rumble.

"In a plane…"

Ymochel's head dropped towards his chest and his fingers slowly clawed deep, angry furrows into the surface of the table as they explained. The world, it seemed, had become far smaller whilst he had been incarcerated.

Chapter Forty

Bitcse – 1611

The trial went ahead without the presence of the main defendant. Erzsébet Báthory had declined the invitation to attend and give evidence in her defence; instead she remained under guard at Castle Csejthe. When Danaan had discovered this she had determined to attend the trial, in her heart she wished to see the consequences of her actions, she also wished to know that mortal justice would prevail. Part of her believed that she should have killed Erzsébet, but only a small part. She knew, deep down, that she was right to vanish into the night with Fenrir.

The obvious difficulty came with the timing of the trial, such events were rarely held at night. It had proved to be an effort to fight the stupor, but not impossible. She had dressed in mourning black, covering her skin as best she could and hiding her features into the bargain. Even so, the pale January sunlight still stung her skin and caused her eyes to ache as she made her way to the courthouse. The sheer act of will it took to fight off the stupor seemed to drain her stolen blood, stopping it from healing her damaged skin. It was almost a penance.

She was confused by her own reactions, her own guilt. Over the centuries she had killed many and felt no guilt or remorse. Yet the actions of Erzsébet both horrified her and caused her to feel a deep melancholy born of the fact that she was the focus, if not the source, of the Countess' insanity. Over the years to come she would examine this dichotomy of emotion. It was clear that she was incapable of feeling regret for the deaths she had bestowed upon mortals; she needed to feed to stay alive. The killing of mortals was natural for her kind. Erzsébet also had a need, though that need was born in the twisted labyrinth of her broken mind. The difference, Danaan would eventually conclude, was one of veracity and excess.

The witches of Csejthe were all tried at Bitcse, their lowborn status not allowing them to stay with their mistress. As Danaan watched the case unfold before her it became apparent that they investigators had searched for a further person, who had been repeatedly mentioned by Erzsébet, a

Katrina. Unable to find her they had concluded that Báthory actually meant Katarina Beneczky, a young maid who had the misfortune to have been employed in Csejthe, though she was not involved in the murders. Indeed she had been unaware of the events, too scared of her mistress to leave her room at night. Her presence at the trial was a further source of guilt for Danaan, the girl stood accused of collaborating in the worst series of murders in living memory simply because she had the misfortune of having a name similar to the one that Danaan had assumed thirty one years earlier. Worse still Danaan knew the truth of her innocence, having brushed the terrified girl's mind.

She had thought, perhaps hoped, that Fenrir would attempt to talk her out of attending the trial. The Concilium spy had stayed close to her since their journey to Csejthe. She had found his company pleasant, indeed she actually looked forward to his visits and their conversations. He had still not described his mortal life to her, but that did not seem to matter. Inside she knew he would, one day, even if a thousand years passed by before he felt that the time was right. But, instead of dissuading her he had actually supported her decision, telling her how important it was that she understood why the Concilium created the rules that governed the Velvet.

So it was that she came, day after day, braving the sun and fighting the stupor. She watched mortal justice play out and heard the disturbing catalogue of crimes that Erzsébet was accused of. The various defendants tried to play down the crimes, making out that only forty or so girls had been killed, as though it were a small number not particularly worth the attention of the authorities. More than this, they claimed that the forty had only been peasants, not girls from the Academy, arguing that the lowborn status of the victims should have ended the trial there and then.

Their evidence was damned, however. The guards who had come to Csejthe the night that Danaan had confronted Erzsébet had found the Countess' journal. Detailed extracts were read to the court and by the end of that session it was revealed that Erzsébet Báthory had detailed the systematic torture and murder of some six hundred girls, high and lowborn alike.

On the final day the guilt of Erzsébet's witches and the Countess herself was pronounced. Danaan sat in silence, physically trembling, whilst Count Thurzo, who presided over the trial, announced his decision regarding Katarina.

"Not guilty," his voice resonated through the room.

The maid broke down in tears of relief and Danaan too shed a blood red tear, hidden behind the black lace of her veil.

The witches were sentenced first of all. Thurzo decreed that their fingers should be ripped out by method of red-hot pincer. Following this the women would be burned to death. Danaan cast her mind to the pyres that the townsmen had been constructing as she had made her painful way to the trial that morning. It seemed that the punishment was to be carried out with all haste.

Thurzo then turned his attention to Erzsébet herself. As a noble she escaped the torture and immolation that her followers suffered. The Count decreed that she would be bricked up in her rooms at Csejthe, only a small gap in the doorway to be left so that her meals might be passed to her.

"There in solitude," he declared, "Will the vile Countess live out her natural life, in that room she will grow old and die."

It was lucky, Danaan mused, that the Countess had not been at the trial in person. She couldn't imagine how the woman would have reacted to the suggestion that she would grow old.

The trial was done and Danaan made her way back to her lodgings to wait for nightfall and Fenrir, she had left him a message saying that she wished to see him. The trial had made her consider her life so far. On the first day of the trial a riot had spread through the town, the commoners angry that Erzsébet Báthory had been granted leave to remain in her castle, believing that justice would not be done because of her aristocratic status. The fools had not even realised that the law of the land had been especially changed in order that the Countess might stand trial. As the riot had spread through the town another vampire had been caught within the disturbance, a freak accident had removed his head from his shoulders and he had died. Danaan had born witness to his final moments. She blamed herself, of course, the riot was a direct result of Erzsébet's crimes and her crimes were a direct result of Danaan's carelessness. Fenrir had calmed her and convinced her that no action would be taken against her, that such a tragic accident would not attract blame. He could not remove her guilt with his softly spoken words, however.

She needed to make amends for both her actions and inactions, and she needed to regain Ariadnne's trust and love. For once in her life she would take responsibility. She knew that Fenrir would come in the night, he would put his arm around her and comfort her and whisper words of solace. Fenrir would know, she realised, he would be able to counsel her on how she might become a Praetorian of the Concilium.

Chapter Forty One

New York City– 2000

The car pulled up towards the gates, which stood open, something was wrong.

Cleaning up after the attack had proven troublesome. Things were not helped by Celeste's reaction. In her first feeding she had taken a life and, when the initial flush of blood had passed, the guilt had come smashing down. It was common amongst Fledglings; in fact Danaan would have been worried if Celeste had not been disturbed by her own actions. There were still the vestiges of mortal morality to deal with, the clash between the newborn vampire's lack of control and the lingering belief that somehow the rules of her mortal life still held sway. The guilt was stronger still as it had been her ex-boyfriend. Danaan didn't blame the young vampire for her reaction, or her crimson tears. It did, however, mean that the girl was useless in the clean up. The problem was that her every instinct screamed that she needed to be as quick as possible.

She had first helped Celeste into her apartment and then dragged the corpse in. She put Steve's remains in the bathroom, out of sight, though probably not out of mind. Next she had cleaned the spilled blood in the hallway.

There was actually very little blood; Celeste had revealed herself to be a very clean feeder and only a small amount of the precious fluid had escaped her hungry mouth. There was also a small amount of blood that had sprayed lazily from Danaan's shoulder wound, now mercifully healed. Cleaning the hallway was, therefore, a speedy affair. In actuality she could have left her blood, within an hour it would be naught but dust. She had to be careful, however, she couldn't risk it being seen before it had corrupted on its own.

Once that was done she selected a couple of bags and a large suitcase. The suitcase she moved into the bathroom and then encouraged Celeste to fill the smaller bags with essentials. She also made the distraught Fledgling find her passport.

Celeste had managed to question that. Danaan explained that her 'disappearance', and Steve's, might elicit questions and investigation. Best they were out of the city. It might be nice, she had suggested, to visit the Concilium Sanguinarius, to put her new life into perspective within the bigger picture. That wasn't Danaan's only motivation, however. She never mentioned the other vampire, there was little sense in worrying the girl, but Danaan was very troubled.

It was clear that Steve had expected this Michael to help him in his attack. More than that, a jealous boyfriend with a gun she could understand, but a machete aimed at severing the head? He had known what she was, of that she was sure. Only this Michael could have told him. She wished she knew who he was. She was painfully aware that he was very powerful, the force with which he had expelled her from his mind bore testament to that. She had never felt anything quite so powerful, though the force of his mental defences had most definitely spared her from the true death. If it hadn't been for his vicious rebuff… It had physically sent her reeling and that was the only reason the mortal had missed his mark.

She was scared. All she wanted to do was get to her home, e-mail Shang-Di, grab some identification and get the Hell to Switzerland.

Whilst Celeste busied herself in the bedroom Danaan moved into the bathroom. She had expected that she might have to dispose of a corpse this evening, she wanted to instruct Celeste with regards the most discreet methods of body disposal. She couldn't ask the poor girl to deal with this though.

She opened the case and then set to work on the exsanguinated body. Fitting it into the case was easy enough, though brutal. Limbs were snapped and the spine pulverised as she folded the body and stuffed it in the case. At least her vampire strength would prove useful carrying the damn thing. She would dispose of it in the furnace at home and that would be that.

In the bedroom Celeste was still not packed. She walked as though she were in a daze. Danaan hurried her along, guilty that she couldn't be more sensitive to the girl's obvious pain but conscious that they needed to make headway into their flight from the city.

Eventually they were in the car heading towards Danaan's home.

The car pulled up towards the gates. They had been left open purposefully and he could tell that the Praetorian knew something was wrong.

Ymochel had slowed to a walk as he passed through the apartment building lobby, he did not want to attract unwanted attention. Once through the doors and onto the city streets his pace quickened as he headed towards the rental car that he had parked a little further down the block.

As he drove he swore softly to himself, the words whispered but full of venom. Words he hadn't used in millennia, the language of his mortal people. He had underestimated the mentalist powers of the Praetorian bitch. If she had discovered his identity then she would inform the Concilium and he would be mercilessly hunted. He wasn't ready for that. It wasn't time.

He reached his own apartment and pulled two thin cases from a locked cupboard, he also picked up a set of keys. It was time to deal with the situation. He had rented the house out of town just in case. It was secluded, hidden in the woods. All he had to do was get the bitch there.

He took the cases down to his car and then continued to the Praetorian's home. He wasn't sure if she would return there or not, but it was his best guess. With luck he would have time to deal with her security before she returned.

He went over the wall, landing in the grounds of the house out of sight of the patrolling guards. After pushing the cases into the undergrowth of the gardens he set about his business.

He was purposefully careful. This was no hunt for food or for pleasure; it was a fight for survival. He approached the first guard, slipping through the night with feline grace, coming up behind the oblivious mortal. His large hands reached out, one smothering the guard's mouth the other cupping the back of the head. He twisted hard, snapping the neck. The guard fell to the floor, he had not had time to make a sound or fire his weapon. Following the same pattern he took the guards one at a time, creeping behind them and snapping their necks in one swift movement. The body would be pulled into the undergrowth and he would move on to the next. Only when he found the last did he allow himself the luxury of feeding. There was a good chance that he would need the blood.

He opened the gates and then went back and retrieved the two cases.

Lost within the dark of the night he opened the metal containers. One contained a high-powered rifle, silenced. The second held two weapons, a hand held taser and a taser rifle. He quickly built the weapons, laying the taser rifle on the floor, slipping the hand held in his jacket pocket and then readying the conventional rifle, waiting for the Praetorian to return.

The car pulled up towards the gates, which stood open, something was wrong. Something was very, very wrong.

Danaan leaned over to Celeste. The girl sat silently, her mind still lost in a turmoil of guilt and confusion. "Something isn't right?"

The Fledgling looked at her, "It's the cops isn't it, they know about Steve." Somehow her words should have been panicky but the Fledgling was too deeply in shock, instead they were soft and dreamy.

"Cops don't leave gates open and make security guards vanish. Besides, they couldn't know about Steve."

"Who is it then?"

Danaan sighed, she reached out with her mind but if this Michael were there he was well hidden, "Another vampire I think. I can't be sure."

"We should go."

She knew that the Fledgling was right, turning around was the safest course of action. She had confidence in the houses internal security, however, once inside their safety ought to be secured. There was a deeper factor at play, however, deeply primal and predatory - she refused to allow her territory to be violated.

"I need to get a message to the Concilium and I need my papers," Danaan explained, "We'll be safe once we're in the house," Silently she added, I hope.

She started to drive towards the house. It was just the reaction Ymochel had hoped for, the vanity of the Concilium drove the bitch forward.

He raised the rifle, ignoring the night sight, his vampire eyes keen enough to make out his target. The kick was meaningless to him, the barrel hissed as the bullet raced towards its target. The tire of the car burst as the bullet ripped through rubber, causing the car to spin out of control. Danaan barely managed to control the skid and bring the car to a halt.

Ymochel dropped the rifle to the floor and picked up the taser. Qutrub had relished experimenting with electricity and the Nubian, who had been the subject of much of the ancient's twisted research, knew the effect it would have on an undead. He stalked towards the car, still carefully shielding his mind.

Danaan managed to force the careering car into a stop. She looked at Celeste, worried at how her lover would have reacted but the incident seemed to have galvanized the Fledgling. Celeste ripped off her seatbelt and forced the passenger door open. The survival instincts of one of the Velvet had kicked in, her fangs extended and her talons unsheathed. Danaan pushed her door open, letting her darkest side free. Whereas Celeste had completely surrendered to her ferocious nature, Danaan, at least, maintained some control. She reached out with her mind but touched upon nothing.

They prowled across the lawn, two young women transfigured into nightmarish figures, then, out of the darkness, he appeared. He held some sort of gun in his hands, moving gracefully towards the two women. His clothes refined, his skin as black as midnight. That part of her that remained in control recognised him, Ymochel.

Danaan ran at the Nubian, an anger welling in her chest. She didn't know why he attacked them, but at that moment it was unimportant. All that was still human within her was gone, only the feral vampire remained.

Ymochel raised the gun and waited. Danaan was within twenty feet of him, she leapt, her hands clawing at the Nubian. Ymochel fired; the compressed air canister forced two electrodes out of the barrel, which buried in her chest. Momentum carried her forward, but Ymochel sidestepped the leap.

A fierce pain passed through Danaan. In mortals the effect of a taser would turn blood sugar to lactic acid. It had a similar effect on Danaan's stolen blood, but Ymochel knew that in the undead the effect was more spectacular. The current took hold of her muscle control; she curled foetal onto the floor. Ymochel smiled, the bitch would be paralysed for at least twelve hours.

Celeste leapt and Ymochel's arm shot out and grabbed the Fledgling's neck. He held her there, his arm at full extension. His fingers were a vice like grip, which she could not escape. She thrashed at his arm with her talons, ripping the suit and scoring long wounds into the flesh that healed almost as soon as they appeared. He dropped the taser from his other hand and nonchalantly reached into his pocket for the hand held version. His finger pressed the trigger button and, with an almost obscene casualness, he pushed the device into her chest, holding it against her until she fell limp.

He picked the two females up, throwing one over each shoulder and walked coolly off the property, heading towards the waiting car.

As Ymochel left the grounds the vampire materialised. His orders were to observe and report, not to take action. Those were his instructions and so he obeyed, though he wanted desperately to rip the Nubian's head from his shoulders. He took the mobile phone from his pocket and began to tap the Morrison County area code. He would have to continue to follow, he knew, but best that the Concilium were alerted immediately.

Chapter Forty Two

Bear Mountain State Park – 2000

The lodge was hidden in the woods on the edge of the State Park. Ymochel had chosen it out of convenience. Bear Mountain was only fifty miles outside New York. It was close enough to run to in an emergency and secluded enough that he knew he would not be disturbed.

The car's headlights illuminated the rustic looking building, whilst the dark depths of the forest threatened to swallow the car and house back into its black embrace. Occasionally an owl would call, its voice haunting in the night.

Ymochel opened a rear door and pulled one of the prone vampires roughly out of the back seat, the Praetorian fell heavily onto the rough mud road. He scooped up her paralysed body and carried her up to the door, his keys in hand.

Danaan was terrified. She was unable to move and yet was aware of everything around her. She wanted to cry, but no tears would come. She wanted to scream, but her voice was trapped inside. The Nubian pushed the door open and carried her inside.

Once Ymochel was out of sight the passenger door opened, though it appeared that no one was there.

Fenrir stalked invisibly to the side of the house. He had alerted Jumlin to Ymochel's activities and, as he knew he would be, had been ordered to continue following the rogue. He had scaled Danaan's wall and, unburdened by bodies, had managed to slip into the Nubian's vehicle before the rogue had reached it. As they drove he had carefully observed their journey and knew exactly where they were.

He pulled out the mobile phone and switched the device back on, relieved when he saw that he was receiving a signal.

Danaan heard the footsteps as Ymochel returned to the cellar, carrying Celeste's prone body.

He had strapped her into a device similar to those Qutrub used to hold his guests; she remembered the device all too well from her Praetorian training. Every Praetorian had tried to escape its immobilising grip. As far as she knew every Praetorian had failed.

Ymochel had seen to its construction on the chance that it might be needed one day. He had not foreseen that he might need two. He searched around for something with which to confine the Fledgling, eventually settling on a set of thick iron chains. He bound Celeste as best as he could to a thick support beam, wrapping the chains tight around her limbs, trusting that the newborn would not be strong enough yet to break her bonds.

The image hit his mind with force. Danaan had pushed and pushed, straining her psyche to break through his defences. The message was clear. She wanted to know why.

He looked at her for a moment, annoyed that she had found the strength to breach his defences, and then answered, "Radu."

She projected again, slipping through the same crack in his mental wall. She showed him the orgy they had discovered in Radu's Schloß, though she knew he had been there, and then constructed a vision of Radu bestowing a Praetorian death upon a vampire. The message was clear. He had been found guilty and had brought his fate upon himself.

Ymochel grew angry. He screamed at her, "Your rules!" In that moment his walls tumbled down and she was engulfed by memories. She saw Radu being groomed by the Nubian. She heard Ymochel explaining to Radu how he might to steal the power of another Child of the Velvet through true death. Then his memories tumbled further back and she saw Ymochel attacking Uriel.

His walls shot back up but she knew. She didn't know what shocked her the most, the fact that he had killed his Bloodfather, the fact that he had encouraged Radu's crime or the fact that he had successfully lied to the Concilium.

Worse, he knew. He was aware that she had seen it all. She could see it in his eyes.

He leaned close and whispered in her ear. "It doesn't matter. You are going to die, you and your little bitch. But I will torture you first, Praetorian, I will let you feel a little of the pain that Qutrub subjected me to. I will give you the smallest taste of the Concilium's justice."

His neck was exposed. She wanted to bite, but her head would not move. She tried to throw her anger and fear at him, but his mental walls were strong again and try as she might she could not break through. Frustration built within her and, inside, she wept.

He pulled back. Outside the sun was close to rising, Ymochel could feel its approach through every cell of his body. He left the two vampires in the cellar and retreated to his room upstairs, priming the security system as he passed through the hallway, unaware that he already had an uninvited guest hidden within the house.

Back in the cellar Danaan felt a push at her mind. She opened herself up and allowed Celeste to touch her. The Fledgling was terrified and, despite her best efforts, Danaan was unable to put on a brave front for her. Instead they allowed their minds to entwine, comforting each other as best they could as the stupor came upon them. The blackness of a vampire's sleep offering the comfort of nothingness and transporting them, for a while, away from their danger.

Chapter Forty Three

Istanbul - 1701

Thick smoke clung in the air as the two vampires sat together, ignored by the milling throng. The men gathered often in these coffee shops, a place away from women. Ymochel and Radu were huddled, talking, choosing a public place rather than a private location. The Nubian vampire felt secure in the public exposure. He had no need to fear mortals; in reality it was his fellow vampires he feared, scared that they might discover his secrets, his hatred and his plans.

Both the undead felt comfortable in Istanbul.

Ymochel did not feel as conspicuous as he did in Europe, where the colour of his skin often caused the observer to view him as a moor or more recently, as the circle had turned full again, a slave. How long had the association with slavery haunted him? For all his long centuries it seemed.

It seemed strange, however, to refer to the bustling city as Istanbul. Ymochel still thought of it is

Constantinople. He had been here when Constantine, the Christian Emperor, had made it his seat of power. So very long ago and yet, in some respects, it seemed like only yesterday. He wondered how Constantine would feel if he saw his city now, probably not as angered as he would have done if he had realised that he had been nothing more than a dupe of an ancient bloodsucker named Qutrub.

For Radu, Turkey was home, more so than the cold grey granite and lush forests of Walachia and Transylvania. It had been since his childhood.

Ymochel had not revealed his plans for two hundred and fifty years; he had felt that his Fledgling needed to learn the patience that had been his constant companion. Not that killing Uriel had been born of patience, it had been an act of opportunism that had nearly proved his downfall and had carried the heavy price of a year of agony as his arm had healed. Ymochel had learnt to act with patience, circumstance had taught him well.

"I have told you," the Sponsor said eventually, "That we may die. That true death can take our kind."

"You have, my Lord." There was no bitterness in Radu's voice, he truly loved his Sponsor and viewed him as his true Lord. Radu knew that he would gladly lay his life down for Ymochel, though he had never felt such a loyalty in his mortal life and knew not where such feelings came from. "I know the danger of sunlight, in large doses, and the peril of fire. You have told me that to lose the heart or the head is fatal to our kind, but all other injuries can be recovered from."

Ymochel nodded, he had not skimped on his Fledglings education, as Uriel had with his. There was knowledge he had kept to himself, however, but he felt that now was the time to pass that on to his pupil.

"What I did not tell you is that when we drink from one of our own we steal their strength, their power." He confided. "It is an act of dominance. If I took you now, drained you dry, you would feel subservient to me. You would bow your head and bend your knee. Not because you love me, but because I had proven my supremacy."

Radu nodded, it was ever the way with animals, he observed, especially, though not exclusively, with predators. Pack predators especially seemed to order their societies by the rule of might. Power was a constant, even in the animal kingdom. Were the vampires not the pinnacle of the predators? Did not the laws that governed the predator species also govern them?

"What you are also not aware of, and I have gleamed that this is kept as a closely guarded secret within the Concilium, is that if we bring the true death to one whose power we have stolen then that power is kept within us. It becomes ours."

Radu smiled, "So If I were to drain you and kill you I would steal your power, my beautiful Lord."

Ymochel frowned, he disliked such thoughts.

"My Lord, I do not threaten," Radu added quickly, "You know I love you more than life itself."

"That I do," Ymochel replied, and added silently, for I have been testing you constantly for two and a half centuries.

Their conversation paused as the boy, of around twelve or thirteen years, brought them both a small cup of thick black coffee. Ymochel nodded politely, such purchases kept them disguised when they sat amongst the mortals, the façade of humanity that they were forced to wear. Radu watched the boy leave, his head bobbing up and down as he watched the boys back. Ymochel looked at his Fledgling and, with a flicker of his eyelashes, indicated his agreement. Radu had grown especially fond of pubescent boys; he claimed their blood contained a fire unfound in any other form of foodstuff. It would do no harm, Ymochel mused, for Istanbul was full of such boys, the disappearance of this one would not cause so much as a ripple.

"I promised you power."

"And you delivered it my Lord."

"No, I have given you a power that no mortal has and introduced you to a hidden world, but true power, no. We are bound, you and I, by the Concilium and their rules. The ancients hold their power and ensure that we are in bondage to it. I wish us to take that power."

If Radu was shocked by the Nubian's words he did not show it, though his response was melodramatic, "A war against heaven."

"A blood war," was Ymochel's response. "We will rest power from the Concilium. No longer will we be their slaves, instead we will be the masters. But…"

"But?"

"Our kind grows stronger as the years pass. I am young compared to the Bloodfathers and mother, though I contain within me more power than they could imagine. You are younger still. We need to accelerate your growth."

Radu understood, "This is why you told me of the way to steal power from our own kind."

"It is the only way to gain our power quickly."

"We hunt our own kind? But you have told me that the Concilium have prescribed such acts as a crime against them."

Ymochel stared off into the depths of the coffee house for a moment. "The boy who brought us coffee," he pointed towards him.

"What of him?"

"What if you brought him to the Velvet, unbeknown to the Concilium, allowed him to evolve and then stole his power."

"Then I would increase my own power and they would be none the wiser."

Ymochel smiled, and the smile melted Radu's heart, "Indeed."

"What would you have me do?"

"I have been told that your ancestral schloß is no more than a ruin, uninhabited, yet there remain many villages and towns in close proximity."

Radu confirmed this, believing he knew where Ymochel's plans were going.

"No-one should think of looking for you there, why would you return to such a desolate place? Why would you consider haunting the lands of your own mortality?

"Return and begin to create our kind, develop them and feed from them, become strong that you and I may, as you say, wage a war against heaven, that we might bring down the old gods who demand our servitude and raise ourselves up into power."

It was done, the plan was in place. As they left the coffee house Radu managed to attract the attention of the boy who had served them. He followed the vampires down the street, hoping to earn an extra coin or two.

Chapter Forty Four

Bear Mountain State Park – 2000

The closet was tiny, but it was shielded from the sun. Fenrir had been in more cramped locations whilst serving the Concilium and, if the truth be known, during his mortal life.

He had fought the stupor, remaining awake through the day. The vampire was comforted by the fact that he could still sense the Praetorian in the cellar. The rogue had not killed her yet. That comfort was not enough to override his uneasiness at what he had decided to do.

Jumlin's instructions had been very clear. Observe the Nubian's actions and await the Emperor's arrival. He could have surrendered to the stupor and still fulfilled his mission.

He opened the door and felt the daylight stream into the closet, brushing his exposed skin with its burning touch. Whilst he could hide from mortal and Velvet eyes alike, he could not hide from the sun. It was an uncomfortable prickling, no more. The sunlight was not direct and, even if it had been, the distance between the cupboard and the cellar would have allowed no more than an uncomfortable reddening of the exposed skin even on the brightest of days.

He had to work fast. The sun would set in half an hour and the rebel would awaken. He went to the panel that Ymochel had used the night before and disarmed the security and then opened the cellar door, heading down the stairs.

In the cellar he went straight to Danaan and began pulling at the bonds. She woke suddenly from the stupor.

"Fenrir?" Her voice was groggy.

"Hush Danaan."

"Fenrir, you have to know. He killed his Bloodfather."

It was as though the spy had not registered her words. He continued to pull at the bonds.

"Fenrir, listen to me… Ymochel… he gave a Praetorian death to Uriel. He knew about Radu all along."

There was still no response.

"Fenrir…" Her voice was sharp.

"I hear you." He stopped and looked at her for a second, holding her glance with his watery eyes. Then he added, his voice filled with the suggestion of melancholy, "I can do nothing about that, can I?"

He gave a final tug and she was free. She flexed her fingers, the paralysis had obviously worn off whilst she slept. Then, as quick as a flash, she was by Celeste. Her fingers tearing through the metal chains as though they were twine. The Fledgling collapsed to the floor, the stupor still gripping her young body.

"Help me with her."

"No." As he spoke he looked at the Fledgling. Ah Danaan, so impulsive still, he thought to himself. So like her, he thought, his memories spinning through millennia.

"Fenrir, you must help me with her. We must get out of here."

"I can do no more." There was an unmistakable edge of wretchedness to his voice.

"Hide us, please, before he returns."

"I have already done too much. The Emperor told me to watch, not to interfere. I shouldn't even have freed you."

This had been the source of his uneasiness. He could not hide her as he wanted to but he could at least free her. Yet doing so was to break his orders. He had never wilfully disobeyed the Concilium before. The Emperor's wrath if he discovered that Fenrir had stepped beyond his remit was of little concern to him. What really bothered him was how Undjit would react.

"You must hide us!"

He turned so she would be unable to see the heartache seared across his face. "I told you, I can't." His words were barely a whisper.

Danaan looked over to him, he wouldn't turn and face her but he could sense the blood tears welling in her eyes breaking his heart. "Then why..."

Outside the sun sank behind the horizon.

From upstairs came the sound of movement.

In her arms Celeste stirred, her eyes springing open.

Fenrir vanished.

"Danaan..." Celeste's voice was tiny, terrified.

"Celeste, my love, we have to get out of here…"
When the Fledgling did not stir, she added more forcefully, whilst pushing with her mind, "Now!"

They moved towards the stairs and then froze. Looming above them on the stairs, silhouetted like a demonic bird of prey, stood Ymochel. Out of the silhouette his eyes blazed red. "How the Hell…"

He leapt and the two girls threw themselves aside one to the left and the other to the right.

He landed in a crouch, his eyes darting from Celeste to Danaan and then back again.

Danaan launched herself at him. His hand shot forward and caught her neck, his talons puncturing the soft flesh. He tore his hand back.

The Praetorian fell backwards, her hands reached for her own throat but only found a gapping hole that was sticky with her own blood. Ymochel had ripped her throat out; his talons had scraped the top of her spine.

Celeste screamed and threw herself at their tormentor. His elbow flew back and caught her cleanly in the face. The power of his blow crushed her nose and threw her back into the far wall of the cellar. The back of her skull smashed against the brick with a sickening thud.

He turned his attention back to Danaan; it was time to finish the job.

Before he had chance to move towards her his attention was drawn to the stairs.

The vampire approaching Ymochel had been Native American when a mortal. His long black hair was braided down his back, his large hooked nose reminiscent of an eagle's beak. Ymochel could feel the power radiating from him like heat from a furnace. Jumlin had come.

The ancient had travelled through the day to get to Bear Mountain. His Praetorian would arrive by helicopter within the hour, but enough was enough. He would take the rebel now.

He allowed his fangs to extend and then soared off the stairs.

Ymochel sidestepped, his speed astounding the ancient. He caught the Emperor's arm and twisted hard. The bones snapped and the ancient howled in pain and shock. It was not right, the ancient thought to himself, no mere two thousand year old should be able to do that to him.

His arm twisted itself as the bones re-set. Pain seared through the limb.

The pain distracted Jumlin for a moment. Ymochel caught hold of the ancient and pulled him down onto his knee, snapping his spine. He knew it was not enough so he did it again and again.

Jumlin reached up and gouged at the Nubian's face. His talons raked through flesh and Ymochel's left eyeball ruptured, spraying its gelatinous fluid.

He dropped the ancient and backed away, a survival instinct overcoming his hatred. He turned and ran towards the stairs. Jumlin clawed across the cellar floor, dragging his body towards the fleeing vampire. Then his spine started to heal and pain racked his body, causing him to halt.

Ymochel was already at the top of the stairs. He burst out of the house and fled into the night.

Fenrir stood invisible in the cellar surveying the devastation. Celeste remained unconscious, her youth and lack of blood had caused her body to collapse into the stupor, though the night was only just upon them. Jumlin gouged long scores in the cellar floor as his back twisted, his spine regaining its shape. The ancient's face twisted into a mask of fury and agony, though his stoic heart would not allow the scream that pressed against his chest to escape his mouth.

For a moment the spy considered pursuing the rogue, of punishing him for what he had done to Danaan. For a moment he pictured himself ripping the Nubian's head from his shoulders, of watching the flesh slough from the bone. A more rationale part of him remembered what Danaan had said. "He gave a Praetorian death to Uriel." If that were the case then Ymochel was possessed of the power of an ancient. Fenrir might have the advantage of invisibility, but as soon as he attacked, as soon as he ceased to be inconsequential, he feared that Ymochel would swat him like a fly.

So, instead of giving pursuit, the spy crouched by Danaan and ran a gentle hand through her hair. She couldn't see him, he couldn't allow it. He was afraid that on seeing him her eyes would contain a brimming pain that would ask the question, "Why didn't you help me?" it was safer to remain inconsequential, safer to remain hidden from her, rather than face the accusation that would brim in her eyes, and yet she could feel his touch through the pain of her body attempting to repair the brutal damage it had sustained. She knew his gentle solace as though his fingers were a light breeze blowing through her hair.

"When you are well again," Fenrir whispered knowing his voice could not be heard, "I will tell you of my life, I will describe my lost Mycenae as you once requested. I promise you that. I will tell you of her"

He remained by her side until he heard the helicopter overhead. By the time the Praetorians reached the cellar he had left the lodge and was making his way down to the interstate.

Epilogue

Alaska - 2000

In the cavern was a giant honeycomb of ice, each comb containing liquid that, somehow, remained unfrozen. In each hexagonal of liquid was an image, each image portrayed a vampire.

It stood by the honeycomb, long unkempt hair flicked back from its dirty, greyed face.

Not all of the Velvet were represented, the honeycomb was too small for that, but those it deemed important were visible. Some images were indistinct, its ability to exert control over that vampire poor at best, other images were crisp and it knew it could exert its will upon that vampire.

In one was Jumlin, his spine now repaired. By his body language, the ancient seemed to be angrily barking orders. The ancient's image was blurred and when it concentrated no sound came, other than an indistinct buzzing. It was like that with the ancient ones, it could observe and no more.

In another there was nothing but blurred landscape, the vampire was not visible. Such was the nature of Fenrir, absolutely removed from its influence. When it concentrated there was only silence.

In another, clear and distinct, was Ymochel. He could see the vampire tumble to the asphalt road. His injured eye had not yet repaired itself; he had focused all the blood on maintaining preternatural speed as he escaped. It had seen the oncoming headlights before the vampire had. If it concentrated it knew that it would be able to hear all, even the vampire's innermost thoughts. Ymochel was its favoured piece in the game. It had bestowed the ability to kill one of their kind without true death, when it so wished, it had bestowed the ability to lie.

The flesh it wore had been a mortal man, but it was a fleshy shell only, no soul had resided within when the spirit had taken him. It didn't think like a man, it had one need, growth, and the time was nigh. Patient millennia had passed and the pieces it had so carefully manipulated were now in place.

It had no need of a name, but the mortals who avoided its mountain called him Mianersiwok, the watcher. They said it was a demon of the snows. The name suited its patience. It reached out with a gnarled talon tipped finger and the dirty, claw like nail pressed into the liquid image of Ymochel. It began to stir. The time was almost right.

Children of the Velvet

Names and pseudonyms

Tracing the history of the Children of the Velvet can be difficult due to both the secretive nature of the Concilium Sanguinarius and the fact that vampires change their names as they make their slow walk through time.

The following should make their history easier to follow.

Ngaut-Ngaut: The first vampire, the source. It is unclear as to whether the Concilium are aware of their pre-history origins

Shang-Di the Child of Golden Skin: an ancient; head of a Bloodline, Emperor of the Concilium in the 19th Century Christian Era (CE)

Susano: a Child of the Bloodline of Shang-Di, died in the atomic explosion at Hiroshima, Japan CE 1945

Ariadnne: a Child of the Bloodline of Shang-Di, Sponsor of Danaan

> **Bronwen**: the name taken by Ariadnne in the 11th Century CE, when she gave Danaan the Velvet Kiss

Danaan: a Praetorian of the Concilium, Fledgling of Ariadnne, Bloodline of Shang-Di, born to the Velvet 1067

> **Dame Mary Startin, Prioress of Kirklees**: an identity assumed by Danaan in 14th Century CE England
>
> **Katrina**: the name taken by Danaan in 16th Century CE Eastern Europe
>
> **Helena**: the name taken by Danaan in the late 19th Century CE
>
> **Juliana**: the name taken by Danaan in 20/21st Century CE New York

Uriel the Leech: an ancient; head of a Bloodline, Emperor of the Concilium in the 1st century CE, died during the eruption of Vesuvius CE 0079

Remus: head of the Bloodline of Uriel (renamed the Bloodline of Remus) following the death of Uriel

Ymochel: a Child of the Bloodline of Uriel, slave of Uriel, born to the   Velvet CE 0074, Sponsor of Radu

> **Little Leech**: a derogatory name for Ymochel, used by the concubines of Uriel during their stay in Pompeii
>
> **Michael**: the name taken by Ymochel in 20/21st century CE New York

Radu: a Child of the Bloodline of Uriel, Fledgling of Ymochel. Unusually Radu was allowed to keep his mortal name by his Sponsor Ymochel (thus we are aware that, as a mortal, he was Prince Radu Tepes), born to the Velvet CE 1473, died at the hands of the Praetorians CE 1819

Laszlo: an illegitimate, fathered to the Velvet by Radu approximately CE 1819, died at the hands of the Praetorians.

Augustine: a Child of the Bloodline of Uriel, concubine to Uriel, died at the Hands of Uriel CE 0079

Mercia: a Child of the Bloodline of Uriel, concubine to Uriel, died during the eruption of Vesuvius CE 0079

Diana: a Child of the Bloodline of Uriel, concubine to Uriel, died during the eruption of Vesuvius CE 0079

Ceres: A Child of the Bloodline of Uriel/Remus, a Praetorian of the Concilium

> **Catherine**: the name taken by Ceres during the 19th Century CE when she acted as the mistress of the French diplomat Charles Maurice de Talleyrand-Perigord.

Undjit the Serpent: an ancient, head of a Bloodline

Fenrir: Concilium spy, of the Bloodline of Undjit. Fenrir has the ability to walk unseen by mortal and immortal alike.

Hephaestus: a Child of the Bloodline of Undjit

Qutrub of the Flesh: an ancient, head of a Bloodline

Baal: a Child of the Bloodline of Qutrub

Huginn of the Morning Star: an ancient, head of a Bloodline

Eshu: a Child of the Bloodline of Huggin, archivist of the Concilium

Jumlin: an ancient, head of a Bloodline, Emperor during the 21st Century CE

www.ingramcontent.com/pod-product-compliance
Lightning Source LLC
Chambersburg PA
CBHW020246030726

47499CB00001B/77